Chasing Ghosts

Also by Lee Driver

Chase Dagger Series

The Unseen
Full Moon-Bloody Moon
The Good Die Twice

Short Stories

Sara Morningsky, Mystery in Mind Anthology
The Thirteenth Hole, Mystery in Mind Anthology

Written as S.D. Tooley

Sam Casey Series

Echoes from the Grave
Restless Spirit
Nothing Else Matters
When the Dead Speak

Short Stories

Solving Life's Riddle, Amazon Shorts

For Middle School/Young Adult Readers

Remy and Roadkill Series

The Skull

www.sdtooley.com
sdtooley@sbcglobal.net

Chasing Ghosts

A Chase Dagger Mystery

Lee Driver

Full Moon Publishing LLC

This book is a work of fiction. Names, characters, places and incidents are the product of the author's imagination. Resemblance to actual events, locales or persons, living or dead, is strictly fictional. Any slights of people, places, or organizations is unintentional.

Library of Congress Control Number: 2008929421

ISBN 978-0-9785402-9-6

Published August 2008

Printed in the United States of America

Full Moon Publishing LLC
P.O. Box 408
Schererville, IN 46375

www.fullmoonpub.com

CHASING GHOSTS

Prologue

The halogen beam sprayed light over stone walls. The shaft was the size of a freight elevator with a metal stairway. He cast a nervous glance at the steel hatch one flight up. A fragile stake of wood propped open the hatch leaching a scant two inches of sunlight into the dark. Leaning over the railing, he aimed the halogen beam down the shaft revealing an endless number of stairs. How far did it extend and what awaited him at the bottom?

With little more than stubborn determination, he continued down the stairs letting the beam of light search for signs on the walls to lend some clue as to what danger he might encounter. He stopped two stairs before the third landing and listened. Silence. Complete silence. Not one hum of a motor or patter of four-legged creatures. Not one hint of a whisper or soft sound of fabric rustling. Just utter silence.

As he stepped onto the third landing a loud bang echoed through the stairwell. The flashlight skipped down the stairs as he dropped the gym bag, pulled his gun from its holster, and flattened his back against the wall. Three flights above the hatch door had slammed shut, breaking the wooden stake. Immediately light sconces on the walls clicked on in succession. His heart pounded in his chest as though trying in vain to escape. He pointed the gun first toward the closed hatch, then down the lit stairwell. He listened for sounds of footsteps running, doors slamming, voices shouting. But still there was only silence, except for the endless clicking of light sconces becoming softer, more distant, until he couldn't hear them anymore.

Looking up he contemplated sanity. Of all the reckless things he had done in his life, this had to be right at the top. He should retreat and trust that the hatch didn't lock when it slammed shut. He should return home and forget about this ludicrous mission. But then the depths beckoned and his curiosity intensified. Insanity had gotten him this far. Why back out now?

He looked down at his feet. What had triggered the lights? His weight on the landing? Maybe a timer after the escape hatch was opened. He holstered the gun, retrieved the flashlight, shoved it in the gym bag, and continued down the stairs. The walls looked like marble or cinderblock that some giant stone polishing machine had buffed to a smooth finish. There weren't any cameras he could detect but for some bizarre reason he felt as though he were being watched.

Dizzy from the endless flights, he collapsed on the stairs and pulled a bottle of water from the gym bag. Climbing down was one thing. Climbing up was a task he wasn't anticipating. Although he should have worked up a sweat, he didn't feel hot. The temperature in the stairwell was relatively mild, not the cold dampness he had expected. The air didn't smell moldy like the inside of a tomb or earthy like a grave. It actually had the fresh scent of the outdoors. It was as though the stairwell were humidity and temperature-controlled, yet there wasn't a sign of a vent anywhere.

His eyes were drawn to a number in black lettering on the wall. It was the second time he had seen the identical number *402*. How many flights since the first time he had seen the number? He had tried counting the lights as he descended but lost track at sixty, or was it seventy? The monotony of the stairwell was getting to him. He could be trapped down here with nothing more than a gym bag of Power Bars, fruit, and water. How long could that last?

He capped the bottle and dropped it into the gym bag. Picking up speed, he pounded down the stairs, no longer concerned about making too much noise. He just wanted to see an end to the metal stairs and stone walls. A third *402* in black letters was painted on the wall at the next landing. Figures bounced in his head — 402 times three equals 1,206. Was that feet? He had certainly descended farther than 1,206 feet. The muscles in his thighs burned. What could possibly be at the bottom of this shaft? Missile silos weren't this deep. Chicago's Deep Tunnel

Project was only 350 feet underground. It took thirty years to build. How long has this shaft been here and how long did it take to dig? He may reach the bottom and find an unfinished shaft. If he had to turn around and run back up, he'd sooner put the gun to his head.

Ignoring the pain in his calves he increased his speed, taking less than one second per flight. He finally caught sight of a stone floor, an actual end to this monotony. Several yards from the last stair was a door. Breathing came in gasps, sweat glistened his skin. On the wall next to the door was the number *1,608*, a familiar number. The number was in meters and equal to 5,280 feet. He was exactly one mile below the surface.

With one hand wrapped around the gun, he grabbed the door latch and slowly pulled. Light burst through forcing him to shield his face. Blinking the burning from his eyes, he rammed the door open and stepped out onto a walkway. Gun at the ready, he checked to the left and right of him but didn't see any movement. Stretched in front of him was a cobblestone courtyard as wide as a four-lane highway. If there were people here, did they run for cover when they heard him coming? Or did something chase them away years before he arrived? Someone or something had to be operating the lights.

One-story buildings served as sentries on both sides of the courtyard, their marble fronts in an assortment of colors, metal doors painted. He ignored the fatigue in his legs while his senses picked up the chirping of birds in nearby trees, the rustling of leaves from a breeze that barely kissed his skin. Billowing clouds hung in a sunlit sky so blue it made his eyes sting. Stone benches lined the courtyard every ten feet. Dazed, he blinked quickly expecting the scene to disappear like a mirage, but it didn't. Slowly circling like a lost tourist, his hand lost its grasp on the gym bag. It slipped from his hand and thudded to the cobblestone. Three-story buildings in the distance jutted toward the sky, chrome facades gleaming in the sunlight. As he wandered into the center of the courtyard he scanned the surrounding buildings, checking windows and rooftops. A variety of sweet aromas filled the air from nearby ceramic flower urns. Yellow petals too yellow, pink petals too pink. The entire area was an amateur paint-by-number scene.

He holstered his gun, stumbled to the curb and dropped onto the nearest bench. He should have been questioning how all this could be happening. After all, he was sure he was a mile underground. Any normal person would have been questioning his sanity, exploring his surroundings, examining all possible explanations. Any sane person would have been mumbling *impossible, ridiculous, absurd*. But only one word came to Dagger's mind:

Home

1

Five Days Earlier

Dagger decided this wasn't going to be a bad day after all. For one thing, all of his organs and bones were intact, despite the throbbing muscles that would turn to huge bruises tomorrow. But more importantly, the man dying on the living room floor hadn't bled on Sara's new area rug. That should win him Brownie points, seeing that he was already on her shit list for not helping to clean Einstein's aviary. Speaking of Einstein, where was the advance warning from his attack bird? The scarlet red and blue macaw poked its head around the corner of the grated door to the aviary. During the melee, Einstein had been noticeably absent.

Dagger struggled to pull himself up on one knee. Maybe he should have extracted a little blood from the intruder and added it to the pink and mauve rug. Sara's bright color scheme made his eyeballs hurt. Now if only he had the energy to bury the oaf before his partner returned.

Too late.

He heard the roar of the truck rumbling down the drive.

"UH OH," Einstein squawked, and flew to his hiding place.

"You're a damn chicken," Dagger yelled, threading shaky fingers through wet hair.

A truck door slammed. Footsteps clicked along the deck porch. The front door opened and Sara took two steps inside before halting. She spent less time studying the body than it took for one perfectly shaped eyebrow to raise. "I thought we agreed not to bring home strays."

Dagger forced one thin smile and said, "Cute," before sliding back to the floor, deciding the scenery was far better from this angle. Sara had one hell of a set of legs. But those weren't her only attributes. Her eyes were the color of Caribbean waters and they were almond-shaped, adding to her exotic beauty. Dark hair sun-streaked in an array of colors hung to her waist.

She shifted the bag of groceries in her arms and stepped over the man who looked as though anorexia would have killed him if Dagger hadn't. Although the man was lying on his stomach, his head was twisted over his right shoulder at a painful angle. Sara studied that angle, winced, and tossed an accusing glare at Dagger.

"He started it," Dagger protested like a five-year-old.

The Caribbean blue turned icy and with an exasperated shake of her head, Sara carried the groceries to the kitchen.

"But don't worry about me," Dagger called out. "I've only got three broken ribs, a ruptured spleen, and a dislocated shoulder."

Several seconds later Sara returned mumbling, "Such a baby."

Dagger grabbed the back of the love seat and hauled himself up on wobbly legs. The intruder couldn't have weighed more than 150 pounds but he had managed to lift Dagger over his head and toss him like a rag doll. How was that possible? He lowered himself onto the armrest and watched as Sara picked up the phone and punched in a two-digit code.

"Good morning." Sara's voice smiled along the phone line. "We need a clean-up in aisle seven. Oh, and we also need the trash taken out." She hung up and marched over to the trash.

"Gee, and how is Skizzy?" Dagger wasn't too surprised Sara knew the programmed code for his schizophrenic friend. Nothing much gets by his partner.

Sara pressed her fingertips to the man's neck. "As usual, you are thorough. She straightened and walked over to where Dagger sat. A bruise was forming on his left cheek. A press of her fingers to the left side of Dagger's chest had him wincing. "Why did you let him in?"

"I didn't. He was already here when I climbed out of the shower. I no sooner slipped into my jeans and shook the water from my hair when I heard the door open. The jerk was standing in the living room."

"I didn't leave the gate open."

"Well, Einstein didn't open it. And the guy sure as hell didn't have the code to the gate."

"So, you said hello and he started swinging."

Dagger staggered to a standing position, pressing a hand to his left side. He didn't think he broke anything but he was as sore as hell. "I stared at him for a beat and he said, 'I need your services.' I asked how he got in and suddenly he changed. I saw something just spark, like my words were offensive somehow. Then he lunged at me. Idiot lifted me over his head and threw me against the wall."

Sara studied the dead man as though mentally sizing him up, then ran her gaze over Dagger's six foot frame. His muscles were toned, shoulders broad. At least 190 pounds of solid power. She dragged her eyes back to the waif of a man lying at her feet. "He lifted you over his head?" That one eyebrow jerked again.

"Hey, you know me. If I had my druthers, I would have shot the son of a bitch but I couldn't get to my gun."

"So instead you broke his neck." Sara knelt beside the body and carefully rolled him over. She patted his jacket pockets before reaching inside. "He isn't even armed."

There was that look again. Dagger had always worked alone and never had to explain or second guess himself. Sara as a partner was like hiring a conscience, but she had talents that were indispensable to his business. Had to take the good with the bad. And right now the way her dress rode up her thigh was looking pretty damn good.

Whenever Sara displayed an inkling of confidence and self-determination, Dagger always pined for the days after he had first met her, when she had rarely left the safety of these three hundred acres of reservation land, when she was frightened of her own shadow and looked to Dagger as her protector and mentor. The good old days were long gone. And his brotherly feelings for Sara were slowly morphing into something that was making it very uncomfortable for him to live under the same roof with her. Not only did he have a very talented partner who was so damn great to look at, but she also provided the living and working space which was saying a lot for a P.I. who used to live above a bar. He had his own bedroom and a cubicle in the living room which served as his office space. The house was a converted car dealership. The adjoining maintenance area, which was originally for servicing cars, served as an aviary for Dagger's rowdy macaw.

"OKAY? OKAY?" Einstein pecked at the grated door.

"Yeah, Einstein. Everything is okay." Dagger watched Sara remove a wallet from the man's pocket.

"Paul Demko. He's from Minneapolis." Sara searched his pants pockets. "No car keys so he must have taken a cab." She checked his inside jacket pocket, then held up a hotel key card. "He has a room at the Embassy Suites." She pulled out a wad of bills from the wallet. "About two hundred dollars, no charge cards, not even an insurance card, no receipts, no airline tickets."

Dagger tested his legs. So far so good. He staggered to the cubicle, pulled out his Kimber .45 and set it on the desk. Next he grabbed an ink pad and a piece of paper, then carefully lowered himself next to the body. "Check him for scars, tattoos, wires." Dagger opened the ink pad and dabbed each of Demko's fingers in ink, then rolled them onto the paper. "We just need to confirm who he says he is."

"Makes no sense. Why would he say he needed your services and then try to kill you?" Once Dagger was done fingerprinting,

Sara rolled Demko onto his stomach, lifted his shirt to look for scars, then pulled the shirt collar down. "Just one scar on the right side of his neck, above the hairline. Nothing else, unless you want to strip him down."

"I'll take a pass." Dagger winced and limped over to the control panel under the alarm system by the door. By punching a few buttons he was able to view the camera recording from the front gate. Sara appeared behind him and together they watched the recording of Paul Demko being dropped off by a cab. Demko looked more like an insurance salesman, slender build with average height and features. If there had been a bank robbery, Demko would have been the first to dive under his desk.

The monitor showed the cab pulling away. Demko walked over to the gate and studied the intercom system, checked the height of the fence. Instead of pressing the keypad to announce his arrival, Demko walked back to the street, appeared to check to see if any cars were approaching, then turned, took a running start and leaped over the ten-foot-high fence.

"That can't be possible," Sara said. "He looked as though he used a springboard."

Dagger replayed the recording. He didn't like the looks of this one bit. Suddenly his muscles no longer ached. Instead an anger and adrenaline coursed through his body. They watched a third time. Demko hadn't brought any type of portable trampoline with him, hadn't used a pole vault of any type, yet he had been able to leap over the fence with little effort.

"As soon as Skizzy gets here, we're going to get over to that hotel room and find out a little more about Paul Demko."

2

Cedar Point, Indiana boasted 100,000 residents and hugged the shores of Lake Michigan in Northwest Indiana. It had its country club and yacht club for the elites as well as the seedy back alleys for the down-and-outs. Sandwiched between the high and low incomes were the struggling middleclass just trying to keep their lawns green, their kids in iPods and their charge card payments down to a manageable level.

The key card envelope found on Demko's body directed Dagger and Sara to the third floor of the Embassy Suites Hotel. Elaborate floral displays were arranged with precision outside the bank of elevators. The carpeting was a thick forest green with an ornate scroll design in cream and navy blue. Two cleaning carts were parked at the far end of the hall.

Dagger and Sara pulled on latex gloves as they approached the door to Room 324. A privacy card was hanging from the doorknob. Dagger pressed his ear to the door.

"Let me," Sara said.

He didn't object. His partner was a shapeshifter. And not only did Sara have the ability to shift into a hawk or a wolf, but she also had the eyesight of the hawk and the hearing and sense of smell of the wolf when in her human form.

"The room is empty."

Dagger slipped the key card in the slot and they cautiously entered. He engaged the safety lock to prevent the cleaning people from inadvertently walking in. They stood at the entrance and made a silent assessment of the room. There was a small bar area and a spacious living room with a desk. A wide doorway led to a sizeable bedroom with a walk-in closet. Sara started with the dresser, checking each of the drawers. She moved to the closet, then stood back, puzzled.

"Dagger." Sara turned from the closet. "He didn't bring anything. There aren't any shirts, suits, not even a suitcase. Who doesn't bring clean underwear?"

"Someone who plans to be in and out quickly."

"So why rent a room?"

Dagger didn't find a toiletry bag nor a toothbrush or toothpaste in the bathroom. The towels were crisply folded on a rack above the toilet as were the washcloths. Since the privacy sign was on the doorknob he knew housekeeping hadn't cleaned. The bathtub didn't show signs of recent use so Demko probably hadn't spent the night.

He walked back to the living area and picked up the remote. "Let's see what kind of charges he's made." He clicked on *MENU* and then *SERVICES*. "The bill claims he checked in three days ago. Meals, dry cleaning, room service, all charged. This doesn't make any sense."

"Is it his bill?"

Dagger glared at her, a look that told her he had been a P.I. for five years and didn't need an uppity nineteen-year-old telling him his job. He scrolled back to the first page. The room had been reserved in the name of Lee Connors. That perfect eyebrow shot up again. One day he was going to peel it right off of her face.

"What about an airline ticket?" Sara rummaged through the garbage can by the bar, then moved to the one by the desk.

He stopped himself from shooting another glare her way and instead unzipped the compartments in a laptop case resting against the leg of the desk. In one of the pockets was a ticket. "Open return in Demko's name. Flew from Minneapolis to Chicago. Probably took a cab or shuttle from the airport. I don't see a rental car receipt." He fumbled through the rest of the compartments but didn't find any car keys or papers. A laptop computer sat on the desk but Dagger didn't want to open it here. Instead he shoved the laptop into the case and zipped the bag closed.

Dagger tossed the bag on the coffee table, then sat down and searched the desk. Stationery and pens were in the top drawer. A phone book lay open on the desk. Dagger fanned through the pages. One of the pages was folded toward the inside in the *P* section of the yellow pages. "Maybe he was ordering pizza." Dagger unfolded the page which listed private investigators. Scribbled in the margin was Dagger's name.

"Is anyone coming? I hear someone coming." Skizzy Borden slammed the tailgate of the truck and scanned the forest with eyes that appeared tethered loosely to his head. Just sixty-eight inches of bone and skin, but Dagger had often said his looks were deceiving. Skizzy was far more deadly than he appeared.

"Ain't nobody coming. Now let's get him the hell out of there." Simon reopened the tailgate of Skizzy's truck. The burly mailman was also far more deadly than he looked. His wife claimed it was his cherub face and twinkling eyes that made him appear more like a black Santa than the Special Ops sharpshooter he was in Nam. He tugged at the blanket-rolled body of Paul Demko and dragged it to the edge of the truck bed. "Grab the other end."

They hefted the rolled blanket off the truck and half dragged, half carried the body through bushes and weeds. The gravel road they had driven on was overgrown with goldenrod and other hayfever-producing plants. The limestone quarry was on the outskirts of town. A half mile wide and a mile long, the quarry had supplied limestone rock and aggregate for a construction company since 1912. It was closed five years ago. What better place to dump a body than in a four hundred foot deep quarry. Once Demko was unrolled from the carpet, the two men stood over him like preachers paying their last respects.

"Sure don't look like a killer," Skizzy said. His wiry gray hair was wrestling itself free from the rubber band. As though on reconnaissance, Skizzy had dressed in camouflage pants and shirt. His eyes scanned the area looking for witnesses, although everyone who knew Skizzy believed he looked for government spies around every bend.

"Let's get a move on." Simon bent down to grab Demko's ankles.

"How's come I always get the heavy part?" Skizzy mumbled. He crouched down to grab the shoulders.

"Guy weighs less than my wife," Simon said.

"You saw that videotape Dagger had. You see how that guy jumped over the fence? That's why I took his jacket." Skizzy had found something unusual about the fabric of Demko's jacket. Although Dagger remained skeptical, Skizzy told him the government was experimenting with a type of synthetic muscle sewn into fabric that adds strength and agility to the wearer. Dagger had told him he was nuts but Skizzy had hacked into enough government project files to know what he was talking about. Skizzy had zoomed in on Demko during his acrobatics and his suit had suddenly puffed up, resembling the Michelin Man. It had deflated just as quickly after he had landed on the ground.

"Hey." Skizzy leaned closer to the body. "Do you hear some ticking? Check for a watch. He might have an expensive Rolex I could sell in the pawn shop."

"Rolex watches don't tick." Simon pulled the shirt cuff back from Demko's wrist. Demko wasn't wearing a watch. He checked the other wrist. "Maybe he has a pocket watch." Simon checked the pants pockets. "Huh. Nothing there either."

"Check the back pockets." Skizzy grabbed a forearm and together they rolled Demko onto his stomach. Dried leaves and dirt clung to Demko's shirt.

Simon shoved his hand into one pocket, then the next. "Nothing."

"I still hear ticking." Skizzy leaned closer to the body. He stared at a spot above the shirt collar. "Is his skin glowing?"

Simon leaned over for a look. There was a red glow flashing under Demko's skin. "I think it says something."

Skizzy squinted, then pulled back a few inches as though readjusting his eyesight. "Fourteen," he announced.

Simon stared, cocked his head. "No, thirteen."

Skizzy studied it closer. "Twelve."

"Eleven."

The two men locked eyes as large as eggs. Both former military, they had a sick feeling what this meant. They didn't waste time trying to rationalize what they were seeing.

"OH, OH, OH," they yelled in unison.

Nine pulsed from under the skin.

"Roll him back, get his shoulders," Simon yelled.

Skizzy fell back on his ass yelling, "Next time you take the head."

"Just start moving." Simon lifted the legs and started dragging the body.

"I'm moving, I'm moving." Skizzy hooked his arms under the shoulders and pulled. "Hurry."

A four foot high rusting wire fence had been mangled from wear, tear, and downed trees. It provided a clear opening into the quarry.

"On the count of three," Simon said.

"Hell, I don't think we have three left."

They made it on two, swinging the body back and forth and sending it through the opening.

"INCOMING!" Skizzy yelled and they hit the dirt as though still in Nam. The explosion shook the ground and rattled their teeth. Skizzy hung onto the grass as though the vibration might tip his body into the quarry.

A metallic sound clanged against a nearby tree and bounced several feet from the two men. They slowly raised their heads, eyes wide in shock. Neither said anything for a few seconds as a pink mist drifted through the air. Their attention turned to the metal object which landed several feet from them. They pushed themselves onto their knees, then stood cautiously, testing the ground. Curiosity got the best of them and they stole a glance over the fence down into the quarry. The pink mist fluttered like a gauze blanket as it spread and settled to the quarry floor.

Simon pinched Skizzy's bony elbow and nodded at the piece of metal that had hit the tree. Stepping closer with a bit more caution, they noticed the metal was the size of a nickel with pieces of bloody flesh attached.

A red light flashed the number *zero.*

3

The gray hawk rested on a cottonwood tree near the limestone quarry, its talons wrapped firmly around the branch. It cocked its head and scanned the area for visitors. It wasn't looking for food since this particular hawk didn't feast. Two-legged mammals were the only ones who should fear this hawk.

A crow diving into the quarry caught the hawk's attention. Sunlight reflected off of the strange color of the hawk's eyes. Although the hawk possessed a visual acuity eight times that of a human's, the color was unusual—a brilliant turquoise, like Caribbean waters.

The hawk pushed off the branch and swooped down into the quarry. With a wingspan of four feet, it circled slowly, letting the wind currents fill its underwing coverts. As it closed in on what remained of the body, the crow scurried away with frantic wing beats. The hawk landed on a boulder several feet from what remained of Paul Demko. Dagger hadn't believed Skizzy and Simon that Demko had a bomb in him. Although Skizzy was on a different planet some days, Simon on the other hand did not contradict Skizzy which made Dagger suspicious.

He was right, Sara said. *There are only bits and pieces of Demko left. Most of the clothing was burned away and what little is left looks singed.*

Whenever Sara shifted, she and Dagger could communicate telepathically. This was something she and her grandmother could do. After her grandmother died, Sara realized she and Dagger could communicate the same way.

Doesn't make any sense. I know he didn't have a bomb on him so it had to be in him. But that should only have separated the head from the body.

It's almost as though Demko were vaporized, Sara said. *There's a spray of blood on the wall. Maybe whatever was triggered in his head released something into the blood stream that was volatile. When the bomb went off, it was like a match touched to a wick and...boom.*

You know, you are hanging around with Skizzy way too much, Dagger replied.

How is Skizzy? I would think something like this would have him building another bunker.

He's too busy with new projects. He can't wait to study the jacket Demko was wearing and he wants to design a new toy to detect microchips. Demko only confirms Skizzy's belief that the government is secretly embedding computer chips in all newborns and every adult who goes in for surgery.

Well, you can assure Simon that what he saw really happened.

He should be here in about fifteen. He's curious about what I might have found on Demko's computer.

Little late for showering, isn't it?" Simon asked, training one eye on the clock above the stove.

Sara's wet hair was pulled to one side and French-braided. Dagger was the only one who knew of her shifting abilities. Shapeshifting was part of Native American mythology. They believed their elders could shift into various animal forms to spy on their enemies. Sara had learned of her abilities at the age of six. According to tradition, there can be no witnesses to her shifting. To avoid exposure, anyone who dares to view her shifting is killed by the wolf. Dagger had saved the wolf's life which is what protects him since he had witnessed Sara's shifting. But he also secretly believed the black leather cord necklace with the silver pendant in the shape of a wolf's head Sara's grandmother had given him also had something to do with protection.

"I was gardening." Sara pulled a pitcher from the refrigerator. "Iced tea, Simon?"

Simon raised his cup. "I need some caffeine."

Dagger stood at the kitchen counter, Demko's laptop computer in front of him. He wasn't as computer savvy as Skizzy and knew the computer would eventually be given to the squirrelly guy.

"Find anything yet?" Sara asked.

"Yeah. A bunch of religious crap that doesn't fit Demko's profile. Skizzy thinks the files might be encrypted so he gave me a decryption program."

Simon rubbed a beefy hand across his face. "You know, I used to think that guy was screwy, but after this morning." He shrugged and shook his head. "Skizzy's beginning to look like the sane one here. What does that say about the rest of us?"

Sara took out a package of cut vegetables and placed them in a colander to rinse. Einstein's squawking was loud and insistent. Just like a two-year-old, he needed new toys to keep him occupied and a variety of foods to satiate him. Brazil nuts and cheese curls were also favorites of his. A grateful client who had been short on funds had given Einstein to Dagger as payment. Dagger wasn't a dog or cat person, much less a bird lover. But Einstein proved to have a photographic memory which came in handy when Dagger was too lazy to look up phone numbers or to write them down.

Sara carried the bowl of vegetables to the aviary. "Hungry, Einstein?" The macaw bobbed its head up and down. "How about outside? Want to go outside?"

Sara opened a second door that led to a screened enclosure. It had several perches at different heights and braided rope toys. They didn't let Einstein out into the open unless either she or Dagger was there to keep an eye on him. His wings were not clipped and there were too many plants in the surrounding acres which were poisonous to macaws.

Sara opened the door to the screened enclosure and rattled the bowl of vegetables. "Come on, Einstein." The scarlet macaw flew to one of the perches and flapped his wings. Sara poured the vegetables into a bowl by the perch. "You be good, okay?"

Einstein belted out another loud screech and settled down on the perch. He trained one yellow-ringed eye on her, then took a stab at her braided hair.

"No!" She shook the rope braid near his perch. "That is your braid, not my hair."

She left him in the screened enclosure and walked back through the aviary, closing both the grated door and the soundproof door.

"You spoil him," Dagger said.

"Someone has to."

"When is that program supposed to kick in?" Simon asked. "We gotta find out about this guy. People just don't blow up. And what was he doing here? Was he supposed to put you in a bear hug and take you with him? How many people have you pissed off?"

Dagger turned from the computer and glared at Simon. "In my estimation? Not enough."

"Simon's right," Sara said. "What if he was meant to explode here in this house? Are you sure you don't recognize him?"

"Never seen him before and I have a pretty good memory for faces."

A square box appeared on the computer screen announcing that the decryption was complete. Dagger clicked OPEN and a dossier appeared on the screen.

Sara asked, "Who's that?"

Simon hobbled over to where they stood. The screen revealed a man in his fifties, light brown hair abundantly sprinkled with gray. Hazel eyes appeared lively and his smile was warm and genuine. The man wore a priest's collar and scarlet sash. The dossier identified him as Cardinal Michael Esrey. He was recently appointed to a position at the Vatican.

"Cardinal Michael Esrey is scheduled to give a speech this Saturday at a conference of Northwest Indiana priests at the Ritz Carlton." Dagger took a step back and folded his arms across his chest. He studied the dossier for several minutes then shook his head. "That can't be right. This guy is dead."

Sara asked, "Is it a current bio?"

"From last week. Maybe Demko was in town to assassinate the cardinal but believe me, Esrey is dead."

"You see his picture right there," Simon argued. "How can you be so sure he's dead?"

"Because." Dagger pressed the heels of his hands to his eyes. Some days he felt like his entire life was a nightmare. "I killed him five years ago."

Simon lifted his cup of coffee. "Got anything to put in this, Sara? Dagger just told me he killed the Pope. I need something a lot stronger than coffee."

"He isn't the Pope," Dagger said. "He wasn't even a priest when I killed him." Dagger braced his arms against the counter and studied the monitor. "At least, I don't think he was."

Sara and Simon exchanged knowing looks across the table. It was Simon who asked the obvious.

"Thought you said you have a great memory. Maybe he just looks like someone you know." Simon took the bottle of whiskey from Sara and added a healthy dose to his coffee. "They say everyone has a double."

"I'm still on the part where you killed him five years ago." Sara's remark hung in the air like an accusation. With Sara there had to always be a good reason for his actions. Her way again of being his conscience. He had always thought her grandmother entrusted him to protect her granddaughter but Sara once commented, "Did you ever stop to think that maybe Grandmother meant for me to protect you?" Those words had proven true on more than one occasion.

Dagger closed his eyes and tried to picture the man, details about his life, where they were when Dagger had killed him. He opened his eyes and studied the picture. "I'm drawing a blank here."

"There been that many that they all blend together?" Simon asked.

Dagger shot his friend a look of irritation. He hated to admit it but maybe there were too many fuzzy areas in his brain. He had memories of his childhood, school, college, military. He could describe places he had visited, people he had met. But if he were pressed to give dates and names, he wasn't sure he could do it. And why was he so convinced he had killed the cardinal but knew so little about why and when?

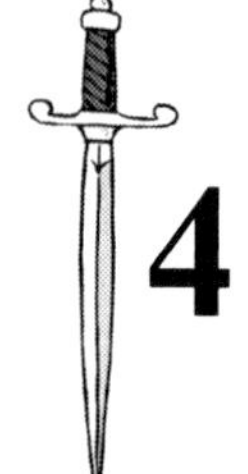

4

Dagger was up early the next morning. Tai Chi out on the deck at six, then a round with the punching bag in the garage until seven. He shaved but it was useless because he always had a five o'clock shadow. With his dark hair, dark eyes, and danger oozing from every pore in his body, it was no wonder he was pulled aside at airports.

In his eyes the world was black and white and the only gray areas you could find were in his bedroom. Gray and black were the colors he lived in and dressed in. Not only did Sara add beauty to his life but she also added color. It was her house so she could pink it up anyway she wanted. There was pink and mauve in the living room, the Florida room, her bedroom. But his bedroom was his domain and it bled chrome, black, and gray.

One wall in his bedroom was mirrored and directly in back of the gym equipment. But the wall was deceiving. Dagger flipped open the lid on a fake thermostat and punched in a code. A door in the wall popped open. Dagger entered a sizeable vault which housed his arsenal, a printing machine that had been known to spit out counterfeit checks on more than one occasion, and a filing cabinet containing paper for such counterfeit purposes. There were also bundles of cash, not counterfeit.

Across from the filing cabinet was a table. Above the table a map lit up with blue lights indicating major towns. But it was the two blinking red lights orbiting the globe that Dagger was interested in. Every day he checked to see if the satellites had shifted their locations. Five years ago there had been just one satellite, one that Dagger had been instrumental in helping plummet from the sky. But within five years BettaTec had managed to install two satellites. These were state of the art.

The government thought they were communication satellites. Dagger knew better. One red light stayed on a trajectory over the Northern Hemisphere. The second red light covered the Southern Hemisphere.

Ever since he saw his name handwritten in the margin of the phone book at the Embassy Suites the first thought that came to Dagger's mind was BettaTec. Had they finally located him? But they couldn't have. Looking at it logically, he had covered his tracks too well. Demko had wanted to hire him, not kill him…at first. Why did it change? He tried to think back to something Dagger had said or did that made Demko snap. Or was Demko just trying to confirm his identity? Dagger's first inclination was to pick up and run. If he stayed on the move, he could keep one step ahead of them. But he was so damn tired of running.

"Dagger?" Sara poked her head in the doorway. "Padre's here."

Sara plied Padre with coffee and cake while Dagger tried to mentally tick through the list of reasons why Cedar Point's top detective decided to pay him a visit. Yes, Padre was a friend but Padre only came to chat or meet him for a beer after working hours. And usually it was because Padre needed his help. Had someone witnessed Simon and Skizzy dumping the body in the quarry?

It was his early years in the seminary that gave Sergeant Jerry Martinez the nickname of Padre. He had felt his time could be better spent in law enforcement making sure people followed the Ten Commandments and received their just punishment rather than simply preaching them. Padre had what he called a high forehead. He would never say he had a receding hairline. Just shy of five foot ten, Padre was one sonofabitch you never dared to cross. Criminals had learned that the hard way. His quick, friendly smile gave suspects the impression he was their friend. Then he swept in for the kill. Padre could smell a lie like bottle flies could smell rotting flesh. He also believed in keeping his friends close and his enemies closer which is why Dagger felt Padre asked for his assistance in certain cases. Dagger not only looked dangerous but he also looked like someone who operated just below the radar. Padre had zeroed in on him not long after Dagger arrived in town.

Padre shoved a piece of gum in his mouth and started chomping and mashing it to death.

"Quit smoking again?" Dagger always knew when Padre was trying to cut down. His gum wrappers increased. He pulled a mug from the cabinet and poured himself a cup of coffee.

Sara busied herself emptying the dishwasher. "I'll be out of your hair as soon as I finish."

"Don't leave on my account, Sara. Matter of fact, you might be able to clear up a few things."

"So this is an official visit." Dagger smiled at the detective. "And here I thought you missed us." He raked his collar-length hair back into a ponytail and wrapped a band around it.

"Sara I definitely miss. But you?"

"I'm deeply hurt." Dagger actually had a fondness for the cop. They had been in a number of scrapes together and Padre was always watching his back. But he didn't doubt for a minute that Padre would toss the book at him if he thought he were guilty of something. Padre was a by-the-book cop. Strange friend for a guy who had tossed out the book years ago.

"Do you know a guy by the name of Lee Connors?"

"Should I?"

"He gave our department a call a couple days ago asking if we could recommend a private detective. I gave him your name. Course, I respect your privacy and didn't give him your address. When I asked him for his number so you could call him, he hung up."

Dagger took a sip of coffee then grabbed the carafe and

refilled their cups. "Guess I should thank you. Did he give any hint what he wanted?" He gave himself a mental pat on the back for ripping out the phone book page with his name scribbled on it in Connors' hotel room.

"I was hoping you could tell me." Padre gave that steely eyed glare Dagger had seen so many times.

Dagger shrugged. "Never saw him."

Sara pulled knives from the washer and dried them with a towel before placing them in the knife holder. Her gaze drifted from Dagger to Padre then back to Dagger.

"Hmmmm." Padre snapped the gum like a truck stop waitress. "What if I told you the cab company has a record of dropping off Mister Connors on your doorstep?"

Shit.

"Oh," Sara said and smiled shyly. "Was that him?" She dried her hands on the towel and said, "I told him Dagger wouldn't be home for a couple hours. He never said who he was, didn't want to wait, and then he left."

"He walked back to town?"

"I offered to call a cab but he had his phone on him and said he would call. He never got inside the gate. Being here all alone I didn't want to let him in."

"No, no. Of course not. Unfortunately, the cab company doesn't have a record of picking him back up."

"Maybe he hitched a ride," Dagger offered.

"Hmmmm." Padre wadded the used gum in an empty wrapper and pulled out a fresh stick. "And this was yesterday?"

"In the morning." Sara went back to emptying the dishwasher.

"Well then." Padre thanked them for the coffee and cake and stood. He started for the door then stopped, one finger raised. "There's just one problem with that story."

"What's that?" Dagger noticed the sound of plates hitting the counter had ceased. He stood to walk Padre out, to keep the cop from zeroing in on Sara.

"Some airport workers found Connors' body stuffed in the trunk of his rental car."

Sara and Dagger both stared at Padre, waiting for the proverbial other shoe to drop.

"He had been dead for two days." Padre chewed, looked from Dagger to Sara and smiled. "Did he look dead to you?"

"Do you have his picture?" Sara walked over to Padre. He handed her what looked like an enlarged drivers license photo.

"Seems to me, if he had a rental car he would have driven himself here," Padre pointed out. "And, number two, how can a dead man appear on your doorstep?"

"That's not the man I saw on the monitor at the gate," Sara said. "Doesn't look anything like him."

Dagger looked at the photo of Lee Connors. He was hefty, a middleweight contender with a broad face and flattened nose. "I've never seen him before." And he hadn't. It definitely wasn't the guy who had died on their living room floor.

Padre tucked the photo back inside his jacket pocket. "I'd appreciate it, Sara, if you could stop by the precinct sometime today and give our sketch artist a description of the guy."

"Is it necessary to involve Sara?" Last thing Dagger wanted was to have a sketch of Demko plastered on the evening news so whoever had sent him would know he hadn't completed his assignment. That could bring all kinds of people into town.

"Got a problem with that?" Padre looked from Dagger to Sara. "Or do you have something to hide?"

Dagger smiled. "Sure, Padre. The guy threatened me, I killed him and had Skizzy dump the body in the limestone quarry, but not before some bomb planted in the guy's neck blew his head off."

Padre threw back his head and roared, a loud, boisterous

bellow. “Oh, Dagger. Always the comic.” He slowly ran his hand from his forehead down to his chin, the smile quickly fading as if his hand were doing the facial transformation. “I’m not amused.”

5

"The forehead was a little higher," Sara instructed the artist. Jimmy Cho pounded the keyboard, a lock of hair falling across his forehead. Sara glanced over her shoulder at Dagger. "You don't have to hover. You didn't even need to come."

Jimmy chuckled at that comment. "If you were my girl, do you think I would let you walk in here alone?" He jutted his chin toward the sea of desks surrounding them. All work had stopped. Men were seated at the desks or perched with one cheek on their desktops, all eyes on Sara. The yellow floral dress she wore brought out the bronze color of her skin. Her dark hair shined with a multitude of sun-streaked highlights.

"How sweet." Sara smiled at her admirers.

Dagger let out a loud huff. "Can we get on with it?"

"I can handle myself, Dagger."

"That's why I came." He nodded toward the hungry males. "To protect them from you."

Jimmy laughed but when he saw that neither Sara nor Dagger was laughing, his laughter faded.

"HEY!" Padre bellowed from his doorway. "Isn't anyone working? Have all crimes been solved? All case files worked?"

The detectives scurried back to their chairs and started making calls or banging on their keyboards.

"Yes, that looks just like him," Sara announced. The computer monitor showed a man with thinning hair, a nose slightly bent, eyes a soft brown.

Padre stared at the screen, then folded his arms. "Sara, that's me."

Sara checked the screen. "You think so?" She looked at

Dagger. "Does that look like Padre?"

"Nah. Padre has less hair."

"He was wearing sunglasses so I'm not sure of his eye color," Sara clarified. "Jimmy put in whatever color he wanted. And I only saw the face briefly on the monitor so I'm sorry I don't remember more distinct features."

Padre was seething. Dagger could tell by the way his jaws were clenched.

"I want to see your surveillance tapes. And don't tell me, Dagger, that you didn't save them."

"I didn't save them." Dagger gave a hapless shrug. "Sorry."

Padre pointed toward a doorway. "In my office. Both of you."

"Did you want me to print this out?" Jimmy asked. His question was met with an icy glare. "Okay. Maybe I'll just save it."

"Sit," Padre ordered. He closed the office door saying, "Let me get this straight. Dagger, you weren't home when this man showed up at the gate. Sara, you thought he looked like me." He sank onto the chair behind his desk and slowly rocked for a full minute while studying them. Finally, he leaned forward and clasped his hands on the desk. "Let me tell you what I think happened. This guy kills Connors, maybe for the use of his room. Robbery wasn't a motive because Connors had his wallet on him. So maybe he needed a place to hide out, use the hotel phone. Although missy here says he had a cell phone and was going to call his own cab."

"Did you trace the cell calls from that…?"

Padre glared at Dagger. "Did I ask you to speak?" He waited through several seconds of silence. "I think my only link to Connors' killer is through you." He looked directly at Dagger. "Now, I can understand you fudging the truth a little, Dagger. But I would have never believed that you would manipulate this sweet, innocent woman to lie for you. That is unconscionable."

"I didn't lie, Padre." Sara's voice didn't display hurt as much as anger. Instinctively her right hand found its way to her mouth and she started chewing on a knuckle, a nervous habit she had acquired since dipping her toes outside of the reservation land. "He did look a little like you in the few seconds I had to look at him. He wasn't much taller than the monitor so he didn't have to bend down to speak into it. That would make him around your height, maybe a couple inches shorter. I didn't see any gray hair but the receding hairline is deceiving. He could be coloring his hair but his face wasn't that lined, not like…"

Padre's raised eyebrows dared her to comment on his age.

Dagger held up a finger. "Can I talk now?"

Padre dragged his eyes from Sara to Dagger.

"What about the cameras at the hotel and the airport parking garage? Besides, the cab company could have lied. Your man could have driven Connors' car with the body in the trunk over to my place, then driven to the airport to dump the car."

Padre punched the intercom on the phone. "I already have a call in for those tapes." When the intercom was answered, Padre told Jimmy, "You can print out a copy of that sketch now." He punched the intercom off just as the phone rang. Picking up the receiver, he barked out, "Martinez…yeah, Chief." Padre leaned back in his chair, the receiver pressed to his ear. His eyes studied the ceiling as he listened. "We told the cardinal's people we'd give him a police escort from the airport to the hotel. They are hiring their own bodyguards for the event…yeah…who's going to bother a cardinal? It's not like the Pope is visiting…yeah… okay…I'm on it." Padre hung up with a shake of his head. "Chief is expecting demonstrators against pedophile priests. Guess some people don't feel the church is doing enough." Padre saw Jimmy through the glass partition and waved him in.

"I made two copies." Jimmy placed the computer sketch on

the desk. "I added sunglasses."

Sara leaned over for a closer look. "Yes, that looks just like him."

Padre studied the image for a few seconds, pressed his lips in disgust, then pulled out an identical pair of sunglasses from his pocket. "Gee, they look just like mine." He glared at his visitors. "Now get out of here. All of you."

Dagger gunned the Lincoln Navigator from the parking lot. He punched the hands-free phone and listened to the phone ring three times, five times, seven times. "Come on, Skizzy."

"Hey, I'm busy here." Skizzy's voice blared from the speaker.

"Just tell me you decrypted the guy's Emails." On their way to the police station, Dagger had dropped off Demko's computer at Skizzy's shop.

"Sure, and I built a high-rise in my spare time. This one ain't so easy. I may have to hack into one of the anagrams to get some assistance."

"FBI, CIA, NSA, I don't care which anagram you hack into, just get me something." Dagger punched the END button. "I don't like the fact that this guy was looking for me."

"Who else would have given out our address?" Sara asked. "If Padre claims he didn't and you aren't listed in the phone book, who else besides Simon and Skizzy?"

Dagger thought about that for several seconds, then swung a U-turn on a busy downtown street eliciting numerous horn blasts.

The Hideaway was a shot-and-beer joint. Dagger had lived in a small apartment above the bar when he first arrived in town. He had operated his P.I. business out of that apartment and it was where he had first met Sara. She had walked in with information about the murder of an undercover cop. At the time he didn't know how she obtained her information, didn't know about her unique abilities, but he followed up on her leads and discovered a jewelry and art theft ring based inside the Cedar Point Police Department. In the melee, a wolf had been injured, its leg shot off. And just as Dagger was preparing to put a bullet in the wolf's head to end its misery, the strangest thing happened. Instead of a wolf, what was lying at his feet was Sara. To say he was shocked was putting it mildly. But his biggest shock came later as Sara lay on her grandmother's bed. Sara's leg had grown back.

Dagger fingered his black cord necklace. He could feel the turquoise stones that served as the eyes in the wolf head pendant and remembered the filmy eyes of Ada, Sara's grandmother who had looked more like a great-great-grandmother. She had been the only family Sara had left and seemed relieved that someone else knew of Sara's gift. Ada promptly died the next day leaving the necklace and a note pleading for Dagger to watch out for her granddaughter, a young woman who had barely left the confines of their reservation land, and was as much afraid of humans as the wolf and hawk were. Dagger had changed all that. Sara now knew self-defense and could shoot a gun as well as he could.

"What are you smiling at?" Sara asked, her smile radiating from the passenger seat.

"Just wondering how many more gray hairs we gave Padre." He parked the Navigator at the curb and they slammed out of the vehicle.

The Hideaway smelled of beer and sweat. If the wood floor ever got a washing it would probably disintegrate. Toby Keith's voice oozed from the juke box talking about loving this bar. Two men swaying at the end of the chipped and bruised bar were bellowing along with Toby. Men playing pool stopped to leer at Sara, their cue sticks hovering over the pool table.

"Well, well. Slumming, Dagger?" Casey stood behind the

bar looking more like a bouncer gone to seed. What might have once been a muscular forty-eight-inch chest had given way to beer and gravity and hung over his belt like yeast-raised bread.

"Your place a slum? Why, it's listed at the Visitors' Bureau as one of the top ten places to see in Cedar Point."

"Ha ha." Casey turned his attention to Sara. There were enough gaps in his teeth to release a whistle every time he breathed. He made a futile attempt at pulling down his Chicago Cubs tee shirt but it didn't help to hide his gut. Tattoos resembling barbed wire circled each of his flabby biceps.

"Who's this? Thought you were engaged to the blonde bitch."

"That ended a long time ago. This is Sara Morningsky. She's my business partner."

Casey laughed. "That what they call them these days?"

"Excuse me?" Sara's right eyebrow jutted sharply. Faster than the bar owner could blink, Sara reached into her purse and pulled out a Kel-Tec P32. "Want to clarify that?"

Casey's eyes appeared crossed as they focused on the weapon. He slowly raised his hands. The men in the bar stopped crooning. Even Toby Keith got the hint as his song ended.

"Sorry. No harm intended. Just having a little fun is all." Casey looked to Dagger. "Can I lower my hands now?"

"Play nice, Sara," Dagger said.

Sara slipped the gun back into her purse.

"Need to ask you a few questions." Dagger moved to the end of the bar, out of ear shot of the other patrons. Sara and Casey followed. "Anyone come in here recently asking about me?"

The big man's eyes grew and a small teletype appeared to play back in his head. It looked as though he were weighing his options – lie and save his skin or tell the truth and walk away with just a few broken bones. Seeing that Sara had slipped her hand back into her purse, he opted for truth.

"Yeah, couple days ago. Looked like an insurance salesman, but a dangerous insurance salesman. Something about his eyes. You just happened to be picking up your cleaning down the street. I pointed out your car," he said, looking nervously at Sara's purse, "and told him he could probably catch you there if he hurried. Did he?"

Dagger shook his head. Demko probably followed him home and decided on a surprise visit rather than approaching him in public. Which means he probably was using Connors' rental car before disposing of the car with Connors' decomposing body in the trunk.

Dagger smiled at the nervous giant. "Guess you can live another day." He led Sara out of the bar whispering, "That thing loaded?"

Sara winced. "Forgot."

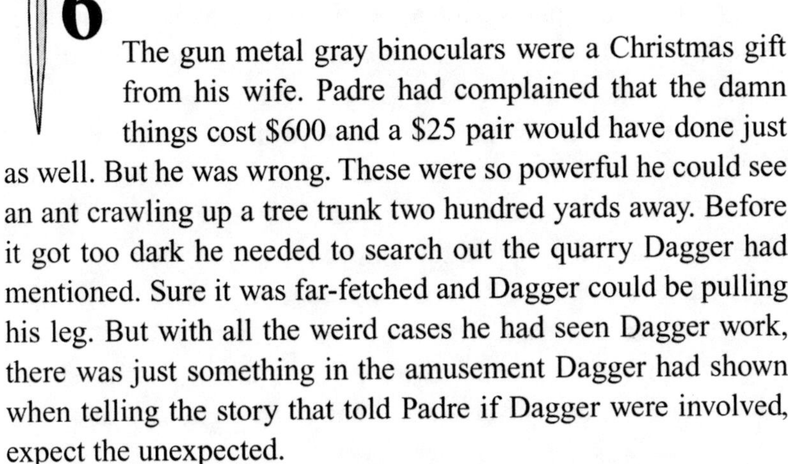

6

The gun metal gray binoculars were a Christmas gift from his wife. Padre had complained that the damn things cost $600 and a $25 pair would have done just as well. But he was wrong. These were so powerful he could see an ant crawling up a tree trunk two hundred yards away. Before it got too dark he needed to search out the quarry Dagger had mentioned. Sure it was far-fetched and Dagger could be pulling his leg. But with all the weird cases he had seen Dagger work, there was just something in the amusement Dagger had shown when telling the story that told Padre if Dagger were involved, expect the unexpected.

The closed quarry dominated the southeast side of town. Padre had been crouched in the weeds searching the area to make sure he was alone. The gravel roads into the property were grown over. So far he hadn't seen any bird watchers or bikers or teens engaged in nefarious activities.

He moved closer to the fence, then trained the binoculars on the floor of the quarry. Small pebbles appeared as huge boulders through the lens. Small bones sprang in front of the lens of the binoculars. Padre figured they were the remains of rabbits and other small animals who had inadvertently fallen into the quarry. A crow cawed from a branch overhead, sending a chill down Padre's spine. He didn't care too much for being out in the woods even in daylight. Ever since the bizarre *Friday the Thirteenth* case he worked with Dagger he hadn't been able to go into the forest at night without an entire arsenal on him. Back then, even an arsenal hadn't helped.

The sun slowly crept across the sky. Padre returned his attention to the floor of the quarry. If Dagger's humor contained one ounce of truth, a body tossed into the quarry would be close to the edge. He swept the floor below him, seeing more small bones, bird wings, a few beer cans. Padre had grown up several miles from the quarry and as a kid remembered his mother yelling every time they dynamite-blasted the rock. All of her knickknacks would fall off the glass shelves.

The lens skimmed the area across from where he sat. Still nothing that looked like a body. There were tires, charred remains of what looked like a car, scrap metal of some type, more bones, shoes…wait. Padre zipped the binoculars back to the bones. He lowered the binoculars to view the area with the naked eye, then back to the binoculars. The bones were fragments but looked larger than rodent bones. Slowly he returned to the shoes, adjusted the focus. The shoes still had socks in them…and feet.

"Tell me again what I'm doing here at eight o'clock at night with my gear and my motorcycle." Luther Jamison pulled the helmet from his head. His close-cropped Afro fit his small frame. There was barely any gray in his hair or lines on his face yet he was pushing sixty.

Padre worked the lock picks in the rusted padlock. He could just as easily have cut the chain but that might encourage others to travel the gravel road down to the floor of the pit. Padre pointed with his chin to the binoculars. "Check it out. Just about two o'clock on the floor of the quarry."

Luther peered through the binoculars and swept down to the approximate area. Puzzled, he adjusted them again, glared at the target, then lowered the binoculars. "This what I think it is?"

"Yep. Shoes and lots of bone fragments. We need to gather what we can and get them back to your lab."

The lock pick finally did its magic. Padre jerked the stubborn lock open and threaded the chain off the gate. "You wouldn't believe it if I told you."

"Huh. That means Chase Dagger is involved." Luther climbed on his bike and nodded for Padre to do likewise. He fired up the engine and tore down the gravel road.

Padre hung on for dear life as the tires slipped and jerked on the gravel. He made a sign of the cross when they finally hit bottom. "Sweet Mary and Joseph. You trying to kill me?"

Luther just smiled, pulled his kit from the back of the bike and moved closer to the battered shoes. He grabbed his recorder, then stopped. "This official?"

"Not yet."

Luther turned off the recorder and picked up his camera. "I need these for posterity. Cases you dump in my lap always make for great plots in the mystery series I'm planning to write about a highly intelligent medical examiner."

"Yeah, you and me both."

Padre waited as Luther snapped pictures and snorted, shook his head, sighed. He walked in a wide circle. There were pieces of bone, clothing, and dried blood spread over a four-hundred-square-foot area. It hadn't rained in days so Padre was sure the rust colored walls were from the victim's blood which told Padre this guy did explode on his way down. He pressed fingertips to his temples and mumbled, "Dagger, I'm going to kill you." A small voice he called his skeptical angel said, "Wait for proof. This may have nothing to do with Dagger."

Once he was done snapping pictures, Luther started to collect the fragments from the outer edges and work his way in. "Hope we have enough daylight left."

"Let me give you a hand so we can move this along." Padre snapped on latex gloves.

"I remember back in 1994 they discovered a meteorite in this place." Luther lifted one of the shoes and sniffed. "It weighed about a thousand pounds and thought to be over four billion years old." He set the shoe in a paper bag saying, "Been dead no more than a day." He sniffed again.

Padre felt his dinner rise as he looked at the bone and muscles jutting from the shoe. The top of the sock had been burned away.

"Anyway, they believe the meteorite hit the Earth about four hundred million years ago and landed in the quarry when it was a coral reef. And this is actually three quarries connected by tunnels. In its heyday it produced seven million tons of rock products annually."

"Thanks for the lesson. Maybe it will come in handy if I'm ever on *Jeopardy*."

Luther picked up pieces of cloth and dropped them in the bag. "Fabric is singed. This guy went up like a torch but the skin isn't black. What the hell?" He studied the surrounding area. "Where's the head?"

Padre shrugged and pointed. "There…there…and there."

The man opened the door and listened. The conference call had started so the representatives from area parishes should be busy for a while. He closed the door then sat at the conference table, the laptop fired up and ready to go. After inserting the flash drive, he waited for the prompts, clicked on EXPLORE and opened DRIVE E. It didn't take long for the detailed list of documents to appear. He opened the first document. Puzzled, he opened several more. Curse words that would have made a longshoreman blush flew from his mouth. Everything was encrypted.

7

"PLEASE MISTER POSTMAN. AWWWKK." Einstein spread his scarlet and royal blue wings as he tap danced on the perch.

"Mornin', Einstein." Simon reached out a hand to Einstein but drew it back right as Einstein snapped at him. Simon roared with laughter.

Dagger lowered the paper and glared at the macaw. "Behave yourself, Einstein. He's one of the friendly guests. We need to keep him around."

Einstein mimicked Simon's laugh which made Simon laugh even harder. The macaw flew up to the catwalk that dissected the living room. Stairs along one wall led up to Sara's bedroom. The catwalk branched out from her door and led to a wall of windows with a picturesque view of their property.

Simon hobbled to the front door and admired the scenery. Sara was watering the flower baskets hanging on the porch. Every time she raised the hose, she exposed more of her tan midrift.

"Um ummmm. Such a lovely thing. One of these days, that young Tyler is going to snatch her right out from under your nose."

Sara had met Nick Tyler during one of her early cases with Dagger. The Tyler family was one of the richest in the Midwest. Women followed Nick around slipping him their phone numbers. He had Hollywood good looks, was currently modeling in Europe, had gone to college in Europe, and had been so taken with Sara that when back in the states, the two were inseparable.

"He's gay."

"Yeah. You wish."

Dagger shrugged. "He's a model, spends a lot of time in

Europe where daddy won't catch wind of his, uh, male friends, and the only reason he squires Sara around is to try to prove to the world that he's all man."

"Squire?" Simon hefted his body onto the loveseat. "No one squires anymore. They hook up. Besides, don't you think those foreign paparazzi would have a field day plastering his face on their front pages? Everyone knows his every move. Except you." Simon pointed a beefy finger at him. "Like I said. One day you are going to wake up and she's going to be picking out wedding gowns."

Dagger folded the paper and tossed it aside. "What have you got for me?"

"Common sense."

"Businesswise."

Einstein swooped back to the perch by Dagger's desk. He bobbed his head as though watching Sara through the window, then belted out a loud screech that had Simon covering his ears. Simon gave up and hobbled out to the kitchen.

Dagger grabbed a Brazil nut from the top drawer of his desk. "Want to go outside, Einstein?" The macaw bobbed his head up and down. "This way." He led Einstein back to the aviary and through the far door to the screened enclosure. Once the macaw was settled, Dagger gave him the Brazil nut.

Simon was cutting himself a piece of coffee cake when Dagger walked in. "Can't talk on an empty stomach," Simon said.

"Oh, hell. You are more trouble than…"

"Hey, no way to talk to a guy who cleans up your messes." Simon slapped the cake on a plate and hobbled over to the kitchen table. Sunlight streamed in through the windows, reflecting off of the chrome and granite counters and fixtures. "Speaking of messes, you figure out how that guy ended up with a bomb in his neck?"

"The guy is unknown and so far no one misses him." Dagger grabbed the carafe of coffee and two cups and set them on the table. "Skizzy has been running the guy's prints through AFIS but so far he hasn't had a hit."

"So you don't know how he knew Cardinal Esrey or why he had him in his crosshairs?"

"Not yet."

Simon reached into his back pocket and pulled out a page from the Society section of the local newspaper. "Thought you might find this interesting, could get yourself an invite." He tossed the page across the table. "The Tyler and Monroe families are hosting a dinner for Cardinal Esrey at the Tyler estate."

Monroe was another of the few elite families in Cedar Point. Leyton Monroe owned a multitude of newspapers across the country including Cedar Point's Daily Herald. Sheila, Dagger's former fiancée, was his daughter. The safest thing would be to go with Sara. Not that he didn't trust himself around his ex, but Sheila usually behaved herself when Sara was with him. Unfortunately, he had other plans for Sara. While the cardinal was busy at the Tyler's and Dagger was there to keep an eye on him, Sara could search the cardinal's hotel room.

Luther and Padre picked up burgers from a drive-through and parked in the cool shade of the stacked parking garage at the shopping mall. Here they could be away from the prying eyes and ears of fellow workers.

"DNA?" Padre asked.

"That will take a few days. Blood is B positive, got some intact fingers." Luther handed Padre a report with prints from four of the fingers. "No scars or markings on any of the slivers of remains we found. No abnormalities in the bones or skull fragments. Wore silk socks." Luther smiled. "Light blue."

Padre glared at the medical examiner as he sipped soda through a straw. "I want to hear how he blew up."

"If it was a bomb, as you say, and only in the neck, as you say, then he would have only lost his head. We should have found an intact torso. I haven't a clue how it was done, maybe some explosive liquid in his pocket. Maybe he set himself on fire. Either way, his entire body appeared to vaporize. But, again, don't ask me how that is possible. It's a little too high tech for me."

Padre chewed his burger slowly. There was a lot of truth to the saying that some people can't think and chew at the same time. High tech was synonymous with Dagger. "You think someone shot him with some type of vaporizer gun? Saw that on *CSI*. Makes more sense, right?"

Luther wadded up the empty burger wrapper and tossed it in a bag. "Like I said, little too high tech for me but I'm working on it. It's a little tough to make phone calls and ask people. They will want to know the whys and the wherefores. Only thing I know is I would never want to meet this guy's boss. He knows how to keep his people in line."

"Find any kind of housing or metal that might have been in or on his body?"

Luther shook his head no. "Not in the bits and pieces we found. We can always go back down there and have another look around."

"No, thanks. I'm done deep-sea diving." Padre gathered up the empty containers and handed them to Luther. As the medical examiner walked over to a trash container, Padre thought, *Damnit, Dagger. What the hell are you into this time?*

Sara set the phone down. "I feel really stupid, Dagger. They will know something is up. I never call Nick."

"Never?"

"No. I'm not a love-sick puppy who follows him around like the rest of the women."

Dagger was glad to hear that. Plan B. "Guess I could just call Sheila and ask if she needs a date." He watched for her reaction. Not a hint of jealousy there. Maybe Sara didn't care. Then he saw her right eyebrow twitch.

"Won't it be a little crowded with Detective Spagnola sitting on one side of her?"

"Oh, is she still dating him?"

Joe Spagnola was a homicide detective Sheila had latched onto after she and Dagger had broken up. Dagger didn't follow Sheila's every move but as far as he knew they were still dating.

The phone rang and the caller negated any need for Dagger to find a creative way to wrestle an invite to the cardinal's dinner.

"Dagger, Robert Tyler here." The voice was broadcaster-smooth and refined.

"Mister Tyler. How is everyone?"

Dagger had helped out the Tyler family during a very public case involving his daughter-in-law, the murder of Tyler's very young second wife, and stolen diamonds. It had gotten messy pretty fast and revealed a gambling problem his oldest son had as well as his youngest son's drinking problem. Now it was just the three men, one grandson, and Lily, the housekeeper.

"Just fine," Robert replied. "What about you?"

"Oh, it's just one explosive thing after another."

Sara rolled her eyes.

"Not sure if you read in the paper that we are hosting a dinner for Cardinal Esrey," Robert explained. "Although I hired security at the doors and the parking lot, I thought having you at the dinner table could add some closer security for the cardinal without him being aware of it. Are you free Friday night? You could bring Sara."

"Unfortunately, Sara isn't available Friday night but I would be pleased to join the dinner party."

Sara motioned to herself, her face revealing hurt and anger.

"What time would you like me there?"

"Cocktails are at six. Come around five and we can catch up on old times."

"See you then." Dagger hung up with a smile until he noticed Sara's stance, arms folded tightly across her waist, eyes drilling him with a laser stare. "I have other plans for you."

"What? Eating a grilled cheese while you have lobster and filet?"

"You don't eat red meat. What I want you to do is get into the cardinal's hotel suite. Find one of the maid outfits, have a look around, plant some bugs."

"Hmmm. That certainly sounds more interesting than listening to Sheila all night. What if he has a guard outside the room who insists on following me into the suite?"

"Then you may have to get creative." Dagger winked.

The printer at Dagger's desk started humming.

"Yo, Dagger." Skizzy's voice bellowed from the computer speakers.

"What did you find?"

"Decrypted a couple Emails in the laptop. It used a very old cipher code created by the Greeks. They used something called a Polybius Square that kinda looks like a five-by-five checkerboard. Number it one through five at the top, same on the side, then run your alphabet A through Z…"

"Break it down, Skizzy. I'm aging as we speak."

"Some lady by the name of Connie sent Emails detailing Cardinal Esrey's travel plans, plane, hotel, dates, times. An Email from Demko to Connie states the amount of security planned for the cardinal and asks how he should proceed. They tell him to hire someone local to get close, someone who would be a dupe.

Use and dispose is how they termed it."

"Use and dispose." Dagger didn't like the sound of that. "Was Demko supposed to report in?"

"His last communication was what I just said. He never reported to them whether he found anyone. There wasn't a mention of your name. But obviously when he didn't report in, it must have made them suspicious."

"Did they give a deadline?"

"He was supposed to report in by ten in the morning. Instead I showed him booking a flight to Vancouver."

Dagger thought about that for a few seconds. Obviously someone was monitoring Demko's whereabouts. Would that someone know Demko had been at Sara's house? "It's a little risky eliminating their man just because he hadn't reported in. What if he had been in the middle of a shopping center?"

"Coulda been a timer, you know, so much time after he expired. Unless they were watching him," Skizzy said. "Big Brother and all."

Dagger didn't like the sound of that. After ending his conversation with Skizzy, Dagger gathered the papers off the printer and carried them into the Florida room. Stair-step tables were lined up in front of the windows where flowering plants were on full display. A large paddle fan droned overhead. It was five hundred square feet of quarry-tiled floor and floral cushioned furniture. Dagger had built it from the ground up. Carpenter projects were his best release valves.

He turned his attention to the papers, thinking it would start with a biography of Cardinal Michael Esrey. It didn't. Other than the cardinal's current travel plans, the only biography Dagger had was the one Sara had printed from her Google search. His suspicious mind started questioning the cardinal's true identity. All Dagger had to do was snatch a wine glass the cardinal touches and, as a backup, have Sara pick up some prints from the hotel room. That was their only starting point.

His mind drifted to Demko. Why did he seek him out specifically? There were other P.I.'s in the area. The more he thought about it, though, he realized they were all high-profile. Their pictures were on billboards, smiling up at you from restaurant placemats, on flyers posted at the local grocery store. Someone would get suspicious if any of them were found dead. But most people knew little about Dagger. His clients were all word of mouth. His obituary would be a tiny blurb buried near the classifieds.

And then there was the cardinal. Dagger studied the face. Could he be wrong? Did Esrey only resemble someone from Dagger's past? Why were some people he had killed so fresh in his mind but Esrey was a blur? There wasn't anything in the cardinal's past that even hinted at corruption or misconduct. Maybe...Dagger shook the thought from his head. That was too bizarre to even contemplate. But the thought nagged at him, kept pushing its way to the forefront until he gave it some structure.

Maybe it wasn't the cardinal's past that had him targeted. It could possibly be his future.

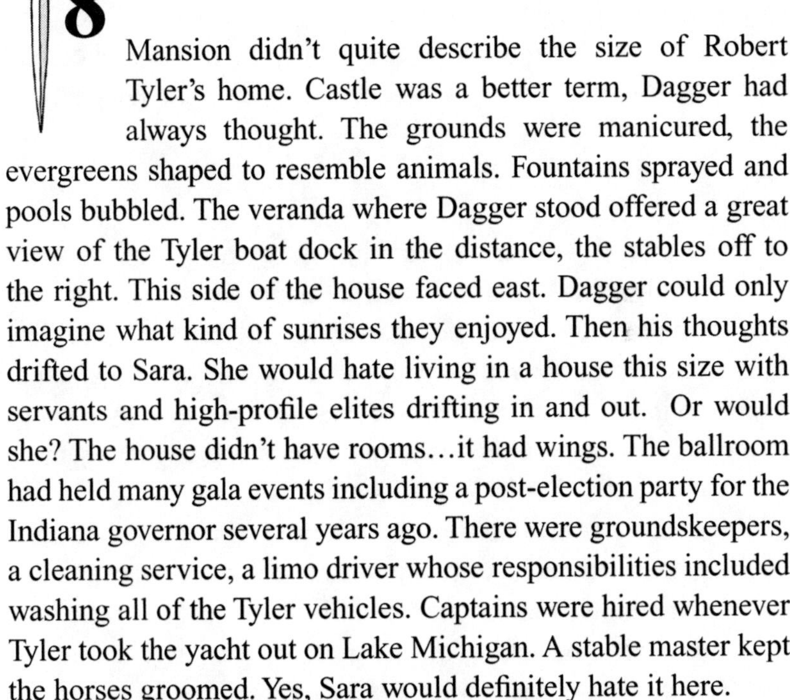

8

Mansion didn't quite describe the size of Robert Tyler's home. Castle was a better term, Dagger had always thought. The grounds were manicured, the evergreens shaped to resemble animals. Fountains sprayed and pools bubbled. The veranda where Dagger stood offered a great view of the Tyler boat dock in the distance, the stables off to the right. This side of the house faced east. Dagger could only imagine what kind of sunrises they enjoyed. Then his thoughts drifted to Sara. She would hate living in a house this size with servants and high-profile elites drifting in and out. Or would she? The house didn't have rooms…it had wings. The ballroom had held many gala events including a post-election party for the Indiana governor several years ago. There were groundskeepers, a cleaning service, a limo driver whose responsibilities included washing all of the Tyler vehicles. Captains were hired whenever Tyler took the yacht out on Lake Michigan. A stable master kept the horses groomed. Yes, Sara would definitely hate it here.

"Dagger, there you are." Robert Tyler stepped out onto the veranda and handed Dagger a beer. "Cardinal Esrey will be coming down in a few minutes." Robert rested one elbow on the railing and watched the guests in the sitting room.

Dagger figured Robert was so used to the grounds that he now took them for granted. Even his string of resorts ran like clockwork so there wasn't a need for him to travel that much. Robert's tanned skin showed few lines which had Dagger wondering if the man recently had a facelift. His hair appeared thicker and more silver. Hair plugs? Was Robert trolling for wife number three? He had always been trim and in excellent shape but having an in-home gym with a weight trainer visiting three times a week would keep anyone in shape.

"I'm sorry Sara couldn't make it. She is a lovely young woman." Robert studied his manicured fingers. "She would be a catch for any man, don't you think?"

Dagger gave a hint of a grimace which he hoped looked like a smile. Maybe Nick was the wrong Tyler he should keep an eye on.

Sara shoved her shorts and top into the gym bag and stashed it in the supply cabinet in the women's washroom. The hardest part was trying to shove all of her hair under the short red wig. The gray and white uniform fit loosely but it was all she could get her hands on in such short notice. She had worn her own gym shoes so hopefully she wouldn't run into a member of management who would notice her lack of adherence to dress code.

Next she put on tinted glasses, more to hide her eyes than anything else. Her eyes were an unusual color and would be the first thing people would remember. She looked at her reflection in the mirror. This would do. The uniform was large enough to hide her curves and she wasn't wearing anything that was too eye-catching to be memorable.

She pulled on latex gloves and walked out of the second floor restroom and down the hall to a red house phone. She dialed the cardinal's suite and listened while it rang several times. After it went unanswered for a full minute, Sara hung up. With luck, his entire entourage was with him at the Tyler residence.

A map on the wall near the employee entrance pointed out the location of all the supply rooms. One was on the floor just below the Presidential Suites. She didn't know how Skizzy did it but he made her a master key card for the Ritz so she didn't have to try to steal one from a cleaning cart.

She rode the elevator to the eleventh floor. Alternatives played in her head. What if housekeeping was in the cardinal's suite now? What if security was posted outside the room? What if the security guard insisted on joining Sara in the room? What if a member of management, knowing that housekeeping shouldn't be working after six o'clock, pulled her aside?

As she wandered the hall, she heard music coming from one of the rooms. Voices from a television set, the news possibly. More voices arguing. Sometimes Sara wished she didn't have enhanced hearing. She concentrated on blocking out the background sounds.

As she approached the supply room, she pulled the master key card from her pocket and opened the door. Cleaning carts lined one wall. Towels and bed linens were stacked on shelves above the carts. Cleaning supplies were on the shelves on the opposite wall. Sara grabbed the closest cart, pushed it out of the room and over to the elevator. Once on the elevator she pushed the button for the twelfth floor. The doors closed but the elevator didn't move. Sara held her breath. Now what? She pushed the button again. Still nothing. Sara inserted the key card into a slot labeled *Suites*. The elevator moved.

The lavish décor on the twelfth floor far exceeded anything Sara had ever seen before. A rain forest of plants surrounded a fountain in the middle of the atrium. She checked the sign on the wall. Cardinal Esrey's was the Cordova Suite. Soft music was coming from one of the suites. Humming, probably from refrigerators. Ice clinking. Someone was making a drink in another suite.

Moving quickly down the hall, Sara located the Cordova Suite. There wasn't anyone standing guard. So far so good. She parked the cleaning cart just outside the door, grabbed a few towels, then shoved the master key card in the slot. A green light flashed. Slowly she pushed the door open, waited and listened. She heard her pulse pounding in her ears. She gently closed the door, then bolted it so no one could enter.

She stepped into a living room with a vaulted ceiling and dark wood furnishings, brocade sofas, and Oriental carpeting. A fireplace was on the far wall with a large basket of flowers set inside. Sara hadn't seen anything this lavish since the Tyler house. Floor to ceiling windows gave a magnificent view of the Cedar Point Yacht Club in the distance. Lights from boats could be seen offshore. A staircase to her right led to a second floor loft, probably the bedrooms. Off to her left was a kitchen and bar area. Further on was a dining room table large enough to seat twelve, and beyond that a separate conference room. Hallways were large enough to drive a car through.

Sara could spend hours admiring the suite but reminded herself she had work to do. She had three surveillance bugs and had to pick the best places to plant them. Dagger was curious to find out more about Esrey that might be hidden from the public. The conference room had an Oriental silk screen painting on the wall. Sara placed one of the bugs on the back of the painting. She stood in the living room and studied the surroundings. She could always place a bug in one of the plants but all of the plants were live and might be watered, repotted, or thrown out. She couldn't chance it. The fireplace had a marble mantel, a perfect place for the second bug.

She headed for the second floor. The staircase was marble with an Oriental runner and high-gloss wood handrail. The upstairs furnishings proved even more extravagant. The bed was on a platform with a velvet canopy. The bathroom had a whirlpool large enough for six people in addition to a walk-in shower. Gold fixtures were just a tad too much in Sara's opinion.

It didn't feel appropriate to bug the cardinal's bedroom. But the loft did have a library and another fireplace. Sara placed the last bug under an end table in the library. A long conference table was in the middle of the room and at one end of the table was an opened briefcase.

She was just about to search the case when she heard a soft creaking, like someone stepping on a wood floor. Sara lifted her head and focused her attention on the source of the sound. It was coming from the cardinal's bedroom. This was a bad time to travel unarmed. She focused her senses on the room as she entered. She didn't hear anything other than her own pulse pounding in her ears and her own breathing. Or was it hers? Was there someone else inhaling? She stopped to listen closer. *Creak.* Her attention riveted to a set of French doors which weren't completely closed. Sara breathed a sigh of relief. It was just the ceiling fan causing a draft. She walked over to the French doors and pulled them open.

A man, mouth twisted in a grimace, tumbled toward her. Sara screamed and stepped to one side. The man fell to the floor with a thud. Sara stumbled away and nearly collided with the bed. Her heart pounded against her rib cage as she stared in shock at what lay before her. Blue face, bulging eyes. The man had been strangled. Thoughts fired through her brain. She had on latex gloves, hadn't left prints anywhere. The bugs were planted. Time to leave.

She ran out of the bedroom, through the library, and right into Paul Demko.

"What?!" Sara's mouth gaped in shock. This can't be. He was dead. But here he was. Same face, same receding hairline, same suit. Demko lunged at her but Sara called on her unusual strength and flung him aside like a rag doll. She dodged his second attempt and tore off for the staircase. A figure appeared in her peripheral vision dropping from the second floor like a suicide jumper. Demko had leaped from the loft and landed at the bottom of the curved staircase. Sara came at him feet first, landing a blow to his head. Something dropped from his hand and scuttled across the floor. He shook off the shock to his body and studied her with renewed interest, cocking his head as though calculating his next move against a 120 pound woman with unusual strength.

Demko took a swing at her but she ducked, flung her feet out and kicked at his kneecap. Bone crunched and he went down with a howl. Sara ran for the door but he hobbled right after her, grabbed a handful of her uniform and dragged her back. He pulled her into a headlock. Sara clawed for his eyes but his other arm held down her hands. She kicked backward, aiming toward his injured kneecap. She turned, moving them in a bizarre circular dance while lights sparkled behind her eyes. She heard pottery breaking and furniture tumbling. Finally her heel connected with Demko's injured kneecap and he folded like a broken chair. Sara stepped away and took in gulps of air. Her vision started to clear as she saw Demko grope for a pen then stumble to his feet, wobbling in front of the tall windows.

"Don't you ever quit?" Sara said. She took a deep breath then ran straight at him, leaped in the air and caught him in the chest with both feet. Her momentum carried them both into the window. Glass shattered as they tumbled out of the twelfth floor. She expected his hands and feet to claw for purchase but instead he was clinging to the pen with both hands. The parking lot below was small and poorly lit. Demko was headed right for the hood of a truck, a vehicle which, even in the dark, Sara recognized. She pushed away from him, then shifted. Demko's eyes grew wide as he witnessed her clothing and wig fall away and the human form change to a hawk. It flew up and landed on the seventh floor window ledge.

Demko's body hit the vehicle with a loud crash. Several seconds later the truck exploded. In succession, several surrounding cars exploded sending up a ball of fire and fumes into the night sky. The hawk used its beak to pull a latex glove from one talon. The glove drifted in the direction of the fire only to be sucked into the flames. The hawk checked the grounds for witnesses. It scanned nearby cars, the back entrance to the hotel, the street beyond. Assured it hadn't been seen, the hawk took flight.

9

Dagger barely listened to Sheila's ramblings about a story she was investigating which had something to do with a refinery dumping waste into Lake Michigan. He was too busy studying the cardinal seated across from him. Esrey had looked familiar in the picture on Demko's computer but up close and personal he was just another priest dressed casually in white collar and black cassock. After spending the last few hours with the man, Dagger was now certain that he had never seen him before in his life. So why had he believed beyond a shadow of a doubt that he had killed him?

"Are you listening to me?"

Dagger shifted his gaze to the exquisite blonde seated next to him. Her silk suit looked as though it were woven with the fine platinum strands of her hair. At least she had the good sense to wear something that didn't expose the breast implants her father had purchased when she graduated from college. Her green eyes blazed with irritation and she pursed her collagen-injected lips into a pout.

"Barely," he replied as he lifted her hand from his thigh. "I'm trying to stay focused here." Dinner dishes had been cleared away and replaced with some type of chocolate mousse and cream puffs shaped like swans. Three platters of desserts had been placed at strategic points on the table. Dagger was sure if he used a yardstick each platter would be of equal distance apart.

Leyton Monroe excused himself, but not before stabbing Dagger with one final glare as a reminder that he was in his crosshairs. Standing up the daughter of one of the richest men in Cedar Point hadn't won Dagger any soft spots in his heart.

Monroe had managed to only lose the security deposit with the reception hall. He had had the foresight to add a clause in the contract to his benefit knowing that somehow the wedding of his daughter to a hooligan like Dagger was never going to take place.

"Sweetheart, come over here and talk to mummy." Anna Monroe patted the chair next to her. She was a short, frumpy version of Sheila. Dagger imagined Sheila would look the same when she reached her fifties. Frumpy for the wealthy was quite a bit different from frumpy for the middle class. Anna's hair was in a fashionable swirl of curls in the same shade as Sheila's hair. Dagger figured they got a two-for-one discount at the salon. Her dress was tailored to hide the middle age spread.

"Oh, jeez," Sheila said under her breath but forced a smile and moved five chairs down.

The dinner guest list consisted of the Monroes, Robert Tyler, Cardinal Esrey, several area bishops, Mayor James Brookins and his wife Bobbie, who had left early because of a nanny problem at home. The cardinal's private secretary, Donald Thomas, was a fidgety priest who made even Dagger nervous. He was a few pounds shy of pudgy with a patch of baldness on the top of his head. Skin as smooth as a baby's bottom, it was difficult to tell the priest's age. If there had been less hair, if it had ringed the bottom half of his head, he would almost look at home in a monastery. He had sat at the cardinal's elbow all night with notepad in hand should the cardinal make a request. Whether bending over his plate or the notepad, Father Thomas was obsessively focused on whatever he was doing. His voice was soft, almost timid and he had waited patiently for the cardinal to finish speaking before interrupting.

Dagger didn't remember Thomas mumbling more than one complete sentence and wondered in what monastery Esrey found this guy. After Thomas left to do God knows what with his notes, some of the guests retreated to the veranda with brandy in hand, leaving the women at one end of the table and Esrey and Dagger seated across from each other at the other end of the table.

Cardinal Esrey studied Dagger over the rim of his brandy glass. Dagger had stuck to coffee through dinner. "You look like a man who might have a lot to confess," Esrey said.

Dagger should have worn a white suit instead of a black suit and shirt with a granite-colored tie. At least he would have looked less like a hit man. He had found the cardinal's dry sense of humor rather engaging.

"My conscience is clear," Dagger said with a smile.

"You have a certain dangerous aura about you."

"It's the suit. I think anyone who dresses in all black makes people cautious."

Esrey chuckled at that comment. "Of course."

Dagger had found the cardinal to be quite knowledgeable on many subjects and able to hold his own when it came to discussing politics with the mayor. When the subject came to the Bible, Dagger had just sat back and listened. It wasn't one of his favorite subjects, seeing that he was an agnostic. His only contribution to the discussion was to say the Bible was a nice behavioral tool but it was too bad not enough people practiced it. This had warranted him a burying of Sheila's nails into his thigh.

"Do you believe in divine intervention, Mr. Dagger?" Esrey asked.

"Would have helped if your quarterback had steered those planes away from the Twin Towers."

Esrey smiled. "I love a challenge, Mr. Dagger, and you are quite a challenge."

"It's just Dagger."

"Dagger." The cardinal took a sip of brandy, then set the glass down and studied the contents of the glass for several minutes. "Haven't you ever seen anything that made you question your lack of belief? That made you think, 'this is the most miraculous thing I have ever witnessed.' You have never felt like that?"

Dagger couldn't help but think of Sara. He couldn't explain her abilities but were they really divine? If he hadn't witnessed them firsthand he would have never believed it. Then he thought of Demco. Demco's abilities, though, were all manmade, he was sure of it.

"Do you believe in evil?" Dagger countered. "And I don't mean the staged exorcisms."

"I noticed you avoided answering my question." Esrey studied Dagger for the longest time. Then he leaned forward, forearms on the table. His tone was hushed so the women at the end of the table couldn't hear. The cardinal's eyes were penetrating when he stared at Dagger. It was as though he were searching for Dagger's soul and couldn't find one. "I have a feeling, Dagger, that you have witnessed both."

Now she was angry. Not only did Sara have to carry the brunt of the hard work while Dagger was eating caviar and drinking champagne, but she had almost been killed. It didn't take her long to shower and change and drive over to the Tyler mansion. She slammed out of the Ford Torino which was still rattling after she turned off the engine. This made her angrier. Dagger had taken the Beemer and left her with the choice of an aging Torino, a black Taurus or the Lincoln Navigator which she felt was too large for her to drive. She would have preferred the Beemer.

The look on her face dared the valet to take her car keys, complain about the eyesore of a car she left at the curb, or look twice at her legs. She gathered the black shawl around her bare shoulders and marched up the stairs. Her P32 was in her purse and it would take all of her control not to pull it out and shoot Dagger.

Security let her pass without even checking her purse. She walked up to the bar set up in the foyer, ordered a glass of white zinfandel, and glared at the bartender when he asked to see her driver's license. She tossed the bartender a five and walked away. It was close to ten, dinner had probably been served hours ago. She could hear violin music playing, probably something to eat dessert by.

The doors to the ballroom were closed. The thought of flinging open the doors and marching in brought back memories of Sheila. That was definitely something Sheila would do. Sara took a sip of wine to calm down. Her hands hadn't stopped shaking and her head was still reeling after seeing a second Paul Demko. Were they twins? Who was the dead man in the closet? And did the truck explode or did Demko explode?

"Sara?"

She turned to find Robert Tyler stepping out of a side room, cell phone in hand. "Sorry I'm late, Mr. Tyler."

Robert Tyler oozed wealth. Distinguished gray hair and fine lines only added to his appeal. It was easy to see where Nick got his good looks.

"I thought you couldn't make it."

"My plans changed."

"Great. We've already eaten but I could have Lily bring you a plate."

"That isn't necessary. Just thought I'd stop in for a few minutes."

"Wonderful." He wrapped his arm around her shoulder and led her to the ballroom. "You're almost like family."

"I am?"

"Of course. If I have anything to do or say about it, Nicholas is going to someday settle down and start a family. And I can't think of anyone more suitable."

Sara didn't like where this conversation was going. "I'm not sure what Nick told you but he and I are just friends."

"Of course." Tyler gave her a wink. "Whatever you kids call it these days."

He led her down the hall to a study. A study in the Tyler mansion was like a single family house at a residential country club. Area rugs separated cozy sitting areas. The local librarian would kill for the number of books stocked on Tyler's shelves. All heads turned as she walked in. Her eyes were immediately drawn to the cardinal whose vestment was trimmed in scarlet. Then her eyes drifted to Sheila who was sitting on the arm of Dagger's chair, her fingers spinning through the hair in his ponytail. There were only six other people in the room. Sheila's mother gushed at Sara's black lace shawl which added a little flash to the conservative black dress. Leyton Monroe chewed on an unlit cigar and gave her a passing glance. Seeing Sara reminded him of the wedding that never happened between Dagger and his daughter. The cardinal gave her a polite nod while Dagger's eyebrows furrowed in confusion.

Sara wandered over to a table of desserts and grabbed a small éclair. Dagger suddenly appeared behind her. He whispered, "What are you doing here?"

She turned to face him, held up her drink. "Getting a glass of wine." Her shawl fell from her shoulders and she saw his eyes move to a spot on her neck.

"Is that a bruise?"

Sara pulled the shawl up, draping one end around her neck. She could still feel Demko's arm against her throat. Dagger moved in closer then turned to scan the room, his back to the table.

"What's happening, Sara?"

Suddenly Tyler's cell phone rang, followed by Leyton's cell phone. Next, two of Cardinal Esrey's security guards were digging in their pockets for their phones. Obviously it took some time for the hotel authorities to first discover there was a body on the burning truck, then determine which floor the victim jumped from.

Sara watched the guests with amusement. “Let’s see. The bugs were planted, found a briefcase on a table, a dead guy in the closet, and I killed Demko.” She popped the éclair into her mouth.

Dagger moved in front of her. “You want to run that one by me again?”

Sara pointed at the rush of bodies nearing the exit. “That is probably the police notifying the cardinal that someone fell out of his twelfth floor window, although it was actually two people but just one hit the ground. Oh, and by the way, he also exploded. It was quite a sight.”

Dagger stared at her for a beat. “You’re wrong, Sara. Maybe it looked like him.”

“I know what I saw.”

“My, my. A lover’s quarrel?” Sheila pried answers from them with her eyes. It was the reporter in her.

“This is a private conversation, Sheila.”

Sheila backed down from Dagger’s glare. “Daddy and I are going over to the Ritz. There’s supposedly a murder/suicide. Thought you’d like to come with. Maybe we can get a drink afterwards.”

“No, thanks. Murders make me nervous.”

She walked off in a huff. Dagger turned back to Sara. Her hand shook as she raised the glass to her mouth. Dagger pulled it away. “Have you eaten anything besides the éclair?”

“I don’t think I can.”

“Robert,” Dagger called out to Tyler. “Can we get Sara something to eat?”

Lily was more than happy to bring out a plate of crab and cocktail sauce, cheese and crackers, fruit, and hot tea for Sara.

Dagger settled her at the end of the table. Either Sara's skin had a healthy glow or anger was radiating from her body. He reached over and pulled the shawl down. The bruise was already starting to fade but still looked tender. He saw a blur of black and scarlet approaching.

"I don't believe I have officially met this young woman." Cardinal Esrey pulled out a chair and sat down. "Mind?"

"Not at all, Your Eminence." Sara introduced herself. The shawl fell from her neck and she saw the cardinal's eyes move to the bruise and then swiftly snap to Dagger as though recognizing his fingerprints. She felt compelled to explain. "Dagger and I work together. Since he was already committed to this dinner tonight, I took a surveillance assignment. My suspect got a bit aggressive."

"I hope you got the best of him."

Sara couldn't help but smile. "You could say he won't be a problem anymore."

Anna Monroe turned on the large screen TV which had on-the-scene camera footage of the burned out vehicles in the parking lot behind the Ritz. A large tarp covered the body of the man who had fallen out of the suite. Speculation was that the jumper had broken the window in order to commit suicide. More speculation centered on a radical group targeting the church over pedophile priests. The victim in the parking lot had yet to be identified. Police were not forthcoming on the body found in the suite other than to say it was one of the security guards hired for the cardinal's visit.

"Your Eminence," Robert whispered. "I believe it is best you and your assistant stay here for the time being."

"I'm going to need some clothes and my briefcase," the cardinal said. "I had worked on my speech on the plane but I need to finish it."

"The police are advising that you cancel your speech,"

Robert said.

"Out of the question. I won't be bullied into changing my plans."

"How about if I send someone to your suite to pick up a few things and your briefcase," Robert suggested. "I know the police chief. I'm sure there won't be a problem getting your things packed up." He immediately turned to Dagger. "Would you go? Maybe you can get an update from Padre."

"Sure. I'm one of Padre's favorite people."

10

"Oh, this is making my night even better." Padre grimaced as Dagger stood in the doorway to the Cordova Suite.

"Nice to see you too, Padre." Dagger had a big smile and a handshake for Padre.

The sergeant ignored Dagger's outstretched hand. "You aren't coming in so get that out of your head right now. I already turned away Sheila and her father. Where were you tonight?"

"Why am I always at the top of your suspect list?"

"Oh, I don't know. Why don't you tell me?" Padre led Dagger away from the entrance and to a sitting area near the elevator.

"I wish you would quit your grudge against me because of that *Friday the Thirteenth* case."

"Oh? You mean because you aged me ten years and turned what little hair I have left grayer?" Padre huffed.

"If you must know, I was having dinner with the cardinal at the Tyler residence. Tyler sent me to pick up a few things for the cardinal since he will be staying with him."

Padre motioned toward a couch by the atrium and took a seat across from Dagger. "Lightning hasn't struck from the sky so I find it hard to believe you were breaking bread with a man of the cloth."

"I break bread with you." Dagger winked at the cop.

The elevator doors opened and two medical assistants rolled a gurney out onto the floor. Padre waited for them to leave before resuming.

"We found a housekeeping cart outside the suite, the door bolted from the inside, a security guard in the upstairs bedroom dead, and a guy who decided to take a flying leap out of the window. And how was your night?"

"Caviar, crab legs, beef medallions, great desserts." Dagger leaned back and fingered his diamond stud earring. There was something in Padre's eyes that told him the cop was holding out on him. He wasn't sure what exactly but Dagger had seen that look in Padre's eyes too many times before.

"Where's the maid?" Dagger asked.

"We thought she might have heard a commotion and taken off. According to management there shouldn't have been anyone working tonight. And why didn't she take the cart with her?"

"What could the cardinal have worth stealing?"

Padre dug in his pocket and pulled out a stick of gum. He took his time refolding the paper for later use. "Looks like there was a fight or struggle of some sort but it doesn't look like robbery was the motive. The wall safe hasn't been tampered with. Hotel security opened it and there's still cash and important papers in there. One of my guys is calling the cardinal to get a verbal list of what he had in the suite. We did sweep the place and found three bugs."

"Spiders?"

Padre just glared at him.

"Sorry. There are just so many food blessings and ring kisses I can sit through in one night. I'm a little slap happy." He watched Padre massacre the gum then start to blow bubbles. "Any suspects?"

"Found some red hairs in several of the rooms. Too long to be a man's."

Dagger cocked his head. "You don't think the cardinal was… you know."

Padre drilled him with another stare.

A female police officer approached carrying a suitcase, a suit bag, and a briefcase. "The hotel manager said they would deliver the rest of his clothes tomorrow."

Padre thanked her and stood. "I have to get back to work."

"Any information you want me to beat out of the cardinal?"

Padre laughed, another boisterous laugh that snapped off as quickly as it had started. "Always the comic."

Before delivering the items to Cardinal Esrey, Dagger had first stopped at Skizzy's to go through the briefcase thoroughly, looking for secret compartments, which proved fruitless. The only item worth copying was the cardinal's travel itinerary. Dagger was curious if it had changed any since the one Skizzy found on Demco's computer. A quick call to Sara garnered him a chill through the airwaves he hadn't felt before. She was still pissed but did manage to steal a glass the cardinal had used. Being an honest and moral person, compared to his own devious nature, Sara had explained to Robert that Dagger needed to exclude the cardinal's prints from any others that might be found in the hotel suite. Sara had left out the little detail that Dagger wasn't investigating the possible theft in the suite. Perhaps he finally was rubbing off on her.

Dagger scanned the cardinal's prints into the computer and zipped them off to Skizzy to check through AFIS to verify the cardinal's identity. Padre had taken pictures of every inch of the suite and planned to show them to the cardinal tomorrow to attest to the contents and confirm that nothing had been stolen.

Sara hadn't said one word to him since he returned home. He could feel eyes drilling a hole in his back. The bruise on her neck had vanished completely, a testament to her rapid healing abilities. His ribs still ached and his bruises looked like he had gone six rounds with Ali. He turned from the computer to find Sara sitting on the couch, bare feet propped on the coffee table. She was flipping through pages of a magazine barely looking at the pictures, her tanned legs clad in floral capri pants. One of his jobs was to keep her safe and she was almost killed tonight. Maybe involving her wasn't the right thing to do.

"I said I was sorry, Sara. If I had known it was going to be dangerous, I would never have sent you." Other than drilling him with those laser blue eyes, she said nothing.

After several additional seconds of chill, Sara tossed the magazine on the coffee table and announced, "I want my own car."

Dagger blinked. "What?"

"I want my own car. You drove the Beemer and left me with that rattle trap you call a classic. The truck isn't something I care to drive in heels nor is my motorcycle, although the truck no longer exists since that's the vehicle Demko Number Two fell on. The Navigator is as long as a limo and too cumbersome for me to handle and I'm not familiar with the Taurus. I want something that's mine."

"So, that's all it takes." Dagger moved her feet and plopped down on the coffee table in front of her. "Bodies fall on you, you fall out of a window, almost get blown up, but all you want is a car. A woman after my own heart." He grabbed her hands and held on tight, thankful that her fear of people no longer applied to him. His patience had paid off and seeing the smile radiating on her face filled him with a thrill that could only be equaled by the purchase of a new weapon. Sara never asked for much. Not like most women. Sheila used to drag him off to jewelry stores for the latest bauble that caught her eye. He felt it was a waste of money. Not to be denied, Sheila would buy it for herself and tell her friends that it was a present from Dagger.

"What kind of car do you want?"

"A PT Cruiser convertible."

"Done."

Sara cocked her head, not sure she heard him right. "Really?"

"Really."

She threw her arms around his neck and kissed his cheek. "Thank you." She jumped from the couch and ran up the stairs to her bedroom.

Dagger started to second guess his motives. Was he trying to compete in some way with Nick Tyler? Would Nick turn around and buy her a Jaguar to show him up? Sheila would have asked for a Mercedes or Lexus but all Sara wanted was a PT Cruiser. Just to see that dazzling smile of Sara's was enough for him. Then he frowned.

"HEY! What about my truck?"

11

Luther pulled his mask off and motioned for Padre to follow. They each had endured three hours of restless sleep last night knowing this was going to be an unusually gruesome autopsy. But they hadn't realized how shockingly gruesome.

Luther's assistant, Gretchen, had completed the autopsy on Hank Hanover, the security guard found dead in the cardinal's bedroom. No surprises there. He had been asphyxiated and his neck broken by a very powerful force.

It was the remains in the hotel parking lot that Luther chose to handle. He loved challenges. When Padre had surveyed the crime scene, there had been something eerily familiar about the victim. Of course the body would be reduced to pieces that could fit in a cigar box. But it was the shoes they had found, the shoes with socks and feet. How many similar deaths had they found in their combined lifetimes? Zip. *Nada*.

Luther settled behind a gray metal desk that looked like a holdover from his grade school days. If they ever had another earthquake or tornado in the Northwest Indiana area, he knew hiding under this desk would save his life. "Maybe my wife has been serving me a dose of psychedelic mushrooms, but this is just too bizarre." Luther snapped up a piece of paper and flung it across the desk followed by a second piece of paper.

"What am I looking at?" Padre asked. "These are fingerprints. You found fingers?"

"The hands did their own walking, or flying in this case," Luther said, eliciting a complete lack of humor from the detective. Luther cleared his throat. "They are identical."

Padre stared at the prints then waited, flapped his hand

repeatedly for more information.

"The prints on the left are from our guy in the quarry. The prints on the right are from our parking lot victim."

"No, no, no. Don't do this to me again. My old heart can only take so much in one lifetime."

The high back leather chair squeaked as Luther rocked. His eyes took on a familiar gleam which told Padre the M.E. anticipated a stimulating case. "Same blood type, same prints, same socks, same damn shoes, and I bet once we get it back it will be the same DNA."

Padre held his head and leaned back to stare at the ceiling. "Why me, Lord? What's wrong with Gary or South Bend? What have I ever done? Are you pissed I quit the seminary? Is that it?"

"If you are expecting an answer, you've got a long wait." Luther rattled more papers. "I've got more."

Padre straightened and glared across the table. "Can my heart take it?"

"Don't know. Those red hairs we found in the suite? Synthetic."

"Wig. So maybe the maid was wearing a wig."

Luther smiled. It was a devilish smile that told Padre he was enjoying this way more than he should.

"Some of the clothing not completely burned looked like a uniform. And there were women's athletic shoes near the wreckage."

Padre pulled out a stick of gum and shoved it in his mouth. He wanted a cigarette so bad that as soon as he left Luther's office he planned to smoke ten in a row. Maybe he would just crumble them up and graze on them. "You've got that shit-eatin' grin on your face. Let me have it."

"No other remains."

Padre paused a beat. "Gotta be. How can you tell with what little was left of the victim?"

"Shoes were empty. Only one blood type on the remains."

"Were the shoes right by the car? Probably unrelated. It's the employee entrance, someone probably dropped her work shoes accidentally. Same with her uniform."

Luther shrugged. "How many red-haired women on the housekeeping staff?"

Padre shook his head. "Only one and she's home nursing a newborn." He could see Luther about to ask another question. After working so many years together he could just about anticipate how Luther's mind worked. "We've gone over the camera footage from the hotel lobby. The employee entrance doesn't have a camera, nor does the Presidential Suites floor. They want the rich and famous to have their privacy."

"What about your crime techs?" Luther asked. "Did they find any fuses? Remains of incendiary devices, something to point to how one body falling can result in such a large explosion?"

"They had to wait for the cars to cool down before transporting them to the lab. They'll let me know what they find." Padre rose from the chair saying, "That it?"

Luther placed what looked like a pen on the desk. Both ends looked melted from the heat. "This was still clutched in one of his hands."

Dagger inhaled the coffee and felt more like mainlining it. They had come up empty-handed when examining Esrey's briefcase. There hadn't been one questionable document. Only speeches, a daily calendar, travel itinerary, and correspondence. Fingerprint analysis also confirmed that Cardinal Esrey was Cardinal Esrey, age fifty-seven, born in Atlanta, Georgia, although he had lost his accent years ago, as far as Dagger could tell. His itinerary over the past five years had him crisscrossing the globe, visiting Rome several times a year, and he had been one of the few cardinals allowed to visit Cuba.

Dagger read Esrey's bio again, tried to piece together why and how he knew him. How could he be so sure he had killed Esrey five years ago when Dagger couldn't remember where and exactly when it had happened? And the proof had been right across the dinner table from him. He had watched the cardinal's eyes for some sign of recognition but if he had ever seen Dagger before, he hadn't let on. And who exactly was Demko and his twin brother? Were they associated with radical groups or was someone else targeting the cardinal? Did Demko Number Two die the same way as Demko Number One?

Sara walked into the kitchen wearing shorts and a floral top tied at her waist. As she reached for the coffee pot, her tanned midriff was exposed. Her sandals wrapped around her ankles like a Roman chariot driver. At the young age of nineteen, she hadn't succumbed to the popularity of tattoos and body piercing. It was easy to understand why she would shy away from such fads. When she shifted, her jewelry, whether it be earrings or a necklace, would look out of place on a hawk or wolf. She didn't even polish her nails. The only jewelry she did wear was one diamond stud earring which was a tracker so if she were ever injured in her shifted form, Dagger would be able to locate her. Her stud earring was a match to the one Dagger wore.

"You are going car shopping dressed like that?"

Sara looked down at her shorts. "What's wrong with it?"

"Car salesmen take advantage of drab married women with three kids in tow. They get one look at you and they will jack the price up and convince you that you need every option they have to offer. You look like you don't know a thing about cars."

"I don't know anything about cars other than what's cute."

"Which is why I'm going."

"No guns."

"No *problemo*."

* * *

“I was hoping to drive it home today.”

Dagger parked the Navigator at the side lot of the Ritz. He had wanted to see the back lot where Demko had taken a dive. “Let them get the pin striping done and add the alarm and better sound system. Then we’ll take it over to Skizzy and have him remove the GPS tracking system. Patience. At least I didn’t shoot the guy.”

And he hadn’t. He had walked into the showroom, Sara had picked out the car she wanted, a shiny candy apple red, and Dagger had told the salesman he wanted to see the factory receipt. The salesman had taken one look at the tall man dressed in black, his dark gaze that was unsettling, the slight bulge at his hip, and nodded in agreement. Dagger opened a suitcase of cash to pay in full. It seemed the salesman couldn’t write up the contract fast enough just to get Dagger out of his showroom.

Crime scene tape circled the back lot. Owners of the remaining cars in the lot had been irate that they couldn’t claim their cars until Padre had cleared the area. The charred vehicles had been removed. The lot looked as though it had been swept clean. Dagger stood back and stared up at the twelfth floor where one large panel of glass was completely missing. Crime techs had obviously removed the entire panel and taken it back to the lab. Workmen were busy inserting plywood, a temporary fix until a new window could be delivered.

Dagger scanned the outer perimeter of the yellow tape, then took a slow stroll. “Keep your eyes out for a piece of metal,” he told Sara.

“Has Skizzy identified it yet?” Sara asked, referring to the metal piece that almost hit Skizzy in the head at the quarry.

“Other than being certain it’s a government implant, no. Hasn’t found anything in the government databases on it.”

Sara stood back and concentrated on the surrounding area.

If one were to get close, they would see that her eyes' irises had become more elliptical in shape. She had called on the enhanced eyesight of the hawk to search the area. She focused on the lot itself, what might have landed under cars, against the curbs, near garbage cans. Then she focused on grass outside the taped area. The police would have no way of knowing how far away the evidence would have landed.

"Looking for this?" Padre had crept up on them. He held out his hand, a round piece of charred metal in the palm.

Dagger tried not to flinch as he saw the familiar piece of metal. "What is it?"

"You tell me." In Padre's other hand was a lit cigarette. He took a long, satisfying drag, blowing the smoke out slowly.

"I knew you'd fold, Padre," Dagger said with a nod toward the cigarette.

"Well, I live to quit another day." He motioned toward the large area within the yellow tape. "Lot of debris over a pretty big area. Five burned out vehicles. Luckily only one fatality, except for the guy upstairs, of course."

Sara asked, "Have you identified him?"

"The diver? Not yet. He was kind enough to leave some fingers behind. Other than that, not much of him left." He held up the metal object for them to see more closely. "Except this."

"He had it on him?" Sara asked.

Padre smiled, the proverbial canary sneaking a peek between the cop's lips. "In him," the detective said.

Sara winced. "How can you be sure? It could have come from one of the cars."

"Skin, brain matter."

"It wasn't all burned away?" Dagger only had to look at the metal once to know it was similar to the one Skizzy had from the first Demko.

"Blown away was more like it."

He and Sara said nothing. But nothing is one of the worst things you could do around Padre. Sara feigned shock. “Do you think he was a terrorist? Who else would strap a bomb to himself?”

“My bomb experts didn’t detect any of the usual bomb-making materials.”

“Have you interviewed Cardinal Esrey?” Dagger asked.

“Headed there now.” Padre caught sight of Sheila rushing across the parking lot toward him. “And it appears I’m leaving in the nick of time.” He moved in the opposite direction of Sheila, flicked his cigarette butt away, and sprinted to his unmarked car.

“Damn.” Sheila smacked her notepad against her thigh. She turned to Dagger. “Did he tell you anything?” Although Sheila had finally faced the fact that her engagement to Dagger was off permanently, the only thing she had officially done was move his ring from her left hand to her right hand.

“No. For some reason he is really keeping this one close to the vest. Maybe having been in the seminary Padre’s trying to protect the cardinal. He’s going over to the Tylers to talk to him now. Why don’t you see what you can find out?” Dagger raked his eyes down her exposed cleavage and short skirt. “Although I think I’d change first before meeting with the cardinal.”

Sheila narrowed her green eyes at him. “And what is your interest in all this?”

“Just love a puzzle.”

She gave an exaggerated swivel to her hips as she strolled back to her car, tossing a flirtatious smile over her shoulder before climbing in and driving off. If she was trying to annoy Sara, it wasn’t working. Sara instead had been concentrating on the charred area where Dagger’s truck had been parked.

Dagger remembered seeing the news reports last night of the cars in flames in the hotel parking lot. Even when Sara had told him she had fallen out of the twelfth floor window with Demko but had shifted, it hadn't dawned on him that she wouldn't have been able to drive home.

Dagger washed his hands over his face. "I hope like hell that the license plates are too damaged to trace. At least the serial number had been filed off."

"I've watched the *CSI* programs. They use something that can raise the numbers."

"Thanks for the encouragement."

12

Skizzy wheeled his chair from one computer to the next. He was in the concrete bunker below the pawn shop. Shelves of canned goods and water bottles could keep him supplied for years should the *big one* come, as Skizzy put it.

"No one is this squeaky clean," Dagger said as he stood by the printer reading additional information on Cardinal Esrey. Dagger picked up the metal plate Skizzy had retrieved after the first Demko's death. He told him about the similar one Padre had shown him and how it might have come from last night's victim.

Without even turning from the computer Skizzy said, "Clone. Government has been cloning assassins for years."

"Padre wasn't too forthcoming. Did you find anything in the medical examiner's database?"

"That's the strange thing. He is treating this as a normal suicide without any mention of the metal contraption or an internal bomb, nothing. Authorities obviously don't know what to make of it so they are keeping their suspicions off the public records."

Dagger set the metal plate down and picked up the Emails from Connie which Skizzy had found on Demko's computer. "Have you found out anything more about these Emails?"

"Not yet."

We have a problem, Dagger. Sara's voice was infused with alarm.

Dagger turned the page to the next Email. *What is it, Sara?* It amazed him that copper wire could block Skizzy's bunker from electronic bugs but there wasn't one thing that could stop telepathy.

All the evidence is gone from the quarry. Not one sign of Demko's remains.

That doesn't sound good. Certainly explains Padre's cockiness lately. What are you doing at the quarry? Dagger asked. There was a long silence. Dagger knew exactly why Sara had gone back.

Are Simon and Skizzy sure that Demko died?

Dagger heard a distinct quiver in Sara's voice. The *Friday the Thirteenth* killer had been a shapeshifter like Sara. Although they incinerated his remains to assure that he couldn't regenerate, even Padre and Dagger himself had second thoughts as to its effectiveness. And now with a second Demko running around, had the first reassembled? Completely outrageous thought but Dagger's life was anything but normal.

Yes. I would have second thoughts, too, except for the strange way Padre has been acting. It's a wonder he hasn't choked on those canary feathers. I expect a call from him the moment he realizes the truck Demko's body fell on was mine. Dagger thought about that for a second. *Oh shit.*

What?

Dagger turned to Skizzy. "Can you get into the police department records of stolen vehicles and fill out a report on my truck? Date the report yesterday morning. You have all the info on it, including the license plate number."

"Good as done." Skizzy smiled a little too devilishly. Any time he could play around in the heads of the locals, he was in his element.

Dagger told Sara, in thought only, what he had asked Skizzy to do.

Of all the vehicles to fall on. I should have parked it on the street but I wanted to blend in.

Don't worry about it. What's done is done.

That's the second vehicle of yours I've destroyed.

You never did like that truck. Sometimes I think you destroy them on purpose. Dagger smiled at that thought.

I liked the '64 Mustang convertible. I LOVED your Mustang convertible.

Dagger sighed. *My '64-and-a-half classic Mustang convertible. It was a beauty.*

"All done," Skizzy announced.

Go on home, Sara. "Thanks, Skizzy. Now all I have to do is wait for Padre to get the heads-up on the identification of all the vehicles destroyed last night."

"And then what? Can't dance around that old tune for too long," Skizzy said.

"Right. Then I'll have to do what I don't do best…come clean."

"I won't take up too much of your time, Your Eminence." Padre took a seat at the conference table in the Tyler mansion.

"I'm just glad to have some quiet time to finish my speech. I understand the hotel is pretty hectic today." Esrey was casually dressed in dark pants and shirt. He set aside his yellow lined pad to give the detective his undivided attention.

Padre waited for Lily to set a tray of glasses and a water pitcher on the table. Once she closed the conference door, he pulled out his notepad and pen. "Had you met Hank Hanover, the security guard who was murdered in your hotel room?"

Esrey appeared to wince at the word *murdered*. "No, I hadn't. My assistant asked the hotel to arrange for security when we realized there might be some disruptions during my stay. I sent a letter of condolence to his family."

"The hotel claims they had not received a call for housekeeping yet a cleaning cart was outside your hotel room."

"Sorry." Esrey shrugged apologetically. "I, of course, was here. I certainly don't want to accuse Mister Hanover of anything but if he was inside of my hotel suite then it wasn't what was understood of his services. Perhaps he heard something and asked housekeeping to unlock the door."

"That's what I had thought, although housekeeping would have had to admit the intruder first and we can't find the employee in order to ask her."

"I thought hotels had surveillance cameras."

"That certainly would make my job a lot easier. The floor you are on has had the cameras removed for guest privacy, which doesn't make sense because these guests are statistically more likely to be victims of crime."

Padre flipped to the next page in the notepad. "Your assistant studied the photos I took of your hotel suite but doesn't think anything had been stolen. Do you have any idea what the thief might have been looking for?"

"Probably for me. Perhaps he was the father or relative of an abused child who wanted to voice his disappointment in the church. I have run into them for a number of years now. Most will sit down and speak rationally. Some are a bit vocal. But certainly no acts of violence."

"There's always a first time. Six radicals disrupted Easter Mass at a cathedral in Chicago. Their issue was the Iraq war."

"Yes, I heard about that. We are living in some very conflicting times. I know the church has a lot of fences to mend, Sergeant." Esrey poured two glasses of water and passed one to Padre. The French doors to the veranda were open and the sounds of riding mowers could be heard, sending the scent of grass clippings wafting through the air. "Have you identified the man who committed suicide?"

"Not yet. If he had any identification on him, it was destroyed in the fire." Padre didn't want to share all of Luther's findings.

"We do have DNA but it will take a week or two to get those results." Padre studied the extremely calm man. For having two people die in his hotel suite, he would have expected Esrey to cancel his speech and leave town. But he was standing firm, either from naiveté or sheer stubbornness.

Padre made one more attempt to change the cardinal's mind. "You can always reschedule your speech. If this man did mean to cause you harm or was so distraught to commit suicide, there may be others out there."

But even as he spoke, the cardinal was shaking his head back and forth. "I know it's your job, Sergeant Martinez, but I'm not going to change my plans. From here I go to Rome for a special hearing with the Pope."

Translation: interview. Padre had heard that Esrey was being considered for an undisclosed post at the Vatican. The secrecy surrounding the appointment made Padre think that Esrey might garner an ambassadorship or special envoy assignment to a country where religion is frowned upon, thus the need for discretion.

"The hotel management can't explain how the intruder gained access to the executive level of the hotel."

Esrey thought about that for a moment, twisting and pulling at one eyebrow. It appeared strange for a grown man to have the nervous habit of a child. "Did you ever think, Sergeant, that maybe the man was a hotel worker? Maybe he had a key to my floor."

"The manager accounts for all of his employees. Doesn't even have a housekeeping employee missing."

"Obviously, it isn't that hard to get a key."

Padre pushed his chair away and stood. Something still wasn't clicking. "You know, it was in the papers that Robert Tyler was hosting a reception for you. I can't help thinking this guy was waiting for you to leave so he could search your hotel room, which tells me you weren't his target."

"So then what was he after?"

"That is the question now, isn't it?"

13

Sheila rushed down the circular drive. "Padre," she called out.

The detective stopped and turned. He gave her a once-over and nodded. "Don't think I've ever seen you dress so conservatively before."

Sheila looked down at her crisp white suit, white heels, white chiffon blouse buttoned to her neck. "Very convent-like, don't you think? And I didn't even get to talk to the cardinal. I was given his underling to interview."

Padre pulled a cigarette from his pocket and lit it. This was the sign Sheila was hoping to see. A pause from Padre was like an invitation to dinner. She pulled her own cigarette from a case and took the light Padre offered.

"The underling is a certified priest. Show a little respect. Did he have anything interesting to say?"

"I don't know. Might cost you."

Padre smiled. "Ahhh, you do know how to hold your cards close."

Sheila smiled back. "You know me. I'll show you mine if you show me yours."

They ambled down the circular drive to the parking lot. Padre's dented unmarked squad car looked anemic next to the shiny silver Jaguar. Sheila changed cars about as often as she changed clothes.

"Let's see," Padre started, "since we haven't identified the man who jumped…"

"Or was pushed," Sheila interjected.

"…or was pushed, the cardinal can't say whether or not he knew him. He had been able to gain access to the executive floor and the cardinal's suite which leads me to believe our jumper might have known the security guard."

"You think the security guard was casing the place out for some secret Vatican jewels and he and his partner had a falling out?"

"Good theory but the cardinal's assistant hasn't reported anything of value missing." They reached the parking lot where Padre stopped to gaze longingly at the Jag.

"Doting Thomas…" Sheila laughed at the look on Padre's face. "I'm sorry. It's Father Donald Thomas but he dotes so much on the cardinal that I just had to peg the guy with a nickname. He moves like he mainlines caffeine with a little obsessive-compulsive thrown in for good measure." Sheila shook her platinum hair and straightened her back as though she were a windup doll. *"I have to iron his shirts twice, lay out fresh socks at noon, he likes two creams, one sugar, and it has to be the real stuff, no fake sugar. His bath is drawn at nine o'clock sharp."* Sheila moved her arms robotically as she mimicked Father Thomas. "Give me a break."

"The man is serious about his duties."

"Whatever." Sheila flicked her wrist as though shooing him away. "Anyway, I asked him about any threats on the cardinal's life in the way of phone calls and threatening letters. Doting Thomas either didn't know or wasn't saying."

Padre ran a hand over the hood of the Jag.

"You're drooling, Padre."

"A man can dream, can't he?"

"I'm supposed to give Dagger an update. Anything you want me to share with him to steer him in the wrong direction?"

"He's asking about this case?"

"I can tell when something piques Dagger's interest. He wasn't just innocently strolling through the parking lot where the man took a dive. He was genuinely curious. Just haven't figured out why yet and you certainly can't convince me you didn't get the same impression," she added with a sly smile.

The throaty sound of a powerful engine echoed down the drive. Sunlight danced off the windshield of a blue Jaguar XKR 100. The convertible screeched to a stop in front of them.

Sheila smiled at the handsome man who leaped over the driver's side door. His sun bleached hair and tanned skin spelled surf and sun. He pulled off aviator sunglasses and smiled at Sheila.

"Like your taste in cars." Nick Tyler wrapped Sheila in a bear hug. "Hi, sis." Sheila wasn't any relation. She was closer in age to Nick's brother, Eric. But the Tylers and Monroes were inseparable when they were growing up. There were few multi-millionaire families in Cedar Point and they all traveled in the same circles.

"Doesn't anyone own a Prius these days?" Padre asked. "You know, good mileage, help the environment, go green."

"When the Cedar Point police department starts giving all their cops Priuses to drive, then I'll buy one," Nick replied. He had a handshake for Padre, then plopped down on the hood of Sheila's Jag.

"Just get back into town?" Sheila asked.

"This morning. There's only so much of nude beaches a guy can take."

"I thought you majored in business management?" Padre quipped.

"I was managing business." Nick grinned, revealing one deep dimple. "Thought I'd check out the Tyler resort in Martinique. Dad's trying to win me over by sending me to the island resorts."

Padre's phone rang. He checked the screen, then flipped the phone open. "Martinez." His face slowly showed shock, then anger. "I'm on my way in." He snapped the phone closed saying,

"Well, some of us have to work for a living."

"Anything I should know about?" Sheila had watched his face with curiosity. She could read just about everyone's face… sometimes.

"Nope." With a wave to Sheila, Padre said, *"Adios,"* turned and walked to his car.

Nick watched the detective climb into the battered car and drive away. "So what's happened that has the police on Dad's doorstep?"

Sheila filled him in on the cardinal's visit and the deaths at the hotel.

"The cardinal is staying here?" Nick looked up at the house as though expecting to see the cardinal watching them from a window.

Sheila followed his gaze. "Nice guy for a clergyman." She returned her gaze to the fading taillights. "Wish I could find a way to get on his good side."

"The cop or the clergy?" That one dimple showed itself as Nick climbed off the hood and carefully wiped the tail of his shirt across the spot where he had sat. "Good as new."

Sheila's lacquered nails drummed on the purse she clutched to her chest. "Are you going to be in town for a while?"

Nick knew Sheila well enough to know when she was hatching a plan. "Why?"

"I thought you could be my eyes and ears around the cardinal, maybe pick up a few words here and there. I'm thinking he is playing down any death threats he's received so as to quell any negative publicity. Maybe he did know the guy who pitched himself out of his hotel window. Maybe not. But he or his handler may slip up."

"Then you can do something for me." Nick walked back to his car, reached into the glove box, and pulled out a small white box.

"For me?" Sheila said.

Nick laughed. "No, but I'd like a woman's opinion."

Sheila set her purse on the car hood and stared at the box with the excitement of a four-year-old on Christmas morning. She carefully opened the lid and gasped. "Oh my gawd!" A dazzling pink diamond perched in a marquise setting sparkled in the sunlight. "Can I try it on?"

"No! It's supposed to be bad luck."

"Luck, schmuck." Sheila slipped it onto her ring finger and gasped again. "This has to be at least four carats." She held out her hand and admired the gem. Then the realization hit her as to the identity of the lucky girl and it was all she could do to contain her feelings of pity. Nick would be an excellent catch for any woman but the woman he was after loved someone else.

"I know what you're thinking."

Sheila realized her face must have read like a neon sign. "What's that, sweetie?" She pulled the ring off and placed it back in the box.

"I have more to offer Sara than Dagger ever could. Dad said he'd give me the resort in Martinique to run. What woman wouldn't love to live in an island paradise? I'd buy her a palace fit for a queen. Her own private plane. Shopping trips to Paris. A second home in France."

Sheila handed him the box, her mind turning over scenarios. With Sara out of the picture, she might have a chance to get Dagger back. Nick was so young and naïve and she hated to see him get hurt. Dagger could claim that he and Sara are just business partners but she had seen the way Dagger protects her, had seen the two of them together. If there isn't something there now, it's just a matter of time.

"You said yourself," Nick reminded her, "that Dagger and Sara are just business partners. I think she may be a little infatuated with him, with his exciting life. But that's all there is to it."

"Nick, players like you can have a different woman every night. But when it comes to marriage, you are always looking for the saintly virgin. And lord knows, Sara is probably the last one in town. Why don't you just sleep with her and nip your curiosity in the bud?"

"How do you know we already haven't?"

Sheila opened her car door and turned toward him. "A big sister knows such things. I can see it in the way you talk about her. The only thing missing is the word *love*."

"God, she's beautiful, smart. Of course I love her. What man wouldn't? She's never jealous. Understands how my schedule and social status puts me in contact with a lot of other women but she doesn't mind."

"And why is that, Nicholas?" Ever since Nick's mother passed away, Sheila had always felt that Nick was missing some sound, motherly advice. Robert was too busy to offer any and Nick was too proud to display any weakness to his father. Eric wasn't an expert on women seeing how his deceased wife tried to sell the family down the river. "Could it be she doesn't mind because she doesn't care?" She could see in his face that her words stung and she had to rein in her criticism. A plan was already formulating in her mind.

"She has yet to turn down a date, even when it's last minute notice. When I call her from Europe she is ecstatic to hear my voice. We have been to so many places and done so many things since we've met."

"Oh, sweetie." Sheila walked back over and wrapped her arms around him. "Sara has been so sheltered from the outside world that she wants to see what's out there. Dagger likes to stay below the radar, believe me. He wouldn't be caught dead going to museum fundraisers, the theatre, or art shows. But Sara wouldn't feel comfortable going alone."

"So you're saying she's using me?" The thought had obviously never occurred to him. He was used to using women, not the other way around.

"I just want you to be prepared for her response. It may not be a direct 'no,' but she may say she needs time." She climbed into her car and started the engine. "In the meantime, I might be able to give you a little help."

She left him pondering that comment as she sped down the driveway. The Lifestyles Editor at the *Daily Herald* was Gabby Goldstein. Gabriella's phone number was on Sheila's speed dial and Gabby was going to love this hot piece of gossip that was going to be dropped into her lap. Gabby may not have a current picture of Sara and Nick but the Daily Herald had some stock photos from one of the numerous *out-and-about* photo layouts that could be pieced together. Sheila couldn't help but smile at her good fortune.

14

He opened the suitcase and checked all the compartments, then unzipped the outside compartments, jamming his hands deep, his fingers probing at the crevices. Next he dumped the contents from the briefcase out onto the bed and pawed through the papers and file folders.

"Damn!" He moved to the bathroom and checked the toiletry bag again, spilling the contents onto the bathroom counter. Nothing. It had to still be in the suite but he couldn't get back into the hotel yet. There wasn't anything he could do now. At least he had already loaded the contents of the flash drive into the laptop. All he needed now was to decrypt the information.

The police weren't sure who the intruder had been or what he had been looking for. The safe hadn't been touched. Had he followed them to Cedar Point to retrieve the flash drive? No one knew where they were headed. It had been a chance encounter at the airport. Or had it?

"Are you sure?" Chief Wozniak rocked back in his plush leather chair, the crime scene investigator's report between thick fingers. Baby fine tufts of red hair sprouted from the tops of his hands, a softer red than what was on his head. Beady eyes squinted at the fine print.

Padre sat across the desk from the chief of detectives, wanting desperately to loan him a pair of bifocals but he knew John Wozniak's ego wouldn't permit anyone to see granny-type glasses perched on the tip of his bulbous nose. Their friendship dated back to seminary school before John chalked up two marriages with the third hanging by an apron string, and Padre began finding more satisfaction in saving the public from criminals than in saving souls.

"As sure as I am that Dagger knows more than he's letting on." The report Padre had shared with the chief confirmed that the truck the alleged suicide victim fell on was Dagger's. "The truck's serial number confirms that it's his even though the license plate was destroyed in the fire." Padre slid another report across the desk.

"What's this?"

Padre just sighed and motioned for Wozniak to read. Any other chief would have hauled Padre and Luther in for dereliction of duty. Since Wozniak was also involved in the *Friday the Thirteenth* case, he would be more open to the details of this case than the average cop. While Wozniak read, Padre studied the walls cluttered with photos, certificates, awards, keys to the city, photos of fishing trips. On the credenza behind Wozniak were pictures of the current wife and his son, Aaron, photos from scout outings where the chief was a scout leader. Padre fingered the gold cross under his shirt collar as he watched Wozniak's eyebrows crawl up his forehead like furry red caterpillars. His eyes flicked to Padre.

"Let me get this straight. A guy is blown to smithereens in the quarry and the same guy or a twin leaps out of the twelfth floor of the Ritz Hotel landing on Dagger's truck."

"Don't forget the part where we have records showing Lee Connors had called a cab to take him to Dagger's place."

"Oh, I read that part where Connors visits Dagger yet he had already been dead for two days, in the trunk of his own car no doubt. But how do you tie Dagger to the guy in the quarry?"

Padre told him how Dagger had jokingly told him, "The guy threatened me, I killed him and had Skizzy dump the body in the limestone quarry, but not before some bomb planted in the guy's neck blew his head off."

"Only thing is," Padre continued, "it was all true." He nodded toward Luther's report.

Wozniak's face lined with worry. "I don't like this."

"Me neither."

"What do you know about the guy in the trunk of the rental car?"

"He's definitely Lee Connors. He's a sales rep for a water filter company. Lives in Boston and was in town for a sales conference. Wife is flying in to retrieve the body."

Wozniak anchored his elbows on the desk, steepled his fingers in thought. "Dagger, this Lee Connors, whoever the guy was in the quarry, whoever the twin…and good God it has to be a twin. What the hell else could it be?" Wozniak shook that line of thought out of his head. "Let's say twin for now, and then we have Cardinal Esrey and the bodyguard. Everything all tethered together and we haven't a clue how, when, or why."

"That about covers it, although Lee Connors was probably an innocent bystander. Our quarry guy needed Connors' rental car and a room to lay his weary head." Padre stood and gathered up the reports. "When you figure it all out, let me know." He turned to leave.

Wozniak's head snapped up. "What do you mean when I figure it all out?"

Padre smiled and sat back down. "I just thought I'd take a few days vacation."

Wozniak waggled a finger at him. "No you don't. You get over to Dagger's and wring it out of him. Talk to that cute assistant of his. She'll give you the lowdown."

Padre's smile faded. "You're kidding, aren't you? In that last case with the art thief she literally threw her body in front of Dagger to save him. You were there. You saw it."

The chief sank back in his chair. "You're right. She's as loyal as a pit bull."

"When she gave Jimmy Cho a description of the guy who allegedly showed up on her doorstep, the damn sketch looked like me."

"Then lean on that squirrelly friend of his. Dagger joked that he's the one who tossed the body into the quarry, right?"

"I'm just starting to get this guy to trust me. I can't go jack boot stomping into his pawn shop and drag him down for questioning. I just can't."

"Then you have no choice. Haul Sara in for questioning."

Padre glared at Wozniak. "On what grounds?"

"Obstruction of justice. Tampering with evidence. Being too damn gorgeous."

"That's not a crime."

"Which one?" Wozniak slowly smiled at that one, the gruff big daddy grin that worked on all of his previous wives. The one that showed appreciation for the female gender which kept him from becoming a priest.

Padre pushed away from the desk and stood. "I'll have to try something else that will shock Dagger into leveling with me."

"What's that?"

"The truth."

15

"Aren't you looking dapper." Sheila stroked the fabric of Dagger's black and gray pinstriped jacket.

Dagger slid onto the bar stool and signaled the bartender. "You hate this outfit, Sheila."

"Maybe it's growing on me."

Dagger doubted that. He shoved a twenty across the bar and studied his reflection in the mirror. So maybe the black crew neck shirt under the pinstriped jacket was a little much. Black was supposed to make him blend into the shadows but with all the loud colors people wore these days he was sticking out like a sore thumb. He also had to quit scanning his surroundings like a cyborg checking for suspicious characters. Sara once said it made him look as though he were casing a place out to rob later. But he couldn't give up his black and gray just yet. There was something about bright colors that repelled him.

He turned away from the mirror and toward Sheila. "So, how's Father Thomas these days?"

"A little stuffy but congenial. I did talk to Lawton Security though. Snippy little receptionist almost wouldn't let me speak to the owner."

"I almost forgot about the security guard." He didn't ask any prying questions. Sheila would spill it all in due time. It was a matter of separating the wheat from the chaff, or the lies from the half truths.

"Hank Hanover was a ten-year veteran with the security firm," Sheila said without referring to any notes. "Great work record. Former Saint Louis cop who was sidelined by an injury. Pretty active in his local church which is why he wanted the security detail for Cardinal Esrey."

"I take it Padre also spoke with Lawton Security?"

"He didn't say." Sheila slapped a silver cigarette case on the bar. Before she had a chance to shove the cigarette in her mouth, the bartender had already flicked a lighter. "Thanks." Her eyes dragged over the bartender's sculpted body.

"And Father Thomas also didn't know who leaped out of his hotel window?"

"Why would he? They are only traveling through town, giving a speech, some meet and greet, then off to Rome. Father Thomas let it be known that the cardinal is up for a Vatican appointment. Of course, I'm not supposed to repeat that."

Sheila took a long drag from her cigarette. Dagger could tell by the way she was pursing her lips that she was just dying to share some hot rumor with him. He concentrated on his drink and wished the smoking ban in Illinois would be adopted in Indiana.

"Your turn. Tell me the real reason you were at the crime scene scouring the hotel parking lot."

"Does there have to be a reason?" He pushed his empty glass to the edge of the bar and motioned at Sheila's glass. "Guess it's the *almost a cop* in me." Dagger had once attended the police academy with the thought of making an honest living. "Since I had been invited by Robert Tyler to attend dinner as added security, I felt compelled to check things out. As you saw, Padre's guys picked the place clean before I got there." He placed another twenty dollar bill on the bar. "I would think your connections could get more details on the coroner's report. Padre has been pretty tightlipped with me lately."

"Yes, I have noticed a bit of a cooling off there. Is the honeymoon over?"

Padre was still straddling the fence between being shocked by the *Friday the Thirteenth* case and intrigued by witnessing the unimaginable. Eventually Dagger knew intrigue and the *blue rush* would win out. Once cops got the adrenaline going, it was hard to deny the rush.

"We're just in a chess game of wits at the moment." Dagger's eyes scanned the faces in the mirror behind the bar, searching out of habit for danger. Maybe subconsciously looking for another Demko. His gaze drifted to Sheila's reflection as she sucked on her cigarette. The foul habit made the lines around her mouth more pronounced, not that she still wasn't beautiful. "I'm more interested in what the *Daily Herald's* ace reporter thinks. What's your take on the jumper? Any buzz in the underworld about zealots wanting to vent their frustrations with the church?"

Sheila stabbed the remainder of the cigarette in the ashtray and fished around for another one. Her cigarette case was empty. Next, she attacked her purse while the bartender waited in the wings with a lighter. "The hotel turned over the incoming phone records to the police department. Padre is checking for threatening messages. In the meantime they have moved his speech from the hotel to an undisclosed location." She sighed when she didn't find a pack of cigarettes in her purse and waved off the bartender's offer to buy her a pack. "I need to cut down anyway."

"What about fingerprints in the hotel room? Padre share any of those results with you?"

Sheila's gaze raked over his body and she leaned back with a look he recognized. "No, Padre was tightlipped but I have a man on the inside who will give me the scoop which I'd be willing to share with you…for a price."

Dagger knew that price. It had dragged him back into her clutches too many times to count. "Thanks, but I also have my sources." In an effort to avoid pissing her off entirely, he added, "But nice try."

This warranted a shrug. "Can't blame a girl for trying."

* * *

Sara was on the phone when Dagger returned home. She sat curled up in a corner of the sectional, a smile on her face that told him Nick Tyler was on the other end of the receiver. He closed the outer door to Einstein's aviary. He had carpeted it which added more soundproofing in addition to keeping out the light from the living room.

He walked over to the bar under the staircase to grab a beer from the refrigerator. He took his time so as to catch portions of her phone conversation.

"I'll be ready. Night." Sara pushed the END button, a smile illuminating her face. "Nick's home."

"Really? For how long this time?"

She uncurled from the couch and set the phone on the coffee table. "What did you learn from Sheila?"

Sara had deftly ignored his question. Dagger didn't consider it prying. He just knew guys like Nick. He was Paris Hilton in pants. Wherever there was a camera or a party, he was there, leaving broken hearts in his wake. Dagger didn't want Sara to be one of them.

"Police don't know anything, although I think Padre was dodging her questions." He took a long pull off the beer bottle, kicked off his shoes, and sank onto the couch, propped his feet on the coffee table. "The security guard, Hank Hanover, had a clean work record, was a cop in a previous life, a churchgoing guy and volunteered for the assignment to guard the cardinal."

"Any fingerprints in the hotel room?"

It scared him sometimes how her mind was starting to click like his. Maybe that was a good thing. Maybe he wasn't giving her enough credit to recognize a two-timer like Nick when she saw one. "She claims to have someone on the inside but we've got Skizzy and he'll let us know when something pops up in the department computers. Speaking of which." Dagger picked up the phone and called Skizzy. "Look over Cardinal Esrey's travel itinerary for the past month. Check airport and hotel cameras and see if you can find anything suspicious."

"What are you looking for?"

"A stalker maybe, someone following him, getting on the same plane, sitting close by at a restaurant, anyone suspicious. No rush. Tomorrow will be fine." Dagger hung up before Skizzy could rant.

16

Dagger gave a low whistle. The macaw peeked out from behind a frond in one of the upper branches of the tree in the aviary. "Fetch, Einstein." Dagger tossed a frisbee in the air. A blur of bright blue and scarlet charged from the tree as Einstein caught the Frisbee in his beak, then landed on a perch by the window.

"Einstein, you are supposed to return it to me." Dagger shook his head. "Training a macaw isn't as easy as they say."

"That's because he's a bird, not a dog. If you wanted a pet that fetches, you should have bought a dog," Simon said.

The Frisbee dropped from Einstein's beak and landed in the birdbath. The macaw pulled a chain then stood under the shower flapping his wings.

Simon cackled at Einstein's antics. "You got some coffee?"

They convened in the kitchen. Morning light splashed across the room. Simon slapped the *Daily Herald* newspaper on the table and shuffled over to the coffeemaker. "Might find the society page pretty interesting."

"I doubt it." Dagger grabbed his cup of cold coffee and set it in the microwave. "If it's about Sheila, I don't care to read it." He punched the one minute button on the panel.

Simon scanned the kitchen counter. "Got anything to eat?"

"Eunie told Sara to only serve you fruit so there's a fruit salad in the fridge."

Simon mumbled something unintelligible and reluctantly dragged out a bowl of fruit salad from the refrigerator. Once they were settled at the table, Simon winced at the fading bruise on Dagger's cheek and tsked. "You should cover that with makeup. People are going to take you for a thug."

"They already do. Besides, it makes people keep their distance."

"Aren't you the social butterfly. Speaking of which." Simon nudged the paper toward him.

"What am I supposed to read?"

"That Gabby lady's column. The one that tells you what the rich and famous are doing."

"And I should be interested because…" Dagger's words caught in his throat as he saw Sara's picture overlaid next to Nick Tyler's. His eyes quickly scanned the article that reported a rumor from an undisclosed source that Cedar Point's answer to Brad Pitt had purchased an engagement ring. Speculation was that a local woman with whom he had been seen with on occasion, would be the recipient of a four-carat pink diamond. Dagger realized his index finger was hot from grasping his coffee cup.

"Didn't I tell you?" Simon stabbed at a strawberry with his fork. "But no. Now Tyler is going to dangle this gorgeous ring in front of her. He's young, good looking, not that you ain't."

"Young or good looking?" Dagger glared at the postal carrier.

"He's got more money than God for one thing. Lots to offer a woman."

"Sara doesn't care about money or mansions."

"She spends a lot of time with him…when he's in town."

"Right, when he's in town." Dagger stalked over to the coffee machine and filled his cup. "Sara knows he dates other women which is why I don't think the ring is for her. They aren't *serious* serious."

"*Serious* serious, like in sleeping together serious?" Simon's eyes twinkled as they followed Dagger back to the table.

"She would have told me."

Simon barked out a laugh. "And why is that?"

Dagger shrugged in response, his eyes drifting to the article again. He and Sara had shared a lot of information in the past. Of course she would come to him…even though she always avoided the subject of Nick in the past. And why was that? He didn't want to think about it.

"You'll see," Dagger said. "The ring is probably for some daughter of a U.S. ambassador he met overseas. Someone with comparable status and a lot of connections."

"AWK AWK. WHAT A BODY."

Dagger heard Sara tell Einstein to shut his beak. He shook his head at Simon as a caution to change the subject, then quickly pulled the paper off the table and put it on the chair next to him.

Sara breezed into the kitchen, her hair a mass of tiny pink papers. "Hi, Simon. I see you are eating healthy." Sara planted a kiss on Simon's pudgy cheek. "I'll be sure to report back to Eunie."

Simon shot a puzzled look at Dagger who seemed just as confused by her appearance. Sara pulled a bowl from the cabinet then settled into a chair next to Simon.

"That all you're eating?" Simon asked as he watched Sara scoop fruit into the bowl. His gaze kept drifting to the pink papers infesting Sara's hair.

Sara unwrapped herself from the chair, pulled a bag from the freezer and popped it into the microwave. Next she grabbed three plates and set them on the table along with napkins. When the microwave dinged she pulled the bag out and shook the contents onto a platter.

"I made ham and cheese crescent rolls last month and froze several bags. Eunie said you can have two." Sara smiled at Simon's grumbling.

"Thanks," Dagger said. He watched Simon's puzzled stare at Sara's hair. He couldn't take it anymore. To Sara he asked, "Did you borrow Skizzy's headset?"

"No," Sara said with a withering glare. "They showed this on

TV. I took small strips of hair and wound them around the pink papers. After several hours, I'll have a head full of corkscrew curls."

"Going someplace special?" Simon asked.

How like Simon to get to the meat of the question, Dagger thought.

"Nick is taking me to dinner at the country club. Said to go all out because it's a special occasion."

Simon's smug smile had *told you so* written all over it. Dagger wanted to punch him silly.

Father Thomas paced in front of the caterer, menu in hand. The event had been moved from the hotel to the Tyler mansion. Robert Tyler had given his name and introduced the timid priest as his staff member in order to keep the caterers from knowing the location of the diocese farewell reception. Father Thomas had obliged by not wearing his clerical collar.

The caterer sat patiently at the table, her starched blouse looked as prim and proper as a cleric's collar. Elaine Godet had catered for the wealthiest families and high-profile functions for over twenty years. She pulled a pen from the twist of salt and pepper hair which obediently remained in place.

"Being that it is summer, you might want to avoid the heavier creamed sauces and dishes," Elaine suggested.

"Yes, yes, Mizz Godet," he agreed.

"It's Go-DAY," Elaine stressed. "Since this will take place later in the afternoon we will need to offer more éntrees."

Father Thomas appeared not to hear. "The strawberry walnut salad will be nice and light as well as the spring vegetable soup." He turned and retraced his steps. "Raspberry iced tea and coffee. The dessert selections look fabulous. I just don't know about the éntrees."

Robert watched him struggle with the number of choices and decided to step in. Any minute he expected the priest to start a mantra about Cardinal Esrey's nap time, digestive problems and allergies. Not that Esrey had any but it wouldn't stop Donald from worrying about them.

"We probably need one red meat, one white meat, and possibly a fish. Maybe a blackened salmon with dill sauce. Do you agree, Father Thomas?"

He bowed his head, the sunlight shining brightly on his bald dome. "Yes, yes. What about a potato?"

"Seasoned rice with mandarin oranges perhaps?" Robert pleaded with his eyes for fear the meek man would offer to ask the cardinal's opinion.

"But the red meat needs a potato." Father Thomas' fingers wound together like plump white worms. "Rice with red meat doesn't go."

The woman seated at the table tapped her pen repeatedly, snatching glances from one man to the other. Father Thomas caught the irritation of the tap-tapping but before he could say anything, Elaine offered, "Boiled pearl potatoes with parsley works fine with the beef burgundy."

"Yes." Robert was relieved to finally end the lengthy menu selection debacle.

"Oh, I'm not sure," Father Thomas whined.

Elaine bent her head and lasered a glare over her bifocals at the timid man. "Beef burgundy over buttered noodles?"

"Perfect!"

Elaine and Robert breathed a collective sigh of relief, but when Father Thomas piped up with, "Then again," they each groaned a little too loudly.

"Maybe we should ask…" he started. "LILY." Robert cried out in relief as his housekeeper appeared in the doorway dressed in her traditional black and white uniform. There was so much black and white in the house this week that Robert was contemplating putting out a moratorium against wearing black after the cardinal leaves. "We were just going to come find you. We need help with a menu. Do you think pearl potatoes or buttered noodles go best with beef burgundy?"

"Boiled pearl potatoes, of course," Lily said. Wisps of short graying hair framed a wise and trusting face. "Buttered noodles would be too heavy."

"Thank you," Elaine said with unabashed delight. She gathered up her papers before anyone could make additional changes. She passed Nick as she headed toward the doorway.

"Did I miss something?" Nick asked, watching as the harried lady rushed out.

"I'll go share this with His Eminence," the priest announced, and hurried out of the room.

"He is a strange guy." Nick placed a small white and gold box on the table. "Tell me what you think."

"Is everything set for tonight?" Robert opened the box and smiled. "You have excellent taste. She is going to love it." He saw a look of apprehension cross his son's face. "Having second thoughts?"

"Who me? Absolutely not."

Robert motioned to the veranda. It was on these beautiful summer days that Robert wished he had a Spanish villa that was open and airy. Unfortunately, being this near the water in the Midwest brought too many insects. "You aren't doing this for me, are you, Son?"

"What do you mean?" Nick sat down, the ring box clasped in his hands.

"I want you to take an interest in the business. So to placate me and also be able to enjoy sun and fun at our Martinique resort, you are going to give the impression you are settling down."

Nick kicked his sandals off and pressed his bare feet against the railing. “Not at all. I’m just trying to snatch Sara before someone else does.”

“Someone like Dagger?” Robert watched his son gaze longingly at the sailboats in the distance. He changed the conversation back to his original question. “You called the clubhouse to confirm all the plans?”

“Yes, and Lily went over the menu with the clubhouse staff.”

“I’m surprised Sara hasn’t called after seeing that rumor in the gossip column this morning. Whose idea was that?”

“Sheila’s.”

Robert chuckled. “That explains a lot.”

“What do you mean?”

Robert rose from the chair and settled against the railing facing his son. “I believe Sheila knows Sara better than you. She knows Sara is too kind to turn you down after all the fuss being made and all the trouble you are going through. And now with that gossip column practically spelling it out for the whole town to know, there isn’t anyway Sara would humiliate you by refusing the ring. This opens the door to Dagger which is all Sheila is interested in.”

Nick gave a shrug. “Is that such a bad thing?”

17

"Oh shit," Dagger mumbled under his breath as he saw the smiling face on the surveillance screen. "Padre's here." He pushed the button for the gate to open.

"Wonder which subject he wants to discuss," Sara said. "Your truck or the remains in the quarry."

Dagger stared at Sara's hair. It was a mass of long tendrils. He preferred her hair straight like she always wore it. Given the weight of her thick hair, he expected the curls to be gone within a few hours.

"Nice," he settled on rather than telling her what he really thought. He wondered what she planned to wear tonight and whether or not he should tell her about the rumor in the newspaper. A knock on the door interrupted his train of thought. "Door's open," Dagger yelled. He tucked the Kimber in the top drawer of the desk and pulled his hair back in a ponytail in an attempt to look clean cut. It didn't work. Danger flowed through his veins and guilt seeped from his pores.

Einstein clamped claws on the grated door and screeched, "UP AGAINST THE WALL AND SPREAD 'EM. AWK."

"Hey my feathered friend." Padre shot a salute at the macaw. "Whoa." He took a step back. "Lookin' good, *mamacita*." Padre walked a 360 around Sara. "Curls galore."

"Thanks," Sara said. "It's different but it won't last long. Do you want a beer, Padre?"

"Nah. I can't stay long. Have to get back to the office."

Dagger eyed him with a bit of suspicion. The shit-eatin' grin was gone so the cop wasn't going to play the *I've got something on you* game. Instead, Padre was wearing his trading card face.

“I have chocolate chip cookies,” Sara said in a sing-song voice.

Padre rubbed the small paunch barely kissing his belt buckle. “The wife has me on a diet.” When Sara flashed a pout, the cop said, “But what the hell.” He cocked his head as he watched Sara walk out of the room, then swiveled his head to the glass window. “Whose PT Cruiser in the driveway?”

“Sara’s,” Dagger said. “It’s a girl car.”

“But it’s a guy color,” Padre added, checking out the bright red paint.

“Doesn’t quite have the power a guy likes.”

Sara carried in a plate of cookies and a bottle of water and set them on the coffee table. “Are you cutting up my car again?”

“Not me,” Padre replied as he settled on the couch.

“COOKIE.” Einstein poked his beak through the grating.

“You get a Brazil nut and like it,” Dagger said, shoving the nut between the grating. Einstein eyed the treat suspiciously but after a few seconds of contemplation, gingerly plucked it from Dagger’s fingers.

Padre popped one cookie in his mouth whole, shaking his head with approval, then washed it down with water. “With all those cars you got, how come you needed to buy another one?”

“This one is all mine,” Sara said. “Besides, Dagger’s truck was stolen.”

“Really? When was that?”

“About three or four days ago,” Dagger replied. “I filed a report.”

“That right? Funny, I didn’t see a report. The only one I saw was the report on your truck being burned at the Ritz the other night.” Padre popped another cookie in his mouth.

“My truck?” Dagger sat on the love seat cattycorner from Padre. He spent several seconds puzzling over the news and hoped it looked sincere. Sara would have been better at pulling it off. "Are you sure?"

"Positive. Where was your truck when it was stolen?"

"I had it at the shopping center," Sara admitted. "I don't know why anyone would want to steal it. The thing was a total wreck."

"Hey," Dagger barked. "The truck was a classic."

"A classic wreck," Sara countered.

Padre took another cookie, this time savoring it in two bites. "You two can argue about its quality all you want. What I want to know is how a dead man ended up on top of it."

"The jumper at the Ritz?" Dagger asked. "Can you tell if the truck was stripped and dumped there?"

"Was there really anything worth stripping on that junker?" Padre asked.

"Hey!"

"Thanks," Sara said with a smile, then tossed a "see?" at Dagger.

Padre pushed the plate away and downed the last of the water. "Anything else you care to share with me? Any new details come to mind on that guy who showed up at your gate several days ago?"

"AWK, DEAD MAN ON THE FLOOR. NEED A CLEAN-UP IN AISLE SEVEN. BROKEN NECK. AWK."

Dagger slowly gritted his teeth at the macaw. Sara gasped. Padre leaned back and clasped his hands across his stomach. And waited. Now the shit-eatin' grin appeared full-time.

After a few minutes of silence, Padre said, "Luther and I have been to the quarry. We scraped up what we could. Thought you might like to know Luther found some pretty interesting things about the man in the quarry and the man who jumped from the twelfth floor hotel window. They had the same blood type and the same fingerprints. We are hoping they were twins because anything other than that would be a little hard to fathom.

I'm hoping you can help sort things out."

Dagger flicked his gaze to Sara who just blinked. Padre was playing a strange game of poker. He just laid all of his cards out on the table. Dagger had the choice of folding or showing his hand. He decided on the latter and started at the beginning. When he was through, Padre just sat there, either numb or trying to determine how much of it was bullshit and just how angry he should be.

"Who are you trying to kid?" Padre stood to leave. "I would have thought you'd be more forthcoming after all we've been through. But lately I get more information from your bird."

"Just give me a minute of your time to show you the video." Dagger retrieved the videotape while Padre reluctantly sat back down. He shoved the tape into the player, and dropped the remote into Padre's lap. Dagger retrieved a beer from the bar as the tape replayed the scene from the gate when Demko had leaped over the fence with little effort. He stood behind the couch as Padre replayed the video.

Padre rubbed his eyes and sank back against the couch cushions. "I'm getting too old for this," he said under his breath. "And you never saw him before."

"Never," Dagger said. "I do have his laptop from the hotel."

Dagger held up a copy of the contents Skizzy had burned onto a CD. "There are instructions from someone named Connie to follow Cardinal Esrey and to get 'the package', whatever the hell that is. Most of the documents on the computer were coded. Since he failed to do whatever he was supposed to do, his twin showed up to probably pick up where the first left off. Maybe the package is the cardinal himself, but I doubt it. Instead of following Esrey to the Tyler residence, he seemed to wait until he was gone so he could search the hotel room."

"Or maybe being from out of town he didn't know the cardinal wouldn't be in his hotel room that night," Padre said. "But that doesn't explain what he wanted with you."

"He was told to hire a private eye to do his leg work and then to get rid of said person." To show he was cooperating, Dagger grabbed a paper from the desk and handed it to Padre. "These are the prints off the guy I killed…in self-defense," he added.

"I thought there wasn't much left of the guy in the quarry," Sara said.

"Luther found a finger or two. Still don't know how that guy blew up so thoroughly."

"I don't either. I haven't seen anything like it," Dagger admitted.

Padre gathered up the CD and fingerprint copy and stood. "I am curious why you aren't surprised that the man who leaped from the window matched your guy's fingerprints. Makes me think you might have been in the hotel room."

"I saw what was left of my truck. It looked too much like the damage done to the guy in the quarry. I don't believe in coincidences."

"Neither do I," Padre said.

Sara looked at the clock above the desk. "I have to get ready." She started for the staircase.

"Hey, congratulations on…" Padre caught the signal from Dagger. "…your new car."

Nick met Sara at the curb. She was surprised he had sent a limo to pick her up. What kind of celebration was he planning? Nick gave her a kiss as she stepped out of the vehicle. He took a step back and held her at arm's length. "Wow, you look fabulous."

Sara had chosen a knee-length turquoise sleeveless dress. A multi-strand necklace in silver and turquoise beads hung in tiers from her neck. She was surprised Nick was dressed in a tuxedo and more surprised that people were snapping pictures. This was normally not seen at the country club. They were strict with security. But everyone appeared to be dressed formally. Out of force of habit, she called on her enhanced hearing and picked up certain phrases: "Beautiful couple…couldn't have made a better choice…"

"What's with the tuxedo?" Sara asked. He did look striking. But then Nick would look great in anything he wore, which was why he was in such demand as a model.

"This old thing?" Nick laughed and led her up the stairs to the canopied entrance. Sara stole a glance over her shoulder at the onlookers who were still snapping pictures. She was starting to get the uneasy feeling that something wasn't quite right.

More guests in formal attire lingered around the lobby under the massive chandelier. Sheila and her mother practically ran up to her in their exuberance.

"Sara, you look absolutely stunning," Sheila gushed.

"Just beautiful," Anna Monroe echoed, clutching a sequined handbag.

"Hey, what about me?" Nick said. He accepted a kiss from Anna.

Sheila wrapped her arms around Sara and gave her a hug. Tiny pinpricks started to dance across Sara's skin. Sheila never touched her, much less gave her a hug. Something wasn't right. Maybe it was the sight of so many people gathering in the dining room that was making Sara nervous. Crowds did that to her. Maybe she could convince Nick to select a table outside, away from the main dining room.

"Where is the ladies room?" Sara asked.

Nick pointed down a long hallway. "Don't be long."

"I won't." Sara hustled down the aisle, past waitresses in black and white uniforms and couples reeking of money. She found refuge in one of the stalls and took a deep breath, closing her eyes to block out the sights and focusing inward to block out the sounds. The door to the lounge opened and voices, excited and bubbly, filtered through. She tried to ignore them and focus on calming her panic attack. But certain words again drew her attention.

"It's such a pity…he is so gorgeous…"

"I know...why does he want to get married?"

"I hear the ring is a shocker."

"He's proposing tonight…"

"In front of God and everyone. Even the press is here."

"Look…today's paper."

Sara's eyes snapped open. They couldn't possibly be talking about Nick! She heard them mention a gossip column in the morning paper. Sara hadn't seen today's paper. But who else could they be referring to? Nick was dressed for a big event and had told her this was a special night. Then again, Dagger would have made sure she had seen the column if it had mentioned Nick.

The women continued exchanging rumors.

"He could have any actress or model…"

"But why a local…?"

"She is pretty. Native American I'm told…"

"But still, she isn't from old money."

The voices drifted as Sara heard the outer door close. She opened the stall door slowly. She was alone. Rushing to the sitting area, she found the newspaper and quickly scanned the column.

"Oh no!" Sara's heart pounded. Yes, Nick was nice. Yes, she liked him. But love? The article didn't name her but did have a dated picture of her with Nick. The last thing she needed was reporters and photographers following her to find out where she lived, then uncovering her relationship with Dagger which would ultimately lead to them trying to find out all they could about Dagger.

She opened the door to the women's lounge and took a quick peek down the hall. She didn't see anyone she knew in the lobby. Staring down the opposite hall she saw a door marked *kitchen* and another door with a red exit sign. She went for the kitchen, grabbing her cell phone from her purse.

Sara dialed quickly and when the phone was answered said, "Can you come get me?"

18

Eunie set a cup of tea in front of Sara and placed one on the table for herself before sliding into the booth across from her. "It's been a long time since I drove up to the back entrance where the hired help go," Eunie said.

Sara didn't say anything, just stared at the laminated table top. The diner was tucked between Cedar Creek Mall and a strip mall. She rested her chin in her hands and finally flicked her gaze to Eunie. The rotund woman was a mirror image of her husband, Simon. They were both a bit top heavy and wobbled when they walked, as though their spindly legs couldn't hold them up. Her hair was a nest of steel wool and hovered over eyes that were the kindest Sara had seen since her grandmother's.

"I had to get out of there," Sara finally said. "I can imagine Nick having an orchestra there, him with the microphone proposing to me and what could I have done? With all those people looking at me I wouldn't have been able to say no. So I just left."

"Just left?"

"Well, I gave a note to one of the cooks to give to Nick asking him to come to the kitchen, that they were having a problem. Then I told him 'Sorry, but the answer is no.' Do you think that was insensitive of me?"

"No, it was honest to tell him."

"He looked so hurt. I felt horrible." A tear made a lazy trail down her cheek but she wiped it away quickly. "I'm afraid if I stayed any longer I would have given in."

Eunie held her cup in both hands, elbows on the table. "Somehow I think he's going to bounce right back."

"But he'll never speak to me again. I sort of yelled at him for blindsiding me. I told him it wasn't a gentlemanly thing to do but he said that wasn't the way he planned it. It was Sheila's suggestion that I..."

"Sheila." Eunie set her cup down and shook her head in disgust. "She must be enjoying this, always telling Nick he could do better."

Sara sank back against the seat. "I can imagine Nick's humiliation when people started asking him where I was. I heard the press was there. I'm sure Sheila made sure the gossip columnist was invited."

"If Nick had proposed and you had accepted, it would be exactly what Sheila would want...you out of Dagger's life."

"She knows Dagger and I are just business associates."

"Hmmmm." There was a twinkle in Eunie's eyes as she lifted the cup to her mouth and took a sip.

"One thing Nick doesn't know, which I'm just going to have to tell him, is that I can't have children."

"That would pose a problem for a Tyler. Robert Tyler can't wait for more grandchildren." Eunie studied Sara with an intensity that made Sara uncomfortable. "I had almost forgot about that case where you were injured. I'm surprised Dagger places you in such danger."

"Did Simon tell you about the killer?"

"A little bit."

"I try not to think about it." Sara would rather not explain the *Friday the Thirteenth* case. Sara's wound had been self-inflicted in an effort to assure no other shapeshifters would be born, especially if one were as evil as Paul Addison. It had been a split second decision she would have to live with.

"I don't plan to ever marry anyway. And telling Nick I can't have children will hurt less than to tell him I feel absolutely nothing when he kisses me."

"Not even when you are out dancing at those fancy clubs, a slow dance when he is whispering in your ear or nibbling your neck."

Sara smiled, surprised at Eunie's playful depiction. "Not even then." Sara grew pensive and frowned. For all the times she had been with Nick, she couldn't remember one time when she could honestly say she responded to him. "Do you think there's something wrong with me?"

Eunie laughed, her eyes twinkling in much the same way Simon's did whenever he was amused. "Not at all. It will happen. One day it will hit you. You are going to feel as though the loss of that one special person will literally pull your heart out, that you would rather die than let anything happen to him."

A familiar scent wafted through the air. Sara didn't have to turn to know who had just walked into the diner. Her enhanced sense of smell and hearing knew he was approaching their table. Sara flashed a look of disappointment that Eunie had shared her problem.

Eunie reached across and patted Sara's hand. "Sorry, child, but I thought tonight of all nights is when you need the one person who knows you best."

Color rose to Sara's cheeks. She slid out of the booth before Dagger could sit down. "I need to use the restroom."

They watched her hustle to the back of the restaurant.

"Oh, dear. I believe she is upset with me."

"Not you, Eunie. She's pissed at me because I didn't forewarn her. That and the fact that I probably wear a perpetual *I told you so* smirk on my face. Nick is a player and Sara refused to see that side of him."

Eunie finished her tea and pushed the empty cup aside. After a quick look over her shoulder in the direction Sara had walked, Eunie leaned across the table and whispered, "I can tell you with firsthand knowledge that child don't love young Tyler, no matter how rich or good looking he is. If she is feeling anything right now it's guilt for using him."

"Using him?" Dagger's concept of *using* was different than Eunie's.

"I don't know why her grandmother kept her secluded for so long but I know she has some serious anxiety attacks—afraid of crowds, unfamiliar surroundings, almost afraid of her own shadow."

Dagger shrugged, knowing far more than Eunie knew but not offering much of an explanation. "Her parents died when she was five or six. Guess Ada might have sheltered her a little too much but she is getting better." A waif of a waitress set a cup of black coffee in front of him and left. He wanted to bring the conversation back to the term *using him* before Sara returned. "Do you know if she and Nick were that...close?" He took a quick gulp of his coffee, burning the roof of his mouth.

"Hmmm," Eunie smiled, a similar grin to Simon's whenever the subject of Sara came up. "I don't ask such personal questions but if you want a woman's intuition..."

"Please."

"Men like the Tylers can play around all they want but when it comes to the women they marry, they want someone unblemished, if you get my drift. No matter what young lady Nicholas marries, if he ever marries, it won't stop his roving eye and he needs someone to understand that. Nicholas is mistaking Sara's aloofness to his roving eye. She doesn't care what Nick does because she doesn't love him." She leaned in closer, training her motherly eyes on him. "Now what about you? Who do you love, Chase Dagger?"

Sara was turning the corner and headed their way, her dress flowing around a set of shapely legs.

"You know me, Eunie. I live the kind of life where I have to be free to leave at a moment's notice. I'm sure you've known guys like that."

"Oh, yes." Eunie slid out of the booth and grabbed her purse. She added with a chuckle, "I married one." She patted his shoulder, gave Sara a hug, and walked out.

"I didn't chase her away did I?" Sara slid into the booth vacated by Eunie.

Dagger pushed her cup of tea across the table. "She thought you were angry with her but I assured Eunie I will be the one on the receiving end of your wrath."

She stirred sugar into her tea, staring silently at the steam. The weight of her thick hair had straightened what little curl she had left. The humidity was causing Dagger's hair to curl.

"It could have been worse," Dagger offered. "He could have invited you to a baseball game and had the proposal flashed on the large screen for the millions in the viewing audience to see." He waited her out, wanting to ask more personal questions but not sure this was the time or the place.

Sara just glared at Dagger, her anger building. "Why did you hide the newspaper article from me? The one that posted a rumor that Cedar Point's most eligible bachelor had purchased a ring. Why didn't you shove the paper in front of my face so I knew what to expect?"

Dagger shrugged, his eyes dissecting her movements, assessing her mood. "I flipped a coin. I could have showed it to you and risked your accusation that I was just trying to diminish Nick in your eyes. Or I could have hidden it, which is what I did, and let things unfold naturally."

"And if I had accepted his proposal?"

"You wouldn't have." Although Dagger didn't smile, Sara could see the satisfaction in his eyes. It angered her that someone knew her so well.

"Doesn't it bother you that I hurt him deeply."

Dagger slid out of the booth. "Come on. I need to show you

something."

They left their drinks and drove back to the lakeshore area. Dagger pulled into a parking space at the curb and pointed across the street. "Take a look at how hurt and upset Nick Tyler is."

The Point was an exclusive club at the marina which had an outlandish cover charge and where one would go to see the *who's who* list of Cedar Point. Nick was sitting on a concrete bench outside the entrance, an arm around the women on either side of him. He was laughing and hugging the women closer.

"I took the liberty of calling the jewelry store which I know had the only pink diamond in the Midwest. They told me Nick borrowed it. He didn't buy it, leaving himself the option of returning it the next day."

Sara said nothing.

"Robert Tyler is eager to give Nick the resort on the island of Martinique but Robert thinks it would look more professional if Nick gave the impression of settling down. Nick was more than happy to have you wear his ring for three or four years while he continued to sow his wild oats."

Sara still said nothing.

"That is why I didn't tell you anything earlier today. To go through my assertions would have had you denying everything I said. Nick is a nice enough guy but he is a playboy. I don't think he will ever settle down."

Without saying anything, Sara exited the Navigator.

The night air was humid but a welcome relief from the Navigator's air conditioning. Sara crossed the street and slowed her walk from an angry march to a slow stroll. She smiled as Nick turned his attention her way. At first he looked pleased, then embarrassed. Both arms dropped from around the two women's shoulders as he stood. Sara couldn't stay mad at Nick. He was like a little boy lost, an adventurer always looking for a new adventure.

"Hey." Nick's smile was genuine. "Change your mind?"

"Can we walk?"

Dagger turned the lights off and slowly steered the Navigator onto the street. The couple moved too far away for him to hear anything. The Navigator crept along as Nick wrapped his arm around Sara's shoulder. Dagger's eyes scanned the area for reporters. He figured Robert Tyler's long arm reached Leyton Monroe and an edict had been set down warning local reporters off of Nick Tyler. It didn't stop the out-of-town rag sheet photographers from trying to snap a few photos, but that was why Nick stuck to members-only night spots.

The couple stopped for an embrace. They kissed, a little too long. "Too much tongue action there, kid." Dagger felt his hands wrap a vice grip on the steering wheel. They broke away with Sara raising her hand to stop Nick's advances. And now she was doing a lot of talking. It didn't appear Nick could get a word in edgewise. Now they were both smiling. "Oh, shit," Dagger said to himself. "Looks like they might have made up."

Sara turned and walked away. A man in a suit and tie clutching a cell phone had to sidestep. He almost dropped the phone and lunged like a juggler to keep the phone from dropping. He yelled out his apologies as he caught the phone but managed to run his eyes over her frame with a look of approval. Sara's smile faded. Dagger knew that look. There was something about the man that bothered her. She continued to stare at the man's retreat while slowly making her way to the Navigator.

As she climbed into the vehicle Dagger asked, "Did you know that guy?"

Sara continued to stare in the direction the man had gone. "No, but something about him reminded me of something. Not sure what."

Dagger flipped the headlights on and gunned the Navigator away from the curb, subconsciously trying to distance Sara from

Nick. "Are you and Nick okay?"

"Sure."

That was it. Dagger was going to have to drag the information from her. He glanced at her left hand. She wasn't wearing the ring. Sara caught him looking.

"I told him I can't have children to which he said we could adopt. I told him his father is looking forward to a Tyler clan to carry the family name. I told him he doesn't love me, he only wants to keep me out of '*circulation*'…his words, not mine… until he is ready to settle down."

"Ouch."

"He said he would never find another woman who understands him so well, who gives him his freedom, who doesn't get mad when tabloids show him with another woman to which I said that's because I don't care because I don't love him."

"Double ouch."

"Well, truth hurts. That's what you've always told me. He admitted the ring was on loan from the jewelry store and that it was Sheila's idea to spring this proposal on me in front of a packed room so I wouldn't back down. He apologized for putting me on the spot. I apologized for using him as a Dating 101 instructor. So we are going out tomorrow night."

"You're going out?" Dagger almost missed the red light. He stomped on the brake pedal and quickly checked the rearview mirror to make sure any cars behind him also saw the red light.

"As friends."

"Friends," Dagger repeated. "You know he's going to cling to that last thread of hope."

"CLING!" Sara clamped a hand around his forearm. "That's what that guy was doing."

"What guy?" The traffic light changed and Dagger burned rubber.

"The guy who bumped into me who was grasping for the cell

phone. Now I remember. That's what Demko Number Two was doing in the cardinal's suite. He was grabbing for something…a pen. I thought it was funny for him to be so desperate not to forget his pen."

"That's all it was? A pen?"

"Yes. I'm positive, Dagger. When I pushed him out of the window he wrapped both hands around it as though it were the Holy Grail. I think that was why he was in the cardinal's suite."

Dagger punched several buttons on the control console.

"Do you know what time it is?" Skizzy's voice blasted from the console.

"You never sleep, Skizzy. Did you go through the cardinal's travel itinerary?" Dagger steered the Navigator away from the marina and toward home.

"Yeah, yeah. I'm still working on it."

"If I told you someone was desperate to steal someone's pen, what would you think?"

"Flash drive."

"A what?" Sara asked.

"I've even got a couple here. It's a real pen but pull it apart and it's a flash drive. You never saw one?"

"Shit." Dagger disconnected the call.

Sara said, "If the Demko clone was there to copy the cardinal's hard drive, I didn't see a laptop there. Only the opened briefcase."

"Obviously Demko lucked out."

"So why was he so desperate to protect the flash drive?"

19

By midmorning the next day, Skizzy reported that he had results.

"Did Skizzy tell you what he found?" Sara asked as she slammed out of the Navigator.

Dagger stepped onto the curb. He felt something slide down his chest and hit his shoe. The black cord necklace lay at his feet, its clasp broken. Dagger froze. He hadn't been without the necklace since Ada died. But why freeze? Was he expecting it to attack him?

Sara reached down and picked it up. "I'm sure Skizzy can fix it." Dagger's eyes remained riveted on the necklace. "What's wrong?" She slowly smiled and nudged him along. "You saved the wolf. That is what protects you. Not the necklace."

Dagger felt foolish as he followed Sara to the opened door where Skizzy was waving them in. But he did remember Ada's warning to never take the necklace off.

"Come on already. I ain't got all day." Skizzy closed the door behind them and slammed the seven locks home. "Hurry hurry." He splayed open the blinds to check the sidewalk before leading them to the back room and down the stairs.

Sara placed the necklace on one of the tables while Skizzy plopped in front of the display of computer monitors.

"Found your bird at a number of locations over the past month but I think the one you might find the most interesting is from the Atlanta airport."

"Bird?" Sara questioned.

"Cardinal." Skizzy tapped several keys. He pulled a chair over and pointed. "Sit."

Dagger sat pressing a hand to his neck. He felt naked without the black cord necklace. Sara was unraveling some of the leather to expose broken wire.

"Pay attention," Skizzy barked. On screen the camera showed Cardinal Esrey and his assistant seated in an executive lounge. Two seats to Father Thomas' left sat a man in a dark suit. A woman behind a counter motioned to the man in the suit. He abruptly rose and strode over to the desk. "Now watch."

"I'm watching." Although Dagger still wasn't sure what was so important. And then he saw it. After the man left his seat, Cardinal Esrey pointed toward the departure board and he and his assistant rose to leave. The cardinal reached down and grabbed a briefcase. The two briefcases had been within inches of each other and looked identical, both black with non-descriptive markings. "I don't get it."

"Maybe he picked up the wrong briefcase. After all, he reached down without looking," Skizzy explained.

"That's weak, even for you, Skizzy. Once the cardinal got on the plane and opened his briefcase, he would know he had the wrong one."

"Maybe that was his plan…to switch briefcases," Skizzy argued.

Dagger wasn't convinced. "Zoom in on that guy again." From a side view it was clear the man was wearing sunglasses. His hair was cut short, though not military short. The suit looked expensive but the man had been careful to appear casually dressed, withholding a tie and keeping the shirt open at the collar. "Does he have a scar?"

"Nope. Already checked that."

Dagger looked for birthmarks, nervous ticks, but didn't see anything that would help him remember the man should he run into him in the future. As the man walked back to his seat, Dagger noticed a slight limp.

"Keep digging, Skizzy."

"Damn slave driver," Skizzy mumbled.

"Either way," Dagger said, "something important must have been on that flash drive, enough to die for. Any of the cameras pick up the guy's face?"

"Not yet. I tried to see what flight he's taking so I can zero in on those cameras."

"How about the camera over that woman's shoulder? Maybe you can zoom in on the passenger list."

"Tried that." Skizzy pounded on the keys. "His name is J. Smith. Fat chance it's his real name. But he wasn't taking a commercial carrier. He's sailing on a private jet."

"Get a tail number," Dagger said.

Sara leaned back to get a look at the man on the screen. "He's not the one who was in the cardinal's hotel room. He's too tall."

Skizzy's eyebrow jerked up. "And how would girlie know that?"

Dagger jumped in. "Camera from the cardinal's room."

Skizzy's other eyebrow narrowed giving his face a comical look. "Paper said there weren't no cameras on the floor or in the room."

Dagger dragged a hand across his five o'clock shadow and winced when he touched his bruised cheek. "Martinez doesn't tell the reporters everything." He turned his attention back to the monitor in hopes of changing the subject. "Padre confirmed the guy at the hotel had the same DNA and prints as the guy you dumped in the quarry."

Skizzy's hands hovered over the keyboard, then dropped to his lap. "Wait a minute." His eyes widened, growing in size like two alien orbs. "I was right! He's a clone. Didn't I tell you?"

"Twins also have the same DNA, Skizzy, so don't start popping pills yet. Just keep on this other guy and see if we can I.D. him and the private plane."

"Yeah yeah. It's going to take me awhile. This facial recognition software I stole isn't as quick as you see on television."

"Skizzy, can you solder this back together?" Sara held up the black cord necklace. "I think if we keep using the metal clasps it's only going to break again."

"Let me see." Skizzy took a seat at the work table and examined the multiple strands of wire under the leather wrap. "Yeah, but it might be best just to solder the thing onto Dagger then wrap the cord around it. That way he won't lose it."

Sara picked up what looked like a small pen light and pushed a button. Nothing happened. "What is this?"

"Detects bugs."

"Thought you already have one of those that checks to see if someone planted a bug in your store," Sara said.

"Not for the store." Skizzy grinned, a self-satisfied smile that lit up his face. He plucked a round metal item from the top drawer and set it on the table. "Point it at that."

Sara pointed it and pressed the button. A loud buzzing and whine was emitted from the instrument.

"That's the tracking chip that was in that guy's head, that Demko guy we tossed into the quarry," Skizzy said.

"What are you going to do, scan everyone you meet?" Sara said with a laugh. She pointed the instrument at Skizzy and ran it slowly down his frame.

"If I have to. Gotta know who you're dealing with. Gotta know who's working for The Man."

Sara turned and pointed the instrument at Dagger, running it from his ankles up to his head. When she pointed it at his neck, the buzzing and whine was loud and persistent. Sara was too shocked to move the instrument as it kept buzzing. Dagger was too shocked to pull the thing from her grasp.

Skizzy bolted from the chair, stumbled back, and fumbled in one of the drawers for a gun. He raised a shaky arm at Dagger, the gun pointed at Dagger's chest.

Stunned, Sara pulled the instrument away and stepped in front of Dagger. "Skizzy, stop."

"Move away from the enemy, girlie." He clamped his left hand on his right to keep the gun from shaking.

"You know Dagger. You know there has to be an explanation. There must be a malfunction."

"Quit hiding behind a skirt, you sonofabitch."

"Sara." Dagger placed his hands on her forearms and tried to move her aside.

"No!"

Dagger thought Sara was taking this protection thing way too seriously. "Skizzy, put the gun away and let's think this through. It's possible it isn't working right. Why and when would I ever get a chip implanted?"

"Maybe in the military. I don't know." Skizzy's eyes welled up and his hands shook so hard Dagger was sure he would drop the gun.

"STAND DOWN, SOLDIER!" Dagger shouted. Something changed in Skizzy's eyes. He snapped to attention and dropped the gun to his side. "RELINQUISH YOUR SIDEARM." Dagger nudged Sara and whispered, "Get the gun."

Sara cautiously approached and pulled the gun from Skizzy's hands.

"AT EASE, SOLDIER."

Skizzy stepped to one side and clasped his hands behind his back.

Dagger eyed all the guns on the wall. Every one of them, he was sure, was loaded. His hand instinctively went to his neck.

"Let me look," Sara said as she shoved Dagger onto a chair. "Skizzy, do you have a flashlight down here?"

Skizzy blinked several times as though awaking from a nap. "Next to the can of pencils."

Sara grabbed the flashlight and snapped it on. She moved

Dagger's collar length hair aside and shined the light. There was a scar starting just above the hairline at the base of his neck and running at least two inches long.

"Oh my God," she whispered, wrapping her arms around his neck and pressing her forehead against the back of his head. "It's there, Dagger. A scar, almost identical to the one Demko had."

20

Dagger felt a cold chill race through his body. This couldn't be right. "I need two mirrors. I have to see for myself."

"Skizzy." Sara looked at the squirrely guy. He wasn't moving, or even blinking. Just frozen in place mouth breathing. "Skizzy, someone did this to him. We have to help."

This snapped Skizzy out of his trance. "Mirrors, yeah, I've got some." He produced two hand-held mirrors. Skizzy held one behind Dagger's neck while Sara pulled Dagger's hair to one side. Dagger held the other mirror and turned it to see the reflection in Skizzy's mirror.

Sara was right. It resembled Demko's. Anger swelled. Who the hell did this? He saw Sara's reflection in the mirror. Silent tears were streaming down her face.

"Are you going to die?" she whispered.

"Better question is, why hasn't he died yet?" Skizzy whispered back. "When's the last time you were in the hospital?"

"Haven't been."

"Prison?"

"No."

"Military?"

"I…" Dagger knew he went through Special Ops training and Navy Seals, but when? "I would have known."

"Right. Put you to sleep and you don't know what the hell they are doing."

Dagger could picture his field training, parachute jumping, reconnaissance. But why couldn't he place a timeline on any of it? He clawed the back of his neck, trying to feel what was under the skin. "I have to get this out."

"Not here you ain't."

Dagger pulled out his cell phone and scanned through the numbers. He punched the one he was looking for. They emerged from the bunker and waited for Doc Akins in the back room of the pawn shop. Very few people knew about the bunker downstairs and Skizzy wanted to keep it that way.

Twenty minutes later a tall man with silver-streaked hair entered the pawn shop. One could have easily mistaken him as a college professor with his wire-rimmed glasses and preppy attire. He placed his black bag on the kitchen table and opened it. "Going to give me a little background info? Not necessary, but might help."

"Yeah, especially if you don't want to blow up," Skizzy snarled.

"What?" Doc's wire-rimmed glasses almost popped off his nose when he turned his head. The streaked hair gave him an older, more distinguished look than his thirty plus years. His lanky body towered over Skizzy.

"Don't listen to him," Dagger said. He gave him an abbreviated version of Skizzy's paranoia and the detector Skizzy had invented that discovered something in Dagger's neck.

"Would have been easier if I could have just X-rayed you at the office," Doc said.

"I'm not sure what an X-ray would have done to it." Besides, he wasn't too keen on stepping outside. What if someone were able to track him? But again, why hadn't they by now or were they just keeping track of his whereabouts and waiting for… what?

Doc jammed a needle into a vial. "Let's freeze this first and then we'll open you up."

Dagger felt a sting in the back of his neck. Thoughts of Demko floated through his head so he tried to shove those aside. "How are the cats and dogs?"

"Doing good. Have a lot of animals up for adoption if you want to add any to your house." Doc Akins' medical license had been suspended when he had admitted to giving marijuana to cancer patients to ease their nausea during chemo treatments. He decided to change to a veterinary practice. He also taught part-time at the local college.

"It would be nice to have a kitten," Sara said.

"Kittens grow up to be cats," Dagger replied. "Although it would be a nice snack for Einstein."

Skizzy laughed at that, a nervous laugh but at least the nutty guy wasn't spouting off about Dagger blowing up in his pawn shop.

Doc was cautious when making his incision. Dagger didn't feel anything but saw Sara and Skizzy edge closer as though curious exactly what was in his neck.

"Just dab the gauze to keep the blood flow down so I can see what we've got," Doc told Sara.

Dagger could feel something touching his neck and unconsciously clenched and unclenched his fists. What if whatever Doc was doing triggered something? His mind raced again, trying to figure out when a chip had been planted. He had never been in a hospital, that he knew of. Skizzy had created such an elaborate background on Dagger that even Dagger wasn't sure where the truth started and the lies ended. How could this have happened?

"Well, well," Doc said.

"What is it?" Sara asked.

"No flashing numbers on it. Not like that other guy's that had a timer," Skizzy added.

"What other guy?"

Dagger winced. He was hoping not to get into the details of Demko. Skizzy was usually tightlipped around people outside of his small circle. Given the unusual circumstances of Demko's death, Skizzy suddenly acquired diarrhea of the mouth.

Doc's scalpel hovered as Skizzy got into the details of the timer, how Demko exploded and a portion of the chip and timer separated from the body. Skizzy pulled Demko's tracking chip from his pocket and showed it to Doc.

"Doesn't resemble this one at all. This one is long and narrow, like a fuse for your car lights," Doc said. "Matter of fact…what on earth?"

"What?" Dagger tensed. He saw Sara and Skizzy move even closer. "What is it?"

"The damn thing is connected to your brain stem somehow. A researcher friend of mine read where they can insert a computer chip into a petri dish of neurons and it just adheres, they become part of it. Then it gets inserted into the brain."

"I knew it!" Skizzy shouted. "Told you they can do this."

Doc straightened. A look of concern clouding his face. "Except he read it in *Future Science* magazine. The article was on genetically engineered soldiers."

You could have cut the silence with a knife. Sara slowly sank onto a kitchen chair. Skizzy wrapped his arms around his chest as though artificially cocooning himself from his surroundings.

Dagger tensed even more. His dark eyes appeared even darker with the irises turning as black as the pupils. "It's impossible. I haven't been to a hospital much less a doctor's office."

"The bizarre thing about this," Doc said, "is that there is a lot of scar tissue here. This chip has been in your head for at least twenty-five years."

The silence dragged on. Only the sound of the scalpel against metal could be heard.

"Twenty-five years?" Sara finally whispered. "You would have been five years old."

"Damn. Big Brother has been busy for longer than I thought," Skizzy added. "Holy sheee-it."

Dagger could feel his pulse pounding in his ears. Twenty-five years? What the hell?

"Got the cover off but it didn't open anything. It's a cover on top of another cover. Everything is entwined," Doc said. "I wouldn't try to disconnect anything if I wanted to." He cleaned off the slender metal lid and handed it to Dagger. "It has some type of serial number on it. I'd like to take it to my researcher friend in California. I wouldn't chance shipping it to him. I'd rather fly out there and meet with him personally."

Dagger wrote down the numbers off the metal. "Get on the first flight you can, Doc. I'll pay for it. Let me know immediately what your friend says."

"Will do. Let me stitch this back up. The stitches should melt but keep the area covered with gauze for at least ten days. Change the bandage every day."

Dagger stared at the two lines of numbers: *41-30-31* and below that *100-47-30*. It didn't sound like a serial number. Not one letter in the bunch but for some reason he thought he should know what they meant.

"Skizzy said they weren't anything alike." Sara's attempts to ease Dagger's mind were proving fruitless. They were seated at a back booth at The Joint, a restaurant owned by a former Joliet prison warden. You had to have a sense of humor just to order. The Sizzle was the best filet in town and on the menu it was suggested that you not order the High Voltage steak.

"At least he fixed your necklace." Sara was having a hard time coaxing words out of Dagger. He said very little since leaving Skizzy's and just kept pulling out the piece of paper and studying the numbers he had written down. "Now that he soldered it on you won't ever lose it."

Dagger instinctively reached behind his neck. He was

beginning to get feeling back where Doc had made the incision. Rather than take pain pills, Dagger was on his second VO and water.

A waitress in a short orange jumpsuit deposited their plates on the table. The top three buttons on her jumpsuit were unbuttoned, revealing an abundance of skin. Dagger barely noticed her.

"Anything else I can get you, handsome?"

Dagger shook his head but winced at the movement. He shoved the piece of paper into his shirt pocket, not even glancing at the blonde babe leaning over his table.

"The name is Roxy if you need anything."

"Thanks," Sara replied although Roxy never paid Sara one ounce of attention.

Metal bars separated the booths. Waitresses sported orange jumpsuits. Waiters and bartenders wore black and white striped prison garb. Beer on tap was dispensed from huge hypodermic needles. Inebriated customers didn't dare argue with the bartenders when they cut off their drinks because Warden Cleaves Jones didn't hesitate to call the cops rather than a cab to drive the drunk home. Jones wasn't about to lose his license much less his business due to a lawsuit. Warden Jones was inconspicuous. Slight build, a bald spot ringed with gray, banker's bifocals resting on his nose. He sat at the end of the bar nursing a glass of fresh squeezed lemonade. He could see the entire restaurant through the reflection in the mirror in back of the bar. Most patrons thought the picture on the wall of a burly guy with tattoos and sporting a scar above one eye was Warden Jones. Few people knew Jones was the mousy guy who looked more like the dreaded tax man.

Dagger picked at his steak. "They are just watching and waiting, Sara."

"You don't know that. Now eat or drink or do something other than agonize over something you can't prove."

Dagger dropped a large dollop of sour cream into his baked potato. He cut into the steak although he could probably have used his fork it was so tender. "It explains why Demko snapped. Maybe his neurons recognized my neurons or whatever."

Sara laughed. "I'm sorry. That sounds so sci-fi, Dagger."

"My whole life is one science fiction novel. I'm beginning to question everything I ever knew about myself."

"Thought you made it all up anyway. Were you really in the Marines and attended the Police Academy as your resume states?" Sara watched as his gaze lifted from his steak to her face. "It isn't real?" She gasped.

"How do I know if this damn thing in my neck has created an entire past for me? I'm probably one minute from being incinerated like that car BettaTec destroyed which, not much to my disappointment, included Mitch Arnosky."

Mitch Arnosky had been a thief who almost succeeded in ruining Padre's career. It was during this case that Sara and Skizzy learned about BettaTec, a company that had something to do with Dagger's past, a dangerous company with laser defense satellites capable of being directed at anything and anyone that proved a threat to them. When Skizzy had tried to hack into their system, it tried unsuccessfully to locate who was doing the hacking. Skizzy cut off communication but not before the BettaTec satellite had destroyed one ranger station in Norway and a lab in New Zealand. Skizzy had masked his IP address so he couldn't be traced but when the secondary servers started to explode, he knew someone was trying to trace his signal. To the locals, it looked as though lightning had destroyed the affected areas.

"Demko was only looking for a P.I. to probably steal the flash drive. When he didn't succeed, they sent his twin," Sara surmised. "Demko has nothing to do with you, Dagger."

Dagger set the knife and fork down and grabbed his drink. "Wish it were that simple."

"Of course it is. What proof do you have otherwise?"

Dagger's grip around the glass tightened. Sara thought for sure the glass would shatter any moment. He quickly set the glass down and reached for the gun at his waist with lightning speed as a shadow appeared at their table.

"Mind if I join you?" Padre set his beer down and slid into the booth next to Dagger. "I do hope that isn't a gun you are reaching for."

Dagger relaxed and reached for his glass. "Sorry. Little jumpy these days."

"Understandable." Padre looked around the restaurant, taking in the décor and dress of the wait staff. "The theme of this place is sick. But I love it."

Sara asked, "How did you know we were here?"

"Who else drives a Lincoln Navigator with a license plate of BITE ME?"

Dagger's lips curled in the first resemblance of a smile Sara had seen all day. "Guess I'll have to be less conspicuous next time. What brings you out on a night made for crime and passion?"

"Following the crime, dreaming of the passion."

Roxy sidled up to the table. "Did you need a menu?" she asked Padre.

"Just another beer, sweetheart." He cocked his head as he watched her walk away. "Did you know Roxy served three years for check fraud?"

"Really?" Sara wondered if the owner knew that.

"The owner hires a lot of ex-cons. Pays for bartender school to give them a skill. Some start at the bottom, work their way up. He's got a pretty good thing going on. Very low repeat offenders."

Roxy returned with a beer. Padre hooked a thumb in Dagger's direction. "Put it on his tab."

"Sure you don't want a steak, too?" Dagger said with

sarcasm.

"Nah. Wife has ravioli in the oven." He cocked his head to look at Dagger's neck. "Cut yourself shaving?"

Dagger's hand instinctively went to the gauze bandage. "I had a growth removed."

"Pity. Thought maybe they added a few brain cells."

Sara watched Dagger's reaction. His mind was in overdrive. She could imagine him contemplating all modes of action. But who does he target? If it were BettaTec, did Dagger know where they were located? Did he know who was responsible? How did he get the map on the wall in the vault which had obviously belonged to BettaTec?

"What's up?" Dagger asked as he pushed the plate away.

Padre pulled a brown envelope from his inside jacket pocket. "Luther found this clenched in the hand of the jumper who landed on your truck." He pulled out what looked like a charred pen from the envelope and opened it. "My geek squad determined it's a flash drive but if I'm jumping, the last thing I would think of clenching would be a pen so there's gotta be something here worth dying for."

"Your people pull anything off of it?" Dagger asked.

"No. I don't think our techs are as good as that squirrely friend of yours," Padre admitted. "Can you have him take a look at it?"

"Sure. Now I have a question for you."

"Shoot."

"Did Cardinal Esrey determine if anything was taken from his hotel suite?"

"Not a thing."

"He isn't missing the flash drive?"

"Surprisingly, no."

21

"Can't you sit your butt down for a few minutes?" Skizzy growled. "You're driving me crazy."

Dagger paced a short path in back of Skizzy's chair. He had dropped off the flash drive last night and told Skizzy to make it a priority. Skizzy looked like he hadn't slept all night. There was a blanket and pillow on the couch against the far wall. A half-eaten bowl of popcorn was sitting on a table.

"For starters you can tell me why a cardinal needs to encrypt his correspondence."

Dagger shrugged. "We're still not sure it was the cardinal's flash drive."

"It's going to take some time to recover what little I can off of a char-broiled stick. Go for breakfast or something."

A loud buzz radiated through the building. "Jeez Louise," Skizzy barked. "Who the hell is that? Sign says I don't open 'til ten o'clock." The buzzing was insistent. It stopped abruptly then a pounding rattled through the store. Skizzy punched a button on the surveillance monitor. Sara was outside the door. "Hope girlie has some coffee."

Dagger pounded up the stairs. He unlocked the bank of security bolts and jerked the swollen door open. "Sara, what is so….?"

"What flight was Doc on?" Sara's words spewed out in a rush as she headed to the back room.

"Why?"

"Haven't you been listening to the news?" Sara hurried down the stairs with Dagger in pursuit. "A plane headed for LAX blew up in the sky over Black Rock Desert."

"What?"

Skizzy half turned from the monitor. "I'm on it." He punched several keys and hacked into the passenger manifest for the airline Doc Akins had taken. It only took several seconds for him to find Doc listed and several seconds more to bring up the news bulletin on the airplane. It had taken off at seven this morning from Chicago's O'Hare Airport and disappeared off the radar over the Black Rock Desert in Nevada. It was estimated that the plane went down in Pyramid Lake.

"Do they think there was a bomb onboard?" Sara asked, tears welling. "I can't believe just when Doc was taking that metal cover to his friend that…"

"Skizzy," Dagger said.

"I'm on it."

Dagger and Sara stood behind Skizzy as he accessed satellite footage from the exact time the plane disappeared off radar. To the unsuspecting eye, nothing seemed out of place. But Skizzy knew how far to slow down the film in order to catch the laser beam. They had to watch closely. It was a brief flash of light from a satellite. An explosion lit up the sky four miles above the Earth.

Dagger's skin felt cold and clammy. No one spoke. Skizzy blinked several times. It was Sara who finally broke the silence.

"Don't you think government satellites would pick up the same thing? Or NASA, the FAA? Or the space shuttle?" Sara asked. "They will know that airplanes just don't disappear."

"Not if they don't know what to look for," Skizzy said in a quiet voice. "They would suspect a bomb onboard first. When the officials don't see what we just saw, then they rely on pilots from nearby airplanes that might have seen an explosion." Skizzy cocked his head over his shoulder and asked, "Want me to send these videos to the press anonymously?"

"No. We can't let BettaTec know we are on to them." Dagger took a step back. Doc Akins was dead because of him. But why?

"This makes no sense. Why now? They had every opportunity since the two satellites have been up and running."

A monitor on the table beeped prompting the printer to start spitting out pages. Skizzy stared for a few seconds and shook his head. "Lotta stuff on Italy, Rome. Hmmm." Skizzy's eyes seemed to dance in opposite directions. "He's got blueprints of the Vatican. Dates, appearances. All kinda jumbled stuff. Too much destroyed to make sense out of it. Who the hell is Joseph Ratzinger?"

"I've heard that name," Sara said. "He's Pope Benedict."

Skizzy looked over his shoulder at Sara, then Dagger. "Damn. They must have some big plans for the Pope. And I bet it ain't good."

Dagger tried to make heads or tails out of the connection but he was coming up empty. He was still trying to wrap his brain around what was in his neck. "I was told Cardinal Esrey is taking a post at the Vatican. Certainly puts him close to the Pope. Skizzy, you need to check more surveillance tapes of the cardinal's flights. Keep trying to identify the other guy. Maybe he and the cardinal know each other."

Skizzy held up another page. "Got some weird numbers here that weren't encrypted…*41-30-31 100-47-30*."

Dagger had engrained those numbers in his head. "Those are the numbers that were on that metal cover Doc was taking to L.A."

Skizzy paced, twig arms wrapped tightly around his body. "That guy broke into your house then his clone steals a flash drive from the cardinal. The flash drive has documents with numbers connected to the thing in your neck. The cardinal is connected somehow." Skizzy spun 180 degrees and leveled a beady eye on Dagger. "Tell me everything you know about this company."

Dagger stared back. "It isn't that easy." When one of Skizzy's eyebrows jerked, Dagger told Sara, "See what else you can find out about Doc's plane." He motioned for Skizzy to follow and Dagger led him up the stairs.

Once at the top, Dagger quietly slid the lock across and closed the bookcase, locking Sara in the basement.

"What are you doing?" Skizzy asked.

"Give me three hours. And whatever you do, don't let Sara out. I don't want her following me," Dagger replied. He rippled his fingers. "I need a car."

"What? You got four or five."

"All that Sara can recognize."

The squirrely guy's eyes narrowed. "What are you up to?" Skizzy slowly pulled a set of keys from a drawer as he whispered, "You know what those numbers stand for, don't you?"

Dagger wouldn't confirm it. All he said was, "Three hours."

Sara watched the tape for the third time. There was no mistaking that the BettaTec satellite shot down Doc's plane. How convenient that they waited until the plane was over the desert, calculating with such precision to guarantee the wreckage would fall into the lake making it impossible for the FAA to retrieve parts to verify what went wrong. Dagger was right—these people were dangerous.

Her eyes were drawn to the numbers again. What could they refer to? Could only be serial numbers. She had seen the metal lid Doc removed. There were two separate sets.

The sudden silence chilled her. Something wasn't right. What was taking Dagger so long? Where did he go? Sara moved to the lit staircase and called out, "Dagger?" She noticed the door at the top of the stairs was closed. Taking the stairs two at a time, she reached the top and tried the doorknob. The door was locked.

"Skizzy?" Sara pounded on the door. "The door is locked." She pressed her ear to the door and listened. Pacing, heavy breathing. Sara pounded again. "Dagger? This isn't funny." And it wasn't a joke. Skizzy was the one pacing. The steps were frantic and in a tight circle…typical Skizzy. Dagger planned to shut her out. But why? "Skizzy, I'm going to twist you into a pretzel when I get out of here."

Sara pressed her ear to the door again. Her enhanced hearing picked up, "Oh boy, oh boy. What am I going to do? Three hours. Dagger said three hours."

"What?" Dagger wouldn't tell Skizzy to keep her locked up for three hours, would he? "SKIZZY, OPEN THIS DOOR." Sara resisted the urge to pound her fist through the door. It wouldn't be hard. She suspected he also closed the bookcase but she didn't want to destroy Skizzy's bookcase.

"I can't," she could hear Skizzy saying. "Can't listen, can't listen."

She could imagine the skinny guy pacing with palms pressed to his ears. This wasn't going to get her anywhere. Sara pounded down the stairs. The person she needed to communicate with was Dagger but she had to shift first. Her eyes were drawn to the cameras. There were four in the bunker, two in the staircase. There wasn't any way she could shift with camera eyes on her.

Three hours. What could he do in three hours? Where was Dagger planning to go? Three hours would allow him a pretty good head start. Her eyes were drawn to the numbers again. "You figured it out, didn't you, Dagger? You know what the numbers mean."

She wheeled her chair over to a second computer and keyed in the numbers in various combinations. This wasn't going to be easy. These could be reference numbers, biblical passages. Was Dagger planning to confront the cardinal?

One of the icons on Skizzy's monitor was for satellite images. She clicked on it and then typed in Skizzy's address. If she could see the satellite image from when Dagger left she should be able to follow him. Estimating the time of Dagger's departure, Sara watched the video feedback. After fifteen minutes she failed to see Dagger emerge from the front entrance. Next she focused on the rear exit. Again, she didn't see Dagger anywhere. His Navigator was still parked in front of the store as was her PT Cruiser. Was he still upstairs or did Skizzy have some secret tunnel? Sara wouldn't put it past him. Skizzy owned a Humvee and a number of other vehicles. They had to be parked somewhere, probably underground. And Skizzy probably had an underground access from the pawn shop.

Sara expanded the satellite search to a surrounding five-block area watching for the appearance of a Humvee exiting a garage. After twenty minutes of scanning, her eyeballs hurt. She was tempted to march right back upstairs and pound through the door and bookcase but then remembered her house. Of course! Dagger would go home first for supplies. She typed in the address for her house and waited for the satellite images. How did Skizzy happen to get live satellite feedback? She didn't want to know. It probably wasn't legal.

Her house came into view. She typed in the time she estimated that Dagger would have arrived at the house and watched for the next twenty minutes. Nothing. Dagger had not returned home. Where could he be?

Sara glanced at the sides of the screen. The top and bottom of the screen had numbers, as did the left and right sides of the screen. She stared at the numbers written on the pad of paper, the ones which were off the metal cover Doc removed from Dagger's neck. Could they be coordinates? How bizarre was that? No matter how ridiculous it seemed, Sara punched in the numbers and waited.

The satellite image shifted and pointed toward a spot in central Nebraska north of North Platte. It was an isolated section near Ringgold. The closest town looked ten miles away. She punched another key and zoomed in on the area. It was a group of buildings with fencing around several large sheds. Not one car was in the area. It looked like a Western ghost town.

By Sara's calculations the abandoned town was close to seven hundred miles from Cedar Point, around ten hours driving time for the normal person. For Dagger, it was probably a seven hour drive. She doubted he would fly because he would need a car, one that couldn't be traced back to a rental company where he would have to show identification.

Sara zoomed in until she could see words on the buildings. One sign on the cyclone fence read *Gemini M.S.* She opened a third window and accessed Google. By typing in *Gemini M.S.* she received tens of thousands of hits, mostly dealing with astrology. She went back to the sign on the cyclone fence. Zooming in again she saw a symbol shaped like a butterfly with its wings closed. A chill swept over her body. She knew that symbol. It wasn't a butterfly at all but a fish…a betta. It was the symbol for BettaTec.

22

"SKIZZY!" Sara pounded on the door enough to rattle the hinges. "DAGGER'S WALKING INTO A TRAP!" She pressed her ear to the door and focused her hearing. Skizzy wasn't pacing. Instead she heard his heart pounding. It was loud and rapid. Skizzy had his ear pressed to the other side of the door. He had opened the bookcase at one point while she was busy doing her searches. But she was sure he was right on the other side. "Skizzy." Sara kept her voice low. "We have to help him. BettaTec owns the buildings where Dagger is headed.

Locks were released. Sara moved down one step. The door swung open.

"BettaTec?" Skizzy's eyes bulged and appeared to wobble in their sockets. "The company with the satellite that explodes things?"

"The company with two satellites that explode things." Sara slowly descended. "Let me show you something." She could have overpowered him if she wanted to and just taken off, but she needed Skizzy's help.

Skizzy slid into the chair and eyed the screen. He went back to the satellite image to check the coordinates. Following the exact steps Sara had taken, he ended up back at the sign on the cyclone fence.

Sara pointed at the symbol of the fish. "That's the same symbol on the map in Dagger's vault, the map he took from BettaTec. I'm sure of it. Did Dagger tell you where he was going?"

"No, but he appeared to know where he was headed. Said he had to do this on his own."

"Those numbers are longtitude and latitude coordinates. It

targets an area in Nebraska that looks like a ghost town. The sign says *Gemini M.S.* Any idea what it means?"

Skizzy let out a whoosh of air. "By the looks of them buildings and the isolated area, I'd say it stands for missile silo."

"Missile silo? What is a private company doing operating a missile silo?"

"The U.S. closed most by 1965. They were focusing more on long range intercontinental ballistic missiles so the missile silos were obsolete. They sold the properties. Some idiots actually turned them into underground bunker homes. Looks like BettaTec bought this one. It's a good cover if a company didn't want people to know what they were doing there."

"I have to help him." Sara charged up the stairs.

"Whoa, wait up there just a minute, girlie. I ain't supposed to let you leave yet."

"Or what?" Sara reached the top of the stairs and turned to face him. "What else did Dagger tell you?"

"Just to keep an eye on the cardinal. There's supposed to be some farewell thing he wants me and Simon to hire on as waiters."

"Well, if you and Simon can't help him, that leaves me." Sara headed for the door but stopped when she saw the Navigator parked at the curb. She whirled on the scrawny guy, forced Skizzy to take a step back. "Where's your garage? I checked satellite surveillance and didn't see Dagger leave the building. So where do you keep your vehicles and what car did you loan Dagger?"

"Oh man." Skizzy kicked at imaginary dirt. "He's going to kill me."

"There won't be anything to kill after I get through with you. Now what car is he driving?"

"An unused utility tunnel leads to my garage a block away. He's driving a turbocharged Chevy Cobalt."

23

Dagger had stayed on I-80 through Nebraska. There were more semi-tractor trailers to pace his speed and, more importantly, a better choice of hotels. He could have picked a small mom and pop motel but with so few rooms, it would be too easy for the owners to describe him. At a larger hotel he could get lost in the crowd.

Just west of Kearney he stopped at a Sheraton Hotel whose marquee welcomed the Nebraska Industrial Instrumentation Association. He didn't request any special accommodations that would make the desk clerk remember him. After taking the room key card, he dumped his gym bag on the bed, showered and changed. His fourth floor room overlooked the parking lot. Several doors down was a pancake house, a steak house, and a large chain family restaurant. Across the street was a gas station with a McDonalds. He would need to stock up on water and protein bars before setting out tomorrow morning. For now he needed one helluva steak.

The lobby was filled with men standing in clusters, some in suits, some dressed casual, all looking like salesmen. Beady eyes appeared to analyze and sort comments. Blackberrys were being punched, cell phones were tethered to ear buds.

Dagger could blend in with this bunch. Black jeans, black tennis shoes, dark gray shirt, a black jean jacket, dark shades, and long hair stuffed under a baseball cap with *Michelin* written across the front screamed *trucker* to all who looked at him. It was too warm for a jacket but Dagger had to hide his Kimber that was in the belt holster. Besides, he doubted there were that many truckers who weren't packing heat.

He slid into a booth in the crowded bar, selecting one in

a corner with full view of the entrance. He pulled a map of Nebraska from the inside pocket of his jacket and unfolded it on the table.

A waiter slouched over. He didn't look old enough to drink let alone serve a drink. He still had the residuals of teenage acne.

"Want something to drink?"

"Have anything on special?"

"Buck-fifty pints."

"That's fine. Coors Light."

"My name's Brad." Brad dropped a menu on the table and left.

The dining room section of the restaurant was filling fast. And although every seat at the bar was filled, there were still a number of open booths. Dagger slid his sunglasses in the pocket of his jeans jacket, then gave the menu a quick scan. By the time Brad returned with the beer, Dagger was ready to order.

"Need to find something?" Brad asked with a nod toward the map. The last thing Dagger needed was for someone to know his destination.

"Just getting my bearings."

"I moved to Nebraska last year, you know."

No I didn't and I don't give a flying fuck. "Really? What brought you to Nebraska?"

"My girlfriend got a job here so I tagged along." Brad glanced over the map again as though looking for arrows or circles.

"How about placing my order?" Dagger tried to be polite about it. A rude customer was one that was easily remembered. He watched Brad disappear into the kitchen. Dagger decided to wait to study the map when he was back in his room. To prevent Brad from making small talk, Dagger pulled out his cell phone and called Skizzy.

"Where the hell are ya?" Skizzy screamed into the phone.

"I'm just one millimeter away from your mouth so you don't

have to yell. How was your houseguest?"

"Mad as hell and threatened to squeeze my neck til my eyes popped out."

"Did she ask you where I went?"

"What good would that do? You never told me where you was headed." After several beats of silence, Skizzy asked, "Where are you, really?"

"On a mission. That's all you need to know."

"Girlie said you needed her help. That you always get yourself into trouble."

Dagger smiled at that comment. He hated leaving Sara in the dark but he had a feeling this was going to be dangerous. "Well, I could be on a wild goose chase so no sense both of us being away from Einstein."

Brad walked over with a tray hefted over one shoulder. He set the tray on the table and distributed the steak platter, baked potato, sour cream, mixed vegetables, and a loaf of bread.

"Anything else?" Brad asked.

Dagger held up the half empty beer glass and Brad took off.

"Does this have anything to do with BettaTec?" Skizzy asked, a bit of hesitancy in his voice.

"Why do you ask?"

"Because of your urgency in leaving, that scarlet red color of rage that was on your face, and your insistence in distancing girlie from you, even to the point of using one of my throw away cell phones rather than taking your own."

"I certainly won't know if BettaTec is involved until I get there, will I?" Dagger spooned sour cream into the baked potato as another waiter, not Brad, set a fresh beer in front of him. He nodded his thanks and then asked, "What do you and Simon have planned for the cardinal?"

"We rented ourselves some fancy tuxedos and we're gonna be waiters at that farewell reception. That will give us a chance to check the cardinal's neck."

"Find any more video footage of the guy at the airport?"

"Yeah. Traced him to the international terminal where the private jets take off. He hopped a sleek streamliner but I haven't a clue where it was headed. Them private jobs don't file a flight plan."

"How about a tail number?"

"Couldn't tell."

"I'll call again the next chance I have. Meantime, give Padre a heads-up on the cardinal."

"Wait. What do we do if the cardinal has one of them scars on the back of his neck?"

"I think you and Simon can come up with something." He hung up before Skizzy could sputter on about his allergy to cops.

Two women entered the bar, one with designer sunglasses and long, brown hair. For a second, Dagger almost thought it was Sara. He could just imagine how pissed she was right now. They had made a promise after Sara had returned from her three-month getaway following the *Friday the Thirteenth* case. Neither one would ever leave. But that was before BettaTec's hit man showed up on their doorstep.

"Aw, jeez." Skizzy punched the END button on the cell phone. "He's gonna kill me."

Simon hefted his body onto a kitchen chair in the back room of Skizzy's pawn shop. "He don't have to know you told Sara where he went."

"That's the point. I didn't. She figured it all out herself but I let her out before the three hours." Skizzy stared at the phone as though expecting Dagger to call back. "Something strange about girlie. She's awful knowledgeable about a lot of things no nineteen-year-old should know."

"Such as?"

"Longitude and latitude. I'da never looked at that."

"Youngsters today pay more attention to detail."

Skizzy shook his head, freeing more strands of hair from his ponytail. "You shoulda seen her on that Mitch case, out at the cemetery. She was like some gymnast twirling in the air, putting herself between Dagger and Mitch, tossing two knives at Mitch with such force they sunk up to the hilt in a tree. Ain't normal."

"Adrenaline. Makes people do unbelievable things. We saw that in Nam." Simon took a sip of coffee and winced. "Damn, that's awful." He shoved the cup aside. "Besides, I would think Dagger would be happy to have Sara's help. He can't do it himself, although the stubborn ass thinks he can."

"Oh, he ain't gonna be pissed if girlie shows up. He's gonna be pissed when he finds out the Chevy Cobalt he borrowed has a tracker on it."

Simon swiped a hand across the stubble on his face. "How much time should we give them?"

"Twenty-four hours. Then we go after them."

The gray hawk swooped down and landed on a light pole near an off ramp on Interstate 80. An intermittent stream of headlights forked out in each direction. A blanket of trees was to the north. A forest would be a perfect place to rest for the night. An unoccupied cabin or ranger station would be perfect. It required too much of Sara's energy to stay in one form for too long. Even a farmhouse with a barn would be nice, some place where humans wouldn't stumble onto her in all her naked glory. With this age of electronics, she had to be more careful to avoid anyone with a cell phone snapping a photo of the hawk shifting.

Sara avoided communicating with Dagger for fear she might slip and let him know her intentions. For now her silence should tell him she was pissed … royally.

24

Dagger took his time the next morning, had a leisure breakfast since it might be the last full meal he had in a while, and then did some shopping to stock up on water and supplies before hitting the road. The sun's heat blistered through his dark clothes. After pulling off to the side of the road, he grabbed a bottle of cold water from the cooler, then sat on the hood of the car, the brim of the baseball cap shielding the sun's glare.

Tumbleweeds whirled and danced across the flat plain churning up dust and grit. It was a stretch of desolate land. Dagger hadn't seen a building in miles much less a road sign. He pulled off the sunglasses, poured cold water onto a handkerchief, and wiped the grit from his face and neck.

Nothing looked familiar to him. If his hunch were correct then something should have looked familiar—a street sign, the name of a town, a hotel, something other than the coordinates. This could be a wild goose chase. But what better place to operate from than an isolated piece of land in the middle of a sparsely occupied chunk of state. Dagger checked his cell phone. No service in this area which didn't surprise him. He climbed back into the Cobalt and checked the onboard map. Leave it up to Skizzy to arm his vehicles with the latest technology. According to the coordinates, Dagger was ten miles south of the target area. The gym bag on the passenger seat was loaded with enough of Skizzy's toys to arm Dagger for a week. He just wasn't sure what he was going to find when he got there. More Demkos waiting on a corner? Both BetteTec satellites aimed over the coordinates? Was he walking into a trap? Did Dagger even bring enough ammo much less food? Fruit, power bars, and water would only last so long.

Dagger slipped his glasses back on and put the Cobalt in gear. He had balked at the sedan Skizzy had loaned him until he got behind the wheel. Skizzy had done quite a bit of work on this particular vehicle. It had been painted silver which helped camouflage the car against the gray sky. But the startling modification was the $3,000 turbo kit.

Dagger slammed the car into gear and the car shot back onto the highway.

"Well, well." Padre crossed the foyer to where Sheila stood. "Shouldn't you be chasing down a story somewhere?"

"I am. Cardinal Esrey is giving his speech today and I'm here to attend the reception afterwards. My photographer will take a few pictures for the front page and you, my dear friend, will give me an exclusive on those three deaths you have been so tightlipped about. They are all connected, right? The salesman in the trunk of the car at the airport, the security guard in the cardinal's suite, and the jumper in the hotel parking lot."

Padre shoved his hands in his pockets and smiled. "Ahhh, my dear Miss Monroe. You may be able to wrap some people around your manicured finger but not me. You will have to go to the police chief for any information since I'm not at liberty to disclose anything. Matter of fact, I think the mayor's office may be handling the press release on that."

"Oh please. The mayor is one of the people I have around my manicured finger and he tossed it back to you. You must have identified the jumper by now."

"All I can tell you is that there wasn't much left to identify. The heat was too intense to leave even teeth for DNA. Until we can compare missing person reports to videotape from the hotel lobby, we have zip."

Thomas crossed the foyer to the study on the right carrying a tray with a carafe. "Now there," Padre said with a nod to the cardinal's assistant, "is one guy I'm sure you can work your charm on."

Sheila rolled her eyes. "You have got to be kidding. The man is an android. He finds it a complete dereliction of duty just to tell me what toothpaste the cardinal uses."

Robert Tyler descended the curved staircase with Lily, giving her last minute instructions. Padre noticed Sheila's eyes dissecting Tyler's movements. He leaned close to Sheila and said, "You know you could do a lot better than that cop you are dating. Tyler's got respect, money."

Sheila tsked. "I have enough money. Besides, he's like a second father to me."

"Women like you prefer the bad boys but some day you will have to grow up."

"Save your pious speeches for someone who asks for them, Padre."

But Padre could see the wheels spinning behind Sheila's green eyes.

Tyler stretched out a hand to Padre. "Sergeant Martinez, what brings you around today?" He gave Sheila a peck on the cheek. "Looking beautiful as always, Sheila."

Padre could swear he saw Sheila blush.

Tyler motioned for them to follow him to the veranda. "Can I get you anything? Coffee? Iced tea?"

"Nothing, thank you."

"Iced tea would be nice, Robert," Sheila said. She stood at the railing and looked down on the gardens. Padre could see her imagining what it would be like to be head of this household, not that her family's estate was a slum. But Padre doubted she could give up her bad boys and Tyler wouldn't settle for a wife with a roving eye.

"I can get a couple uniformed officers to check I.D.s outside and a couple more to stand guard if you'd like," Padre offered.

"Two officers outside is all we'll need. Dagger is sending two men to work undercover inside."

"Dagger won't be here?" Sheila's voice didn't mask her disappointment. "Did he say why?"

"Something about paying respects to the family of a friend who died in that plane which fell into Pyramid Lake in Nevada."

"Friend? What friend?" Sheila demanded.

Lily brought a tray with three glasses of iced tea. Padre checked his watch and decided he had time for iced tea. He wondered what two friends Dagger planned to send over in his absence. More importantly, he wondered what coincidence it was that Doc Akins' plane fell from the sky. Homeland Security was all over the case but Padre didn't believe in coincidences.

"I'm not sure," Robert replied. "I don't make it a habit of prying into other peoples' lives. I leave that up to you reporters." Robert motioned for them to have a seat. "I really don't anticipate problems today, Sergeant, and Cardinal Esrey feels I'm imposing on the police department for no good reason, but, to be safe, I think it best to have some show of caution."

"I agree."

"Dagger's two associates will pose as waiters," Robert added.

"Associates?" Sheila asked. "What associates?"

Padre looked quizzically at Sheila. "For having once been engaged to the guy, you certainly sound surprised that he has friends and associates."

Sheila's face flushed. "Dagger always was very private. I know he refers to Sara as an associate," she added with a bit of cynicism. "Does she plan to be here, too?"

"Only two men from what I understand." Padre was curious,

too, if Dagger really was paying his respects. If not, exactly what was he doing?

Robert refilled Sheila's glass with iced tea. "I understand you had a hand in that engagement party fiasco. Nick is a bit more distressed than he is letting on."

Sheila's face flushed again as she pressed her hands across her linen skirt. "Sometimes people just need a little push. I miscalculated Sara's feelings for Nick, that's all."

"In the future," Robert said, his gaze locking onto hers, "I would appreciate it if you would leave your pushing to the Monroe family."

"I meant no harm, Robert. I hope you believe me."

Padre thought if Sheila's face got any redder, she'd need an ice pack.

"Of course. I've done my share of meddling in my sons' lives so I know how much harm can be done. I have to admit I'm guilty of miscalculating their relationship, too. I was also guilty of trying to manipulate him. I dangled one of our island resorts in front of Nick, hinting that it would look far more professional if he exhibited a serious commitment to business and his life. Believe me, I see the errors of my ways."

"Why? What happened?" Sheila placed a hand on Robert's arm. Padre was getting pretty good at reading Sheila. She was like a chameleon being jealous and manipulative one minute and a concerned friend with motherly overtones the next.

"He flew to Hawaii to do some surfing. At least Eric is there so he can give him some brotherly advice. Matter of fact, tomorrow morning after the cardinal leaves for Rome, I'm going to head there myself. We are going to have a Tyler family R and R. Try to get back on track. It will be good to spend some time with my grandson."

"I would think if you were going to be upset with someone, Robert, it would be Sara, not me." When Sheila bristled, it wasn't a pretty image. She didn't wear jealousy well.

"Sara was the victim in this, as was Nick. I was trying to control him for my own benefit and you were trying to control the entire situation for your own benefit. Neither one of us was innocent in this."

Padre felt like an intruder in a family spat and desperately wanted to change the subject. "I'm glad I'm here should you two take the gloves off, but if I might interject a question here regarding the cardinal, Mr. Tyler."

"Sure, I'm sorry."

"After the break-in, did the cardinal notice if his briefcase had been tampered with, maybe documents stolen or perhaps noticed that someone logged onto his computer while he was at the dinner?"

"For one thing, the laptop was here. It wasn't at the hotel. More importantly, I don't think he would be the person to ask any questions regarding the computer."

"Why's that?"

"He writes everything in long hand. Hasn't stepped into the electronic age, in his words. Thomas types all of the cardinal's notes into the laptop."

25

Dagger glanced at the satellite image on the monitor as he sped past several buildings. Up ahead was a fenced in area as far as the eye could see. He slammed his foot on the brake and spun the car 180 degrees. He checked the monitor again, the car idling. A rusted sign on the fence said *Gemini Missile Silo*. And just below the name was the symbol for BettaTec.

Out of force of habit, his eyes scanned the fencing for cameras, but what did it matter? BettaTec had the biggest eye in the sky. Thankfully, according to Skizzy's findings, the two satellites weren't pointed over this area, which made Dagger wonder, why not?

He studied the ghost town stretched out in front of him. An asphalt street without curbs made it look as though some Hollywood studio had thrown up a backdrop overnight for a movie scene. The buildings were wooden, some windows broken out, some doors yawning open in the hot wind, banging incessantly against the doorjambs. Weeds and litter tumbled across the asphalt. Dagger watched for any signs of movement, listened for voices, music. He punched a button on the grid and checked for cameras, then rolled the Cobalt slowly down the street letting Skizzy's toy scramble any cameras he hadn't detected that might still be in operation.

He parked the car in front of a building with a striped pole. Cautiously he climbed out of the car and slammed the door. His eyes scanned rooftops, the narrow alleyways between buildings. He opened the door to the barber shop and stepped inside. Three chairs faced the doorway waiting for their next customers. Carcasses of bugs and birds scattered a dirt-covered wooden floor. Towels lay across the tops of chairs, one towel tossed on a counter.

Dagger stepped back outside and entered the next building. Shelves were stocked with canned goods and torn boxes which looked as though animals might have had a feast. What was missing was a cash register, or perhaps that was the only thing anyone thought of taking. A rack by the door had a stack of newspapers. Dagger pulled one from the middle of the stack to avoid all the dirt and grit. It was dated five years ago.

A scratching sound came from upstairs. Dagger froze. Slowly he pulled the Kimber from its holster and stood silently for several minutes, listening. The tapping and scratching were coming from directly above him. A staircase in the back ran along the side of the wall. Dagger moved cautiously, his finger twitching on the trigger. The scratching intensified as he climbed the wooden stairs. He stepped on the outer edges of the staircase to avoid weak spots in the middle that might creak under his weight.

Daylight fell across the top of the stairs. This town was in the middle of nowhere. He hadn't noticed any cars parked anywhere, although one could be hidden in back or in a garage. Perhaps he should have walked behind all the buildings first before venturing inside.

The wood groaned under his foot. Dagger stopped as did the scratching sounds. He didn't recall any fire escapes on the outside of the buildings so whoever was up here would have to go through him. With the gun at the ready, he peered over the railing, then rushed to the top of the stairs.

A flash of feathers and loud cawing charged up from the floor. Dagger stumbled backwards, his finger almost firing off a round at the crows feasting on what looked like a dead rodent.

The birds rushed through the open window leaving Dagger to chase his pulse back to normal. "Damn." He avoided the rat as he crossed the floor. Two chairs sat in front of the window as though lookouts had been positioned here at one time. What were they watching out for? Or whom?

There was another door to his right. Dagger should have brought a flashlight but he had left the gym bag in the car. He used the Kimber to tap the door open. He felt the wall for a light switch and flipped it on. It was a bathroom. The tub and sink were water stained. The toilet seat was up. He opened a cabinet above the sink. It had several toothbrushes and a used tube of toothpaste, some bandages, and antiseptic spray. A narrow closet behind him contained two towels and washcloths. One towel was draped over a towel bar by the tub.

Dagger returned to the first floor and found the back door. It, too, had been left unlocked. He stepped out into a backdrop of more sand and empty prairie. The next building had also been left unlocked. The back room had scales for what might be used for weighing packages. He threaded his way to the front to find mail slots and a counter. The mail slots were empty. They had been careful not to leave any mail lying around.

He stepped through the front door and made his way into the street. This couldn't be a town. There were only eight buildings resembling army barracks. It was more like a guard station. A building at the end of the block confirmed his theory. Five stories high with an enclosed stairway, it resembled a watch tower. Was it a control tower for private planes? Dagger climbed the stairs two at a time. The top floor was walled with glass on four sides. A desk and one chair were against a wall. If he had hoped for a log book or notes, he was sorely disappointed.

Dagger should have brought binoculars with him. His own well-stocked gym bag was at home but he had avoided going home first, preferring to grab what he could from Skizzy and get on the road. From the watch tower he could see a fenced in area the size of a dozen or more football fields. Short, round silos were spaced hundreds of yards apart. Gemini Missile Silo. Abandoned, forgotten. There were also several flat metal objects, what looked like square manhole covers. Escape hatches? Only one way to find out.

"Open up. I know you're in there." Padre squinted through the blinds in the window. He pounded his fist on the door again. "HEY! Do you want the Health Department inspector to pay you a visit?"

The door was pulled open a scant two inches. One hazel-colored eye stared somewhere over Padre's shoulder, although Padre was sure it was supposed to be aimed directly at his face.

"You know it's polite to call and request an appointment," Skizzy growled.

"I have an appointment." Padre held up his badge. "Now open up." The cop pushed his way through. The door was immediately slammed shut and locked. "You owe me a report. Since you aren't coming to see me, I'm coming to see you."

"Yeah, yeah, yeah," Skizzy grumbled. "Did you ever stop to think that maybe I don't have anything to tell you?" He weaved his way around the counter and barked, "Stay there."

Padre scanned the shelves lining the walls, his expert eyes looking for anything suspicious. He knew Skizzy was too smart to leave guns sitting out. Instead the showcases held jewelry, ivory-handled knives, colored glassware that he remembered his mother calling *carnival glass*, lamps with carved bases, pocket watches. "Hey, I thought you had a pawn shop here," Padre called out. "It looks more like a garage sale or flea market."

Skizzy emerged from the draped doorway, paper in hand. "Are you disparaging my establishment?"

Padre stifled a smile. "How the hell do you make a living selling this junk?"

One bulging eyeball jerked up, making Skizzy's face appear distorted. "I get by. Whazzit to you?" He slid the piece of paper across the counter.

"That's it? One sheet of paper?" Padre scanned the report picking his way through a crossword puzzle of words. "Not so surprising that the Pope is mentioned."

"It isn't unless…"

Padre tossed a withering glare and waited. But then his cop brain kicked into gear. "Nah." He re-read the words. "You don't think these are threats against the Pope, do you?"

"Oh, so now I'm a psychic?" Skizzy snatched the paper from Padre's fingers. "Dagger, being of the ever suspicious mind, thinks it might not be the cardinal's flash drive. Did the cardinal mention his got stolen?"

"He swears nothing is missing from his hotel room." Padre wasn't sure what he could do with this information. He couldn't exactly call the Vatican. "No city, no date, no specifics."

"Yeah, pretty cryptic. Almost reads like a to do list—*pick up the laundry, gallon of milk, kill the Pope.*"

"Dagger tell you the jumper had the same DNA as the guy dumped in the quarry?" He was fishing, he knew it, and Skizzy's face was hard to read. The squirrelly guy's one eyebrow lowered while the opposite one raised, like two flagships passing each other.

"Government clones. I've been warning you people for years."

You people? Padre would have better luck talking to the residents of the Cedar Point Mental Hospital. "When's the last time Dagger saw Doc Akins?"

"You'd have to ask Dagger."

"I would but he left town."

"There you go."

There I go? "He's not answering his cell phone."

"He's probably on a religious retreat, maybe getting his inner *feng shui* recalibrated."

Padre didn't have an answer for that. He just shook his head, waved his thanks, and left.

Dagger crossed the field to the closest escape hatch. The gym bag he retrieved from the car contained weapons, the pick gun, and provisions. Unfortunately, the pick gun had been useless on the outer fence's rusted lock. He had to shoot it off instead. Skizzy's toy was clipped to his belt. It would scramble any surveillance cameras. Although the black sleeveless tee shirt provided some relief from the heat, the color seemed to absorb the sun's rays.

He gathered his hair into a ponytail as he studied the metal lid. It was much larger up close. The lid was split with two handles. He pulled on the handle and one half of the door opened with ease. Below him were metal stairs into darkness. He shoved the sunglasses in his pocket, flicked on the flashlight, adjusted the strap of the gym bag on his shoulder, and entered. Although Dagger welcomed the outside light, leaving the hatch open might draw unwanted attention. He wasn't sure if anyone patrolled the area, but he didn't want to take the chance and also didn't want to get locked in. A piece of wood lay several feet away. He used it to prop open the hatch before proceeding down the stairs.

The halogen beam sprayed light over stone walls. The shaft was the size of a freight elevator with a metal stairway. He cast a nervous glance at the steel hatch one flight up. A fragile stake of wood propped open the hatch leaching a scant two inches of sunlight into the dark. Leaning over the railing, he aimed the halogen beam down the shaft revealing an endless number of stairs. How far did it extend and what awaited him at the bottom?

With little more than stubborn determination, he continued

down the stairs letting the beam of light search for signs on the walls to lend some clue as to what danger he might encounter. He stopped two stairs before the third landing and listened. Silence. Complete silence. Not one hum of a motor or patter of four-legged creatures. Not one hint of a whisper or soft sound of fabric rustling. Just utter silence.

As he stepped onto the third landing a loud bang echoed through the stairwell. The flashlight skipped down the stairs as he dropped the gym bag, pulled his gun from its holster, and flattened his back against the wall. Three flights above the hatch door had slammed shut, breaking the wooden stake. Immediately light sconces on the walls clicked on in succession. His heart pounded in his chest as though trying in vain to escape. He pointed the gun first toward the closed hatch, then down the lit stairwell. He listened for sounds of footsteps running, doors slamming, voices shouting. But still there was only silence, except for the endless clicking of light sconces becoming softer, more distant, until he couldn't hear them anymore.

Looking up he contemplated sanity. Of all the reckless things he had done in his life, this had to be right at the top. He should retreat and trust that the hatch didn't lock when it slammed shut. He should return home and forget about this ludicrous mission. But then the depths beckoned and his curiosity intensified. Insanity had gotten him this far. Why back out now?

He looked down at his feet. What had triggered the lights? His weight on the landing? Maybe a timer after the escape hatch was opened. He holstered the gun, retrieved the flashlight, shoved it in the gym bag, and continued down the stairs. The walls looked like marble or cinderblock that some giant stone polishing machine had buffed to a smooth finish. There weren't any cameras he could detect but for some bizarre reason he felt as though he were being watched.

Dizzy from the endless flights, he collapsed on the stairs

and pulled a bottle of water from the gym bag. Climbing down was one thing. Climbing up was a task he didn't anticipate. Although he should have worked up a sweat, he didn't feel hot. The temperature in the stairwell was relatively mild, not the cold dampness he had expected. The air didn't smell moldy like the inside of a tomb or earthy like a grave. It actually had the fresh scent of the outdoors. It was as though the stairwell were humidity and temperature-controlled, yet there wasn't a sign of a vent anywhere.

His eyes were drawn to a number in black lettering on the wall. It was the second time he had seen the identical number *402*. How many flights since the first time he had seen the number? He had tried counting the lights as he descended but lost track at sixty, or was it seventy? The monotony of the stairwell was getting to him. He could be trapped down here with nothing more than a gym bag of power bars, fruit, and water. How long could that last?

He capped the bottle and dropped it into the gym bag. Picking up speed, he pounded down the stairs, no longer concerned about making too much noise. He just wanted to see an end to the metal stairs and stone walls. A third *402* in black letters was painted on the wall at the next landing. Figures bounced in his head — 402 times three equals 1,206. Was that feet? He had certainly descended farther than 1,206 feet. The muscles in his thighs burned. What could possibly be at the bottom of this shaft? Missile silos weren't this deep. Chicago's Deep Tunnel Project was only 350 feet underground. It took thirty years to build. How long has this shaft been here and how long did it take to dig? He may reach the bottom and find an unfinished shaft. If he had to turn around and run back up, he'd sooner put the gun to his head.

Ignoring the pain in his thighs he increased his speed, taking han one second per flight. He finally caught sight of a stone actual end to this monotony. Several yards from the last stair was a door. Breathing came in gasps, sweat glistened his skin. On the wall next to the door was the number *1,608,* a familiar number. The number was in meters and equal to 5,280 feet. He was exactly one mile below the surface.

With one hand wrapped around the gun, he grabbed the door latch and slowly pulled. Light burst through forcing him to shield his face. Blinking the burning from his eyes, he rammed the door open and stepped out onto a walkway. Gun at the ready, he checked to the left and right of him but didn't see any movement. Stretched in front of him was a cobblestone courtyard as wide as a four-lane highway. If there were people here, did they run for cover when they heard him coming? Or did something chase them away years before he arrived? Someone or something had to be operating the lights.

One-story buildings served as sentries on both sides of the courtyard, their marble fronts in an assortment of colors, metal doors painted. He ignored the fatigue in his legs while his senses picked up the chirping of birds in nearby trees, the rustling of leaves from a breeze that barely kissed his skin. Billowing clouds hung in a sunlit sky so blue it made his eyes sting. Stone benches lined the courtyard every ten feet. Dazed, he blinked quickly expecting the scene to disappear like a mirage, but it didn't. Slowly circling like a lost tourist, his hand lost its grasp on the gym bag. It slipped from his hand and thudded to the cobblestone. Three-story buildings in the distance jutted toward the sky, chrome facades gleaming in the sunlight. As he wandered into the center of the courtyard he scanned the surrounding buildings, checking windows and rooftops. A variety of sweet aromas filled the air from nearby ceramic flower urns. Yellow petals too yellow, pink petals too pink. The entire area was an amateur paint-by-number scene.

He holstered his gun, stumbled to the curb and dropped onto the nearest bench. He should have been questioning how all this could be happening. After all, he was sure he was a mile underground. Any normal person would have been questioning his sanity, exploring his surroundings, examining all possible explanations. Any sane person would have been mumbling *impossible, ridiculous, absurd.* But only one word came to Dagger's mind:

Home

26

The man known as Donald Thomas stared at the strange numbers and letters on the computer screen. All he had done was run a decryption program and now it looked as though the characters on the screen were eating through every document. Somehow someone had sent a virus through the computer, destroying everything he had loaded off of the flash drive. They knew. They were onto him. He tried to quell the panic building. If only he could find the flash drive. It had to be somewhere. Then he remembered the news of the man who had jumped from their hotel suite window. Were the papers correct? Had the jumper been someone protesting the church's handling of the abuse charges? Or had he been sent to retrieve the flash drive? Did the flash drive burn up with the body? Had to. The orders would have been to destroy it at all costs, even if it meant self-sacrifice.

There was always a problem when there were too many chiefs, especially if they weren't in agreement on actions to take, programs to pursue. The organization was fractured and people were taking up sides. Negotiation had never been part of the corporation's tenet. Now their small splinter group had been compromised. Their leverage was gone, burned up in a parking lot and eaten up by a computer virus.

Checkmate.

"You ever see such posh digs before?" Skizzy moved in a circle, his head levered back like a Pez dispenser as though he were studying the artwork at the Sistine Chapel.

"Just don't knock anything over." Simon set a silver tray on a cart and moved toward the dining room. "Stay close to me. God forbid they notice you don't know what the hell you are doing."

"Whoa." Skizzy's head snapped forward as he saw the long buffet table, the glistening wine glasses illuminated by the chandeliers. His finger dug at the knot of his bowtie. "Feel like a penguin in this suit."

"You look like a penguin." Simon set the tray in the center of the buffet table. "Awful lotta hoopla for just ten guests but the Tylers don't do nothing small."

The floral arrangement in the center of the buffet table was four feet long and included some of the most exotic flowers Simon had ever seen. He watched as Skizzy started to light the candles on the table. As Skizzy's shirt sleeve rode up, Simon saw something duct taped to his wrist.

"What the hell is that?"

"Huh?"

Simon pointed at Skizzy's wrist. "That."

"That detects people who have trackers in their bodies."

Simon rolled his eyes. "It's a wonder you haven't checked me out."

"Already did," Skizzy replied with a grin. "When I was helping you on with your tuxedo jacket. You're clear."

"Who do you plan to scan here? The cardinal?"

"Yep, and whoever else gets near me."

Simon set individual crystal butter dishes at each place setting. He shook his head at the amount of wealth in this house, the furnishings, the grounds. "The rich and famous. All this wasted butter. All this crystal. Must be nice."

"That's who you'll find out is behind this BettaTec company. The richest people in the world. They pool their resources like all those medieval organizations—the Masons, Knights Templar, Skull and Bones, Illuminati, 33 Degree."

"You're going pretty far back, aren't you?"

"Probably still around today. Just changed their names but they are behind everything that happens. It's like they sit at some big chess game with the world map in front of them, moving all them chess pieces around."

"Don't make no sense," Simon said with a huff. "If alls we had to do was make a list of the ten richest people in the world, you'd know the players. But those ten aren't interested in anything but making more money. No. Power is what drives people, power and some global plan for humanity. A man with a vow of poverty can move mountains if he has the will to achieve his goals and enough like-minded people supporting him."

"What are you two up to?" The men turned in unison. Sheila stood in the doorway, hands on narrow hips, jewels dangling from her wrists. She strolled on heels sharp enough to be registered as lethal weapons. Her head shook back and forth like a hall monitor who just caught two pupils out of the classroom. Well-coiffed platinum hair swung in a synchronized rhythm, each strand obediently returning to its rightful place. "I know you two aren't butlers."

"Some of us need a second job as caterers," Simon sniffed. "We aren't like some rich folk who can support a third world country with their salaries."

"Right." Sheila struck a thoughtful pose, left arm across her stomach, left hand propped under her right elbow while a manicured nail tapped repeatly against bright veneers. "I had expected to see Dagger."

Simon knew when someone was fishing for information and it was probably killing Sheila not knowing Dagger's whereabouts.

"He's outta town," Skizzy barked as he sidled up behind Sheila and waved his right hand across the back of her neck.

"What are you doing?" Sheila dodged his waving hand.

"Checking if you are wearing a wig. Hair looks too perfect." Skizzy's toy had remained silent.

Sheila flashed a smile, taking his remark as a compliment. "Where did Dagger go?"

"Didn't tell us." Simon placed salt and pepper shakers on the table.

"What about Sara?"

Simon smiled. "Not sure but I think Sara went out of town, too." He watched disappointment cloud her face. "Guess your plan to get her hitched to young Nicholas didn't work." If Simon had expected her to deny any involvement, he was wrong.

"Can't blame a girl for trying. Nicholas is more Sara's age. Besides, Dagger likes refined women who know how to keep a man satisfied."

"Guess that's why you ain't with him no more," Skizzy mumbled in a voice too low for Sheila to hear.

"What do you think of Cardinal Esrey?" Simon asked.

"He's nice," Sheila replied in all sincerity. "Pretty down to earth. Padre likes him so I guess the Martinez seal of approval goes a long way. Have you met him?"

"No," the two men replied in unison.

Guests started to file in. Simon rubbed his hands together. "Show time."

"HEY, YOU MUTT!"

The gray wolf tore off for the woods, a piece of fried chicken in its jaws. The farmer had just set his plate on a picnic table in the backyard when the wolf jumped onto the table, snatched the chicken and sped through the cornfield. It had been careful to make sure the farmer didn't have a gun anywhere around.

The gray wolf made a quick survey of the wooded area. Confident there weren't any witnesses, it shifted to the hawk and flew to a high branch of a cottonwood tree where it shifted to Sara. She grabbed the fried chicken with both hands as she leaned against the trunk of the tree. She had gone too long without food after expending a lot of energy. The foliage was dense this high up but she still felt exposed as leaves caressed her naked body. When she finally reached her destination, she was going to have a problem with clothing. Houses were getting fewer and far between. Although the farmer's wife had laundry on the line, it would be difficult for Sara to travel carrying the clothes. And she would have to find shoes. At least if Dagger had taken one of his own cars, Sara would have had no problem finding clothes. She kept shoes and a change of clothes in the trunk of each of Dagger's vehicles for just such an occasion.

"Mmmmmm." The chicken tasted just like her grandmother's. Crispy and not too greasy. If she wasn't already in the farmer's crosshairs, she'd go back for another piece. Now she needed a bath. She shifted quickly and with the bones in its beak, the gray hawk shoved off the tree branch. It watched for small animals below and then dropped the bones for them to pick clean. A lake was off in the distance. Before emerging from the safety of the woods, the hawk swooped down, shifted back into the wolf and charged toward the water.

The wolf took a tentative step at the shore, padded in, then dove under the surface. It shifted to Sara. With eyes open she dipped and swerved in the murky water, barely able to see beyond six feet. Muck covered the bottom along with beer cans, what looked like railroad ties, and an automobile covered with green algae. Sara moved closer to the side window, peered inside, then pulled back in alarm. She shoved off toward the surface and came up gulping air amid a crowd of cattails.

"Why me?" She breathed in deeply trying to erase the image of the remains she saw in the car. All this time she had thought it was Dagger who attracted trouble. Now she wondered if she was the culprit, or was it just Dagger's influence on her.

She used her hawk vision to study the opposite shoreline.

Two young boys were fishing off of a pier. Ducks paddled a safe distance from the boys. A no trespassing sign was clearly posted to Sara's right. A no swimming sign was nailed below the trespassing sign. What to do.

The farmer's house was less than a mile away but she was not exactly dressed for walking much less for swimming up to the boys to ask if they had a telephone. She gulped air and sank back down to search the car. The license plate was hanging on by one screw. Sara tried unscrewing it but it was rusted on. She tugged, wrenching it from the bumper then swam back to the surface.

The gray wolf emerged from the water, dropped the license plate on the grass, shook the water from its body, snatched the plate in its jaws, and tore off across the field, through the woods. As it approached the farmer's yard, it halted. A police car was in the driveway. It tensed when it saw the gun in the cop's holster and the rifle in the farmer's hand. It crept closer.

"I tell you, Sheriff, it was a wolf."

"Woody, wolves want fresh meat, not something cooked to order. It was a wild dog, that's all. You didn't get harmed none. And I don't want to hear of you tempting wolves or coyotes here so you can earn a bounty." Sunlight reflected off the sheriff's mirrored sunglasses. The name *Olsen* was on his shirt pocket. He worked a toothpick around his mouth as he looked toward a pen of alpacas nearby. "If it had wanted to, it could have gone after the alpacas, but it didn't."

"Still don't mean it won't be back. I got little ones. I can't send them out to play if..." Woody saw the toothpick drop from the sheriff's mouth. "What?" He turned to see the wolf creeping toward them. Woody shouldered his rifle but the sheriff clamped a hand on his arm.

"Hold it up there. It don't look menacing. Look." He motioned toward the pen with his chin. "The alpacas aren't even agitated that the wolf is near. Strangest damn thing I ever saw."

"What's it got in its mouth?"

The gray wolf stopped, looked from one man to the next. Cautiously it moved forward, then dropped the license plate on the ground. It looked over its shoulder once, took several steps back and waited.

"What the hell?" Sheriff Olsen took several cautious steps toward the license plate. The wolf retreated, then approached, retreated again. "I think it wants us to follow it."

"Right. Lead us right to the pack where it will rip the skin off our bones."

"Woody, you been watchin' too much television." Olsen picked up the license plate, swiped a hand across the mud and muck. "It's wet. Been in the water."

"Hey, does that say Rosegard?"

"Why…I think you're right." Olsen pulled out his hankie and wiped the plate dry. "A lady who owned that flower shop over in Mitchell County went missing over five years ago. That plate number went through a statewide broadcast for at least a year. Was real foggy that night from what the report said."

"You don't think she went way out of her way and ended up in our county, do you?"

Olsen looked at the wolf and cocked his head. "Unusual intelligence for a four-legged animal, if you ask me."

"Well, we'll just see." Woody grabbed the license plate and called out to the wolf, "Hey, where'd you find this?" He waved the plate in the air.

"Set the rifle down so it sees you don't mean it no harm. Lord knows, I don't need PETA parked on my doorstep."

Woody placed the rifle on the picnic table and took a step toward the wolf. "Show us where you found it." The wolf took off across the field.

"Climb in, Woody. We'll take my Blazer."

They sped off across the field in pursuit of the wolf. Woody said, "The only water close by is over on the Bishop property. Got a ten acre pond. If someone were to take a wrong turn off that cloverleaf and mistake that tractor road for a street, they could very easily end up in a whole lotta trouble."

The pond came into view. The wolf was standing at the edge looking at the water. It cocked its head as the Blazer skidded to a stop. Sheriff Olsen stepped out of the vehicle and stripped off his gun belt, hat, shirt, shoes, and socks.

"May as well get a little wet." Olsen approached the edge of the pond. The wolf was just ten feet away. "That is a beautiful animal. Look at them eyes, Woody. Just beautiful." Olsen stepped in and gasped. "Feels good. Been so hot lately." The water crept up to his waist. "Get a rope out of the back of my truck in case I need a pull out of this muck." When Woody returned with the rope, the sheriff tied it around his waist and then dove into the water.

Woody stared apprehensively at the wolf. "Hope you enjoyed that chicken of mine. If you'da stuck around you coulda had some peach pie."

The sheriff broke the surface, his hair plastered to his head. He clambered out breathing heavily. "It's there. Gotta car and a body. I gotta call it in, get the state officials out here. Let them drag the car out."

"Well, that closes a huge case thanks to…" Woody turned. "Where'd the wolf go?"

27

Padre found Cardinal Esrey pacing the walkway between the fountains and garden, hands clasped behind his back. It reminded him of his seminary days when he would catch John Wozniak pacing the seminary grounds, contemplating his desire for the priesthood and Renee Banasiak, his college sweetheart. Padre had learned several months later that Renee's pregnancy had a lot to do with John leaving the seminary.

There could be a lot weighing heavily on Cardinal Esrey, Padre tried to convince himself. After all, he represented millions of people and a 2,000-year-old faith. The child abuse scandal was just starting to subside. He had met with a number of area priests concerned about school closings as well as representatives of Catholic charities. Although careful to show only his serious side to the press, how many people, Padre thought, would be surprised to see the collection of books which accompanies the cardinal on his travels? Besides poetry, the cardinal was a big fan of science fiction.

Cardinal Esrey stopped in front of a stone bench and sat down slowly. Padre didn't have to be a cop to know that something was wrong, more than school closings and child abuse allegations. The cardinal leaned forward, elbows on his knees, hands clasped, but not in prayer.

Padre approached slowly, then stood for several seconds waiting. The cardinal finally looked up and pointed toward the bench. "Please," the cardinal said.

"Forgive me for the intrusion, Your Eminence," Padre said, taking a seat next to the cardinal. "But you look like a man in need of confessing."

* * *

"Don't look so depressed," Simon said. Skizzy had made a point to place each guest's napkin on his lap, allowing the bug monitor to pass behind the guests' necks but not one person set off the monitor.

"Don't seem right. Thought for sure the cardinal woulda set this thing to beeping and humming, but nope." They stood in an alcove watching the caterers refilling platters of food. The cardinal had given a short speech of gratitude for Robert Tyler's hospitality but all in all the event had been stiff and boring.

The cardinal's secretary had refused to join the guests and taken a tray to his room. Even Skizzy had found the guy squirrelly, which was strange coming from Skizzy. Now Father Thomas was back, showing papers to the cardinal and talking about flights.

"The cardinal has the patience of a saint," Simon whispered. "Trouble don't follow a man like that."

"Except for the break-in at his suite, the dead security guard, and the clone jumper," Skizzy reminded him.

"Good point."

Father Thomas had his hands full of papers as he headed for the alcove. Not watching where he was going, he bumped into Skizzy sending papers flying.

"Father Thomas, are you okay?" Simon said as he bent down to help pick up the papers. Simon looked up to see Skizzy's eyes growing in size. He half expected them to pop out of his head at any moment. Without any warning, he saw Skizzy pass his hand across the back of the priest's neck. The monitor started buzzing and beeping.

Skizzy jerked his hand up and clasped his ear just as the priest straightened, papers clutched to his chest.

"Sorry, it's my hearing aid," Skizzy blurted.

The normally congenial priest glared with righteous indignation at Skizzy, then stalked off.

"What kinda hair-brained idea is rolling around in that head of yours?" Simon asked.

Skizzy pounded away on the keyboard, his face a combination of anger, fear, and maniacal devilishness. After excusing themselves from waiter duty, Skizzy had rushed back to the shop to check further into the videotapes from the airport. An hour before departing for their terminal, Father Thomas had confronted the man on the videotape while the cardinal made a stop in the restroom. It had been a heated discussion with Father Thomas blocking his way. The two men appeared to jockey for position. That was when Father Thomas slipped his hand into the man's pocket.

"Crap. Did you see that?" Skizzy said.

"Yeah. He stole something from him."

"The flash drive. It was in the man's pocket."

Simon stood back and studied the man for several seconds. "Zoom in on the tall guy. See if he's got one of them scars."

Skizzy said, "Already checked. He's clean. Obviously a big honcho."

"A dead honcho," Simon said. "If that flash drive was important and he lost it on his watch, he's good as dead."

"Maybe Father Thomas wanted more money for whatever it is he was hired to do."

"What money? If Thomas has the scar then he's a genetically engineered soldier. He does what he's told."

"Unless he went rogue. That's what I think happened to Dagger. Maybe he went rogue and the powers that be can't have that."

Simon didn't have an answer to that. It all made sense. "So

what are you doing with the cardinal's IP address?"

"Mr. Tyler said the cardinal isn't up on all these new electronics, that only Father Thomas has access to the computer."

Simon looked over Skizzy's shoulder as he accessed a number of porn sites. "What the hell? The church has enough trouble with child abuse," Simon argued.

"No children. These are lovely ladies, escort services, and anything else I can find. This should keep the assassin out of Rome."

28

Dagger had been sitting on the bench for what seemed like hours trying to make sense out of everything. Buildings were tethered together, all doors and windows and the same marble running up the faces of the one-story structures. He inhaled deeply and closed his eyes. The aroma from the flowers was strong. Dagger reached over and fingered the petals of one of the plants. They weren't real. They were silk. Another sound made him spin around. Children laughing, dogs barking. Dagger dashed from pillar to pillar, making his way toward the noise. His eyes scanned the windows for images as he moved. He made his way down the street, then turned a corner. A block away there was a park but there weren't any children. He heard dogs barking but didn't see any dogs. Swings moved back and forth yet no one was on them.

"What the hell?" Dagger didn't believe in ghosts but this was like an underground city whose residents refused to leave. He checked the door to one of the buildings, tried the knob but it was locked. He pressed his face to the window and saw office furniture, computer equipment, what looked like a lab coat across the back of a chair. Using the pick gun, he unlocked the door just as a new stream of noise from the park erupted. Dagger turned to see the park filled with people.

"Shit!" He slipped into the office, locked the door, and watched the park from the window. Assured no one had seen him, he turned away from the window and studied the office. There was a flat screen monitor on the desk but no keyboard. There wasn't a desk calendar or a scrap of paper anywhere. A stained coffee cup was once full of something that had long since produced its own penicillin. The occupant didn't even have time to finish his coffee before vacating the premises. Dagger studied the park again. People were jogging, children were swinging on the swings, mothers were sitting on benches talking.

Dagger moved quickly to another door at the far wall and cracked it open. There was a wide corridor leading to other offices. It appeared the exterior buildings were just a false facade to the large office complex within. He turned his head to listen for sounds in the outer offices. It was silent. He returned to the window. The park was empty.

Dagger felt dizzy and wondered if the depth he had descended was screwing up his head. Maybe he needed to eat. He closed the window blinds partway then settled behind the desk. He pulled out one of the protein bars and a bottle of water from the tote bag. While he ate, he rummaged through the desk drawers. A stained paper bag was in the bottom of the drawer. He carefully lifted it and peered inside. Someone had left a lunch to mold and petrify. The top drawer held the typical office paraphernalia of paper clips, staples, pens. There wasn't a clock or calendar in the room.

Furniture was wood and chrome or a metal of some type. A couch against the side wall was leather and looked inviting. He dropped the gym bag on the floor, stretched out on the couch, and told himself he would just rest for a few minutes.

The gray hawk settled on top of a utility pole. Across the street was the silver Chevy. The hawk had scanned the area enclosed by fencing after locating the car. So far its visual acuity had not detected any human movement.

Unsure if there were cameras around, the hawk wasn't about to take any chances. It flew across the street to another building and through an open window where it quickly shifted to the wolf. The wolf immediately picked up Dagger's scent. He had been in this building. It followed the scent down the stairs and out the back door. The wolf paused at the bottom of a stairway which led up to a tower. It picked up the scent again and tore off toward the missile silo. There were danger signs on the fence but the gate was unlocked and pulled open several feet, just enough for a man to pass through. The wolf retreated, made a slow circle, looked at the area beyond the fence, then returned to check out the rest of the buildings.

Unlocked doors yawned open in the breeze. The wolf listened for movement, voices, tilted its head to catch any scent of danger. The air was as vacant as the small outpost. It passed what looked like a post office then darted into a clothing store. There were racks for clothes with little more than frayed rags and empty hangers. But one glass case held out hope. The wolf quickly shifted to Sara. The warm air licked her bare skin. Although Sara was sure she was alone, she didn't like the exposed feeling of walking around nude. She pulled out one of the garments and unfolded it. All of the garments were blue in color and resembled one piece janitorial suits. But it would have to do. Most of them were in a large size. Settling on the one lone medium size, Sara slipped into the suit. Six inches of fabric flopped past her toes. This wouldn't do at all.

There were drawers by the counter. Searching through them, Sara found a pair of scissors. She slipped out of the jumpsuit, folded it in half, laid it across the counter, and cut off the sleeves and half of the length in the pant legs. With this heat, the last thing Sara wanted was anything long. She slipped back into the suit and zipped it up. Deep pockets were on the sides of the pant legs. Now she needed shoes. The doors below the counter opened up to a mixture of dust, dirt, and dead snake carcasses. Sara shuddered and checked the cabinets on the opposite wall. Success. Several boxes were stacked in the cabinet. Sizes were stamped on the boxes. She selected a size seven and opened the box.

"Yuk." Black work boots were not a girl's best friend. She moved to the next cabinet. "Yes." These boxes contained blue and white athletic shoes. Sara shuffled through the boxes until she found a size seven.

A search of the rest of the store didn't yield socks. After lacing the shoes and plaiting her hair, Sara turned to leave. A door in the back had a sign which said, *Authorized Personnel Only. Do Not Enter.*

Her curiosity piqued, Sara walked over and pressed her ear to the door. Nothing. She tried the doorknob. Warped from the heat, the door was wrestled free from the lock by brute strength. The door opened to a round room, no more than six feet across, with what looked like chrome walls. She stepped into the room and the door snapped shut. Sara jumped. This side of the door was paneled in chrome, like the walls. And there wasn't a doorknob.

Vertical lights flashed on opposite sides of the tubular room. Then she heard a sound, a whooshing, like air escaping. Her ears started to feel strange. The room was dropping.

"What's happening?" Sara braced herself against the side, palms flat against the wall. Her heart pounded in her chest and she felt panic set in. She tried to count the seconds. How far down did this chute go? How many floors? Was it really descending or was it an illusion?

At the count of ten, Sara felt the room slowing down. She was surprised she didn't have to yawn to pop her ears. It was as though this makeshift elevator were pressure-controlled. She heard a hiss but nothing happened. Was she stuck in this tiny place with no way out? But then the chrome door slid open. Sara stared at the room beyond. It was as large as her living room at home. All chrome and glossy wood with a floor...where was the floor? It looked like she was stepping out of a spacecraft with nothing more than the universe under her feet. There were stars and comets, distant universes. Another illusion? She tapped one foot where she thought the floor should be. It was solid. Sara smiled. It was a glass floor and underneath it was a map of the universe.

"Neat." She emerged from the elevator and made her way to the doorway. She stared down a long hall to her right. It was empty. There was a shorter hallway to her left with a door. She went for the door. It opened out to a short set of concrete stairs.

Dagger leaped from the couch, gun in hand as a sharp alarm blared. "What the hell?" Checking his watch, he saw that he had slept for almost two hours. Shadows passed beyond the closed blinds. He scrambled on all fours to the closest window and splayed the blinds. Hordes of people were walking down the cobblestone street. Kids in baseball caps, mothers pushing strollers, men casually dressed, others in lab coats.

"Shit." Dagger opened the door and peered out. Staying in the shadows, he waited until the last of the group passed, then he moved along the overhang.

The alarm died as people stood around in clusters. Dagger found shelter behind one of the large concrete pillars and watched from a distance. The workers were talking, laughing. Were they doctors? He doubted it. Something told him they were researchers. There wasn't a clipboard among them though, much less a briefcase. It was like the town of Stepford. An alarm sounds and they all walk out in unison. What comes next?

A straggler approached close to the pillar. Dagger pulled back and waited. There was something familiar about the way she walked. It couldn't be! Just as she passed close by him, Dagger reached out, wrapped the gun arm around her waist, clamped a hand over her mouth, and pulled her behind the pillar.

She tensed and he could feel her start to struggle. "What the hell are you doing here?" he whispered in her ear. Sara relaxed against him and he took his hand away.

"Saving your ass."

"Yeah, right. I thought Skizzy had you under lock and key."

"Nice try, big guy."

"Sara." Dagger tried to keep his anger in check. "This is dangerous. You have no idea what you are walking into." He jutted his chin toward the courtyard. "As you can see, we are a bit outnumbered."

Sara gave her patented eye roll, said, "Oh, jeez," and pulled away from him.

"Sara!" Dagger whispered as she slipped from his grasp and strolled over to the closest cluster. He aimed the gun, ready to shoot if necessary. He watched as she approached a group of five people. Not one person acknowledged her presence. She turned back to Dagger, smiled, then walked through them…literally. It was as though they weren't even there. Sara turned and walked right back through them as though they were wisps of air.

Dagger shook his head in amazement as he joined her. "How did you do that?"

"They are holograms." She nodded toward the ceiling. "Just like the sky. Everything is fake, Dagger. The dogs and kids playing in the park, the cricket sounds. I was able to see partially through the people." Sara's enhanced eyesight could detect things Dagger couldn't. "I spent time walking the area. The horizon isn't even real. It's just made to look like wide open spaces."

The crowd started to disperse, fading into various doorways or dematerializing, it was hard to tell. Within seconds the courtyard was abandoned again leaving Dagger and Sara gaping after their transitory visitors. Sara did a slow turn, studying the buildings, much the same way Dagger had when he first stumbled out of the stairwell. "Want to explore?"

Dagger shoved the gun back into the holster and moved toward the bench. "I need to rest my legs a bit more after trekking down one mile of stairs." He saw the look of utter amusement lighting up her eyes. "What?" He plopped down on the bench next to her feeling every muscle scream for relief.

"You walked down one mile of stairs?"

"Yeah."

Her smile spread brightening her eyes even more. "I took the elevator."

"What?"

Sara laughed, that carefree laugh that sometimes made him feel as though he brought some joy into her life. Other times, like now, he felt like the ass end of a very bad joke.

"The clothing store had a closet or storage room. I was curious because it was completely empty and was a strange, tubular shape. Once I stepped inside, the door slid shut before I could stop it. There weren't any buttons or controls but I felt it plummeting. I ended up here." She placed her chin on his shoulder and stared up at him with those gorgeous eyes. "And you walked down over five thousand feet?"

He held up a hand in warning. "Don't. I may be tired, but I'm still armed."

Sara stifled a laugh, grabbed his hand and placed it palm down on the bench with her hand on top of his. "Feel it?"

"So? It's marble, slightly warm."

"No, the movement. I can feel the ground, the bench. Everything has a slight humming or vibration."

Dagger concentrated, tried to feel what she was sensing. And then it hit him. It felt as though some mild electrical charge was arcing through the air. "Yeah, I do."

"There's an electrical source somewhere. The holograms, the sounds, the movement of the clouds in the sky, something is controlling everything."

"Or someone." Dagger lifted the silver tube clipped to a belt loop. "Skizzy's invention has scrambled any cameras in the area if there are any."

"You haven't seen signs of life, have you?"

Dagger shook his head. "It's as though everyone left in a pretty big hurry. They didn't even take time to empty coffee cups." If he had found coffee cups with warm coffee he would immediately suspect everyone was holed up in some large panic room somewhere sealed off from everything yet with a screen to monitor what he and Sara were doing. It wasn't a far-fetched idea.

Sara stood abruptly. "You've had enough rest. Let's go check out the neighborhood. There are houses down the block."

"Damn, my Kimber for a car." His legs protested as he stood.

An overhead door across the courtyard started to roll open. Dagger grabbed his gun and he and Sara darted for the nearest pillar. They waited as the door ended its ascent. "Check it out," he told Sara.

"Sure, I'm the one who gets her head blown off." But it was Sara's enhanced eyesight that he needed. "All I see are motorcycles of some sort."

Dagger peered over the top of her head. She was right. From what he could see, it appeared to be a garage. "No humans, animals, or holograms?"

"No."

They crossed the courtyard, eyes scanning the buildings, windows, looking for signs of life. Once inside the garage, they saw close to twenty vehicles resembling motorcycles but without wheels. They were made of a steel gray metallic construction, built for two people with a platform to place the feet but without pedals.

"Strange. I don't even see a start button."

"What's stranger," Sara added, "is that you no sooner mentioned needing a vehicle when we suddenly have a choice of vehicles."

Dagger let that slide right off the logical side of his brain. He was too busy trying to figure out how to turn the damn thing on. "Bizarre. No key, no gas cap." He slipped the sunglasses on and studied the front panel.

Sara climbed on the back and wrapped her arms around Dagger's waist. "Maybe you just have to tell it to go." The vehicle started humming and Sara let out a yelp as it rose six inches off the ground.

29

The vehicle moved silently through the streets, passing what appeared to be a commercial area and into a residential compound. The vehicle was so quiet they didn't have to scream to hear each other, not like when they road Dagger's Harley.

"It's hydrogen or steam-powered or something." Dagger turned the grips on the handlebar and realized he could control the speed. Not everything was out of his control. "This is like a Hover," Dagger said. "Skizzy found a print out for an experimental vehicle on a government web site. If the price of gas keeps going up, we'll all be driving these."

"I wouldn't mind. These are fun, as long as they don't take total control."

Dagger didn't like the sound of that and the logical side of his brain grasped for the significance of Sara's previous point: that he no sooner needed a vehicle and one was provided. Maybe he should have tested whatever was controlling this small town and asked for a medium rare steak. Perhaps if he said it aloud the Hover would zip right over to a restaurant.

He steered the Hover down a tree lined street of cookie cutter houses. Each house had the same type of fencing, the same evergreens placed in identical spots, and identical front windows.

He decelerated and said, "Stop." The Hover stopped, then settled down to street level. They climbed off. Dagger took a step back and lowered his sunglasses, as if for the first time assessing Sara's legs, the firmness of her calves. "Where did you get the clothes?" He popped the sunglasses back in place. "I know you didn't haul them all the way from Cedar Point."

"If you had taken one of your many cars instead of Skizzy's, I would have had something of my own to wear since I keep a change of clothes in each trunk. I had to settle for what was in the outpost clothing store. Not much to choose from. Had to do some of my own tailoring."

Dagger glanced at the zipper that stopped a hair's breadth above her cleavage. "I like your method of tailoring." He turned his attention back to the houses and out of force of habit, pulled his Kimber from its holster. "Are the houses holograms?"

"No," Sara replied. "But they look more like upgraded Army barracks. You would think they would have ultra-modern housing."

Dagger reached down and pulled a Kimber sub-compact from an ankle holster. He handed it to Sara but she refused. "We're the only ones here. I'd probably end up shooting you," she said.

Dagger kept a gun in each hand as they crossed the lawn to one of the houses. He stopped and ran his foot across the grass. "Astroturf, or something like it."

"No need to cut the grass."

They moved cautiously down the sidewalk with Dagger watching the houses for movement while Sara scanned the houses across the street.

"You will let me know when you see someone who isn't a hologram, right?"

Sara smiled. "Thought you didn't need my help."

A movement in one of the windows had them running to opposite trees.

"I'll take that gun now," Sara said. Dagger tossed the sub-compact to her.

Sara caught the gun then waited several seconds before stealing a glance at the house and the person standing in the window. She called on her advanced sight and studied the window closer, then the area around the window. "Dagger, there isn't any glass in those windows. They are empty." She stepped out from behind the tree. "Those pit marks around the windows are bullet holes and the people are fake."

"What?" Dagger moved cautiously from behind the tree and approached the house.

Sara turned and studied the houses across the street. "This is like some type of military practice range. Look." Across the street another figure popped up behind the window. This one was a child.

Dagger moved quickly up to the front door and kicked it in. The wood frame splintered, spraying wood into an empty room. It wasn't even a completed house, just a front with one room. Sara came up behind him so quietly he almost turned his gun on her.

"Little jumpy there." She walked over and kicked at the figure. It clanged and clattered against the floor. "Seems to be made of metal." Several other figures lay in a corner, their metal frames melted and twisted.

Dagger knelt down in front of the remains. "Something had to be pretty hot to melt these."

Sara ran her hand over the window frame. "I thought they were bullet holes but they aren't. The house looks like it's made of stone or marble. A bullet would have shattered it, right? Not made a clean hole through it."

Dagger joined her at the window. Everything about this place was a little too high tech and he expected any moment to wake from a bad dream.

"Come on. Let's get out of here."

Sara was several steps ahead of Dagger. They were a few feet from the Hover when Sara stopped dead in her tracks. "Do you feel that?" she asked.

"I don't feel anything."

"Right. Something turned off. I don't hear the humming.

Don't feel the vibration."

As though someone had hit the dimmer switch, the sun started to disappear, slowly fading on the horizon. Street lights clicked on and a full moon rose in the sky as though pulled by some invisible string. Sara slipped her hand into Dagger's and held on tight.

"Did it rain while we were in there?" she whispered. Water puddles glistened under the glare of the lights.

Someone or something was messing with their minds. Dagger shoved the sunglasses in his shirt pocket and checked his watch. "It's only six o'clock." They walked trance-like into the center of the street, keeping their backs to each other as though waiting for something to jump at them from dark alleyways. "I think now would be a good time to return to the courtyard."

Sara slipped the gun into the pocket of her jumpsuit. Dagger holstered his before climbing back onto the Hover. One bright halogen beam lit up their route. "Courtyard," Dagger called out and the Hover took off.

"Where does everyone live if these houses are fake?" Sara asked.

"Like you said. These streets are more like a training camp. Maybe the sleeping quarters are another floor below." Dagger had a feeling they did more than just military training here, he just wasn't sure what. He hadn't seen enough of the compound to get a feel for what had been going on. Even the office he had slept in didn't have much in the way of office equipment. Whatever prompted the evacuation was serious enough that they dropped everything and ran.

"Food," Dagger yelled. The Hover took a sudden turn at the courtyard and stopped several doors from the bench where Dagger's gym bag lay. They climbed off the Hover and watched as it returned to the garage. Once inside, the garage door slid shut. The building where the Hover deposited them was a bright yellow which almost appeared to glow in the dark. A neon sign of a glass and a platter of food flashed in the window. It looked like any downtown eatery they might find at home.

"I wish the sun would come out again," Sara said. Immediately the moon started a descent and the sun rose above the three-story buildings. Street lights snapped off and water puddles disappeared as quickly as they had appeared.

"This is just too weird." There was an intelligence here that made Dagger a little uneasy. The neon sign in the restaurant's window snapped off but suddenly music and laugher spilled out along with the scent of grilled beef. Dagger pulled open the door and halted. People were seated at tables, standing at a stone bar. Waitresses were delivering platters to tables. "Holograms?"

Sara sighed. She would even eat a steak about now. "Yes, even the food."

"Damn." Dagger released his hold on the door and stepped back into the courtyard. "Well, my lady, I can treat you to a power bar, a banana and a bottle of water." Dagger started across the courtyard.

Sara held him back. "Do you hear something?"

Dagger didn't hear the usual insect sounds nor birds. He didn't hear dogs barking or children playing. "No. What do you hear?"

They wandered to the middle of the courtyard, eyes scanning the buildings, bodies slowly turning in a circle yet they kept close enough for their fabrics to touch. Like mirror images, they each slowly pulled their weapons and held them down at their sides.

"Whining," Sara whispered

"Kids?"

"No, gears. It's coming from something small and its moving closer."

"Never a dull moment," Dagger whispered. "Home sweet home."

From one of the entryways appeared an army tank in camouflage paint. It was a replica, like a remote-controlled toy a kid would own, chugging across the walkway onto the courtyard and toward them.

Sara smiled and leaned down as though it were an approaching puppy. "Isn't it cute?"

A turret popped out of the top and turned toward them. Dagger yelled, "NO, SARA," and pulled her toward a pillar. A blast exploded from the tank pulverizing the pillar just as Dagger and Sara moved to the next one.

Another tank appeared from another entryway. Dagger pulled the slide back on the Kimber and told Sara, "There's a red light on the underside. It's a power pack. Aim for it."

They separated, Dagger moving to his left, Sara to the right. Soon, four more tanks appeared. Another pillar exploded showering Dagger with pieces of marble. He hit the ground and rolled to his left, aiming for the underside and losing his sunglasses in the process. He fired. One bullet bounced off. The next one hit the power pack. The tank ground to a stop. Dagger ran for the bench and dove for the gym bag. He grabbed it just as a blast shattered the marble bench. He fumbled in the gym bag for a clip and hoped he brought enough ammo. After shoving a clip in each pocket, he slipped his arms through the straps of the gym bag and carried it like a backpack. More blasts and gunshots echoed through the compound.

"What the hell? These are nothing more than toys." Dagger slipped behind one of the tanks and kicked it against a wall. It bounced off and turned its turret on Dagger. "Shit. Damn thing is armor-plated." Dagger didn't have a move that wouldn't put him in its crosshairs. He saw a movement to his right. Sara leaped in front of him, rolled to her left and fired. The tank ground to a halt. Sara flashed a look of sheer enjoyment at him. For a brief moment he wondered if someone were testing their capabilities.

Testing. Why did he pick that word?

Dagger ran for the next pillar with a tank in pursuit. He saw another tank bite the dust as Sara succeeded in hitting the power pack. He marveled at her accuracy enhanced by her visual acuity. What was even more marvelous was how the jumpsuit she wore hit every curve of her body. She couldn't possibly be wearing underwear.

A tank appeared to his right having somehow snuck up on him as he was admiring Sara's attributes. He dove to his left, rolled several times and came up shooting, stopping another tank. "The stairs." He pointed to a short flight of stairs and waited until she was safely down and into the building. Dagger followed close behind, a blast showering him with stone fragments before he pulled open a door and lunged to safety.

"It can't come down stairs, right?" Sara asked as she tried to catch her breath.

"I highly doubt it."

A clanking sound came from the stairwell.

Dagger frowned. "Well, at least it can't open doors." He studied the room they had entered. It was an elaborate maze of cubicles. Lights from the ceilings were almost too bright. "We should be safe now."

A blast hit the door blowing a fifteen inch hole making an opening for the tank to chug through.

"Oh, shit." Dagger tore off down the hall and through an open doorway into the labyrinth. They wove their way around cubicles, stopping a safe distance from where they had left the tank. They sat on the floor behind one of the desks. Dagger wiped rock dust and dirt from his skin and clothes. Sara looked as though she had just stepped out of the shower and slipped into clean, crisp clothes. Not a mark on her. How the hell did she do that?

Sara reached up and touched the bare desk. "That's strange. No keyboard."

"Computer is probably voice-activated." Dagger unzipped the gym bag and handed Sara a bottle of water and took the same for himself. "Why aren't those tanks holograms?" Dagger whispered. "And who sent them?"

"I was going to ask you the same question."

"Me?"

Sara stared at him as one perfectly arched eyebrow crawled up her forehead. "How did you know it had a power pack and where it was located?"

Dagger shrugged. "It's mechanical. Everything has a power pack."

"And the bright colors outside that look too artificial? Certainly explains why you prefer boring black and gray. You've been here before."

He unscrewed the cap on the water bottle and chugged half of the contents, ignoring her prodding. Truth was, Dagger didn't know why some things seemed familiar. Neurons must be firing up in the back recesses of his brain. Worse yet, he had a vague recollection of not only the tanks but also the residential target range. They were fleeting memories, flashes that were there and then disappeared. He shook it off, jammed the water bottle back into the gym bag and moved quietly through the maze with Sara close behind. Chairs were turned as though someone had just run out to get a sandwich and would be returning soon. Dried sticks of what must have once been flowers jutted from vases, remnants of dried petals scattered on the desk, the water long evaporated from the vases. Cubicle walls were free of posted notes, family pictures, and schedules.

"What's that?" Sara pointed at a round hole in the floor about the width of a coffee can.

"Individual incinerators. You noticed there aren't any garbage cans. I haven't been able to find one scrap of printer paper to give me a hint what the hell they were working on down here. My only guess is that they were careful not to print anything, that everything might have been kept on a hard drive somewhere."

"So we have to find a mainframe."

30

Dagger leaned against the wall and washed his hands over his face. Sara had followed him into what might be a trap. Neither one may make it out alive.

Sara's eyes narrowed and she cocked her head as though sizing up his response. She wasn't going to let up. "Why did you say home sweet home? Is there something you're not telling me? The numbers on that metal piece in your head had the coordinates to this place."

Dagger stared at her for several seconds. Yes, her skills came in handy, but how could he live with himself if something happened to her? "I know. I thought once I got here everything would fall into place. Bits and pieces look familiar but that's it. I remember standing on the cobblestone and staring up at the sky at some point in my life. Descending that mile of stairs didn't seem familiar until I reached the bottom and looked up." He raked strays hairs back. In the melee he not only lost his sunglasses but also the band around his ponytail and the bandage from his neck. His fingers gingerly touched the stitches. He wanted more than anything to rip the computer chip from his body. Dagger rustled through the gym bag and pulled out a couple power bars and handed one to Sara.

"Thanks. I haven't eaten since I had chicken earlier today."

Dagger stared at her. "You walked into a KFC nude?" He tried to slap that vision out of his mind.

"No," Sara said with a laugh. "The wolf stole it and I ate it in a secluded place. I also found a body."

"What?" Dagger tore off a piece of the power bar.

Sara kept her voice low as she told him about bathing in the pond and finding a car at the bottom with a body in the front seat. "I took the license plate, or rather the wolf took the license plate, and dropped it at the foot of a sheriff who was called out by the farmer whose lunch I stole."

"The farmer calls out the authorities because his food was stolen?"

"The farmer thought I was a coyote or something I guess."

Dagger started to speak but Sara held up one hand. She cocked her head. The intense look in her eyes told Dagger she was using her enhanced hearing. She placed a hand on the floor, as though feeling for a vibration.

They quickly finished their power bars. Dagger dropped the wrappers into the hole in the floor. "Where do you think it is?"

"It sounds like it's idling, like it's waiting for us to make the first move."

They moved cautiously to the opposite side of the room and stepped out into the hallway. The tank was waiting for them.

"MOVE!" Dagger pushed Sara back into the room as a computer and desk behind them exploded in a barrage of wood and metal. He fired off a shot but the bullet bounced off of the armor. They wove around cubicles as debris rained down around them. Dagger couldn't stop long enough to get a shot off.

"How is it tracking us?" Sara yelled.

"Probably thermal imaging."

They tore down a hallway, around a corner, and into another large room with cubicles.

"Wait." Dagger counted the floor tiles from the point where they were standing to the hallway. He handed the gym bag to Sara, pulled out a knife and pried the tile up. Sliding it aside, he said, "Wait here." He jumped down the four feet into the utility space beneath the floor. Dagger counted the tiles overhead. When he reached what he thought was the hallway, he removed the tile, leaving an opening in the floor. Dagger returned to the office, climbed out, and replaced the tile. "Now let's see how badly it wants us."

They moved through the office to the next doorway. Dagger peered around the corner. The tank was waiting near the first doorway. "Wait here." He moved out into the hallway at a run. A loud whining erupted from the end of the hall as the tank tore off after him. He darted through the next doorway as heat from a blast rushed past him. A quick peek into the hallway revealed that the tank hadn't slowed down any. It was headed toward the opening in the floor. Dagger had the Kimber ready. The panel to the right of him exploded. "Damn. I'm going to rip that fucker apart screw by screw." But the tank stopped. It had detected Sara's thermal image. But where? Dagger stole another peek to see that the tile behind the tank had been removed. Sara was in the utility space. He had to smile. Her mind was always clicking. Next, the tile to the right of the tank dropped away. Slowly the tank's turret turned. It was searching for Sara. Would it be smart enough to check beneath it? At some point the tank had to run out of ammo. The tank's turret made a sudden 180 degree turn.

"SARA!" Dagger called out. He hesitated not wanting to fire for fear of hitting Sara. The turret turned back to him. Fire erupted from the tank's gun. The tank advanced oblivious to the opening in front of it and just as it tipped into the empty space in front of it, Sara fired at the power pack. There was a crash and clatter as the tank hit concrete.

Sara pulled herself out of the utility space. "One less energy pack." She replaced the tiles that had been removed.

"Good job but a stupid move. I could have shot you." Dagger turned and stalked away. He pushed through an exit door and back out into the courtyard where he dropped the gym bag onto a bench under the overhang and sat down. A soft rain dotted the cobblestone as angry clouds drifted across the sky.

Sara took a seat next to him. "How can it be raining?"

"Sprinkler systems. Gives the illusion of the outdoors so everyone who was trapped down here didn't suffer from reality withdrawal. Pretty clever."

"Can I have my water bottle, please?"

Dagger downed two aspirins with his remaining water, then opened another bottle. He rationed out two more protein bars and settled back. He could feel Sara's eyes silently prying answers. She was patient to a point. His hand again moved to his neck, feeling the scar from the incision.

"Whatever is in your neck, I think the answers are here," Sara said. "Doc said the scar tissue is at least twenty-five years old. You don't remember being here as a kid?"

Dagger shook his head.

Sara reached out and pulled his hand from his neck. "You aren't sure of anything prior to five years ago?"

Dagger said nothing.

"Maybe these holograms are your memories triggered when you entered the facility," Sara suggested

Dagger said nothing.

"And I think you suspect the same thing."

Dagger still said nothing.

Sara studied the buildings across the street, the potted plants, the skies which lit up with artificial lightning. "It feels like the entire place is alive. But it appears to be for someone else's amusement."

"Well, I hope we run into whoever it is." Dagger's bottle hovered before his lips.

Sara studied the buildings more closely. "Do you think we are being watched? After all, someone sent the tank outside, right where we were standing."

"Cameras don't work, remember? I scrambled them all," Dagger said. He tilted his head back and checked the overcast sky. "Of course, maybe it isn't a sky at all but a window."

"How big do you think this town is?"

Memories flashed through Dagger's brain. Just entering this underground city appeared to have opened up wounds he didn't know he had. He wasn't sure if the memories were his or if he was being bombarded with illusions of memories.

A rainbow stretched across the sky as sunlight broke through the clouds. The drizzle quickly ended and the sounds of birds and insects filled the air.

"It's like someone is sitting in front of a control panel pushing buttons. Cut the rain, start the birds. Even the temperature seems to be controlled, not to mention the oxygen." Sara stood, folding the wrapper from the protein bar into a neat square. She looked around for a garbage can. There was a marble pillar nearby, its opening as wide as the opening in the floor they had found next to the desk. She peered into it. "Think this is an incinerator?"

"Yes." Dagger stood, slipped his arms through the handles of the gym bag, and hefted it onto his back like a backpack. "Let's check out the rest of the town, but this time, let's walk."

Although the sun shone brightly overhead, there was no mistaking they were below ground. Perhaps it was the dark cobblestone or the stone walls in the distance that made them feel confined.

Sara said, "I may not like crowds but there is something about one mile of rock on top of my head that leaves an uneasy feeling."

Dagger searched the courtyard behind them. They hadn't been to the park yet. Then he looked ahead where the large chrome and marble buildings stretched three stories high. "Just don't know where to start."

A large lit screen appeared to drop from the sky a few feet in front of them. It was a computerized map of the area. They took a step back and waited.

"This is really bizarre. I am not liking it at all." Sara slowly approached. "How is this happening?"

A flashing red dot on the map marked *You Are Here*. The underground city was no more than five square blocks. They were currently in the central part of the city. Dotted throughout the map were residential areas, training camps, schools, the park, restaurants, a gym, clinic. A small inset map revealed that one floor below was *The Lab*.

"The Lab," Sara said.

"Very strange. Everything down here is identical to a normal town. It has streets and a sewer system." Dagger's finger tapped a spot on the map that marked the *Director's Residence*. "Let's go check out this guy's life."

"Sure."

They dodged puddles as rain water trickled down to grated drains. The street had that just-washed smell to it. Dagger remembered seeing a waterfall in the park but that might have been a hologram, too, for all he knew. Except for the intermittent sounds of nature, the area was desolate and quiet. There was a rhythm to the birds and insect noises, as if the sounds were taped on a loop and replayed. Maybe Sara was right. Someone was pushing the right buttons, someone who knew they were there. He didn't like that feeling.

They passed marble buildings with chrome railings, passed what looked like back alleys. For all the brightness that the sun churned out, there still were pockets of shadows.

Butterflies swarmed planters filled with flowers. Dagger opened his mouth but before he could ask, Sara said, "Holograms." They turned a corner and stretched in front of them was a flat marble building that looked more like an elaborate mausoleum. Marble statues watched over a garden. Birds dodged around a bird bath. Flowering trees sprouted from marble urns.

"So this is how a director lives," Sara said.

Dagger felt a cold sweat prickle his skin. His eyes immediately riveted on a second floor window. Why that one? He had the image of a gun in his hand pressed to a man's forehead. He shook the picture from his mind and trudged up the walk.

"What's wrong?" Sara asked. "Your pulse has elevated."

There wasn't much he could keep from his partner. It was a curse and a blessing. "I don't know."

"Think you've been here before?"

They reached the front door but there wasn't a doorknob. Dagger pressed his hand to the door but before he could give it a shove, the door hissed open.

"That was weird." Sara stepped closer. "Wait." She listened for sounds from inside. "Something is running, something electrical, maybe a refrigerator or air conditioning."

They stepped into a marble foyer that was the size of a basketball court. Sunlight streamed in from windows on the roof. They were too large to be skylights. A curved staircase led to a second floor. There was something clinical about the house. Everything was white and chrome.

A whirring sound came from a hallway. Dagger pulled his Kimber and waited. A robot about four feet tall whizzed across the floor. "Hologram?"

"No." Sara grabbed his arm. "Wait." The metal machine had a round head and feet that were round disks. Flashing lights circled the round disks, blinking in rhythm to its movements. "It's a vacuum cleaner."

"A what?"

"I know that's a peculiar word for you," Sara said with little humor. Dagger wasn't known to do much in the way of housecleaning. "It's obvious the last person out of this town not only didn't turn off the lights but didn't deactivate the toys."

"I just need to know if it's armed." Dagger pointed the Kimber at the robot. It halted and slowly turned its head in Dagger's direction.

"I would say to put your weapon away, Dagger," Sara said, her voice strained. "As soon as it stopped moving, a red light appeared in that square of glass where its eyes should be. It thinks you pose a threat."

Slowly, Dagger put his gun away and held his hands out. "This is stupid," he whispered. "Having to show some piece of metal that my hands are empty." The red light faded and the robot went about its business, disappearing through a doorway, the hum and swishing of the vacuum growing fainter, replaced by voices, whispers, coming from the upstairs.

Dagger took the stairs two at a time, again pulling his Kimber from its holster. He briefly wondered why he hadn't found any high tech weapons in this town. Did they keep them locked up or take them with?

With her lightning speed, Sara reached the top stair before he did and placed her hand on his chest to slow him down.

The voices were louder now, but they sounded intimate, soft murmurs, something sounding like kisses.

Dagger and Sara hugged the wall as they made their way to opened French doors. From the hallway they could see a platform bed, drawers in the marble wall which probably served as a dresser. They reached the doorway and peered in. A woman was cuddling a baby and smiling up at a man who vaguely resembled Dagger. The man's hair was military short. The woman had long, dark hair and a face that could grace just about any magazine cover.

Sara gasped when she saw the similarity. "You have a wife and baby?"

31

"Not to my knowledge." Before Dagger didn't trust his memory. Now he had a hard time trusting his vision. Yes, the husband did resemble him somewhat, but married? The woman didn't even look vaguely familiar. "Holograms?"

"Yes," Sara replied.

They ignored the obvious family display of affection and searched the room. If there was a desk it was pretty well hidden as were any indications of a closet or nightstand.

"Wow." Sara walked over to the shelf which was lined with individual fish containers. Their bright colors were striking—royal blue, scarlet, bright red, with long, flowing fins.

"Holograms?" Dagger barked out as he aimed his gun at the shelf.

"YES." Sara stared at him in shock. "They are only fish. Chill." She turned back to the shelf and read from a gold plate on the wall. "Betta splendens. Native of Thailand and very aggressive toward other male bettas." As each fish maneuvered in its container, it would catch sight of the fish next to it and go into a frenzy. Its fins ballooned and the fish darted at the reflection in an attempt to get to the other betta. "Aren't they beautiful?" Sara took a step back, her face reflecting realization. "I remember my research. Scientists have been studying these fish since the 1930s as it relates to the aggressive nature of man." Sara repeated things verbatim as she recalled details from her memory. "They believe it is linked to an endocrine disrupting chemical and at one time the military thought of duplicating it in man to create a super sol…"

Soldier. Dagger didn't have to finish her thought.

"Oh my God," she whispered. "Is that what BettaTec is all about? Is this where it all started?"

"Let's get out of here." Dagger stalked out of the room and rushed down the staircase. A wife and baby? Why didn't he remember? And why did seeing the fish bring back memories of small fingers, his fingers, tapping the glass? And was Sara right about someone creating super soldiers? Demko's abilities were still fresh in his mind. Skizzy did mention genetically engineered soldiers as Doc Akins was removing the cover to the chip in his neck. And how Demko changed after looking at Dagger reminded him of the betta fish.

He was out the front door and down the walk before Sara caught up with him. Five years ago he had succeeded in destroying BettaTec's one satellite. Then a year ago he found out they not only had one but two satellites in orbit, more sophisticated and capable of destruction. But what happened before those five years? The military training, Special Ops, police academy— was all of that fabricated?

Sara was surprisingly silent as they stalked back to the courtyard. He wasn't sure if that was a good sign. The possibility of having a family somewhere was enough to silence him let alone Sara. But more importantly…where were they now?

Dagger stopped in the center of the courtyard. "Map," he called out. The map materialized in front of them. "Lab." A bright yellow light pulsated on the map. The lab was the next building over from the maze of cubicles. "Can you find your way back to the elevator you used?"

"I think so. Why?"

He turned to face her. So young, so innocent. So fragile. "I want you on the elevator and out of here."

"No way."

"It's not open for discussion."

"I'm not leaving you."

"I'll drag you there if I have to, now get out of here."

She stepped in front of him, hands on her hips. "You and how many Demkos?"

Dagger almost barked out a laugh but it caught in his throat as he remembered the two men Sara had flung fifty feet and over a truck cab. It pained him to do it but the only way to get her out of harm's way was to knock her out and put her in the elevator. His fist came out with lightning speed but was met by her opened palm. Before he could blink, she had his arm behind his back and twisted up.

"I don't want to hurt you, Dagger. You won't be any good with a broken arm."

Dagger struggled to pull his arm free, tried grabbing her with his left hand but she pinned that one, too. He winced as she pressed his arm further up.

"Promise me you'll behave."

Dagger heaved a sigh. Maybe to get her out of here he would just have to shoot her. "I promise."

She released her hold but played it safe by stepping several feet away.

Dagger shook the blood flow back into his arms. "Let me put it another way," he said. "When and if I get out of here, I won't go home, unless you leave now. Your choice." He turned his back on her, expecting her to plead, shed some tears. But all he heard were footsteps. Dagger turned to see Sara stomping off. He hated being a bastard. He was so good at it when he directed it toward Sheila but with Sara it hurt. She didn't understand that he was trying to protect her and she sometimes overestimated her ability to protect him.

Sara stormed down the stairs, through a passageway and pounded her way into the building. She took angry swipes at the tears blinding her. "That arrogant S.O.B. If it hadn't been for me Mitch Arnosky would have stabbed or shot him. Dagger would still be hanging by his thumbs from the catwalk when those jewelry thieves robbed us. But no." She stalked down a wide hallway, glass walls on her right. The rooms beyond the glass appeared to be surgical rooms. What looked like robotic arms hung from the ceiling. The walls and tiles were constructed of the same white marble in the hallway.

Her pace slowed as she realized no matter what Dagger threatened, she couldn't leave him. Not here. Not like this. Not without knowing that he ever made it out of this place. She stopped and took in her surroundings, not sure if anything looked familiar. She didn't remember passing the surgical rooms when she first arrived. The elevator had emptied into an office, not a hospital wing, and she had turned and immediately found an exit door. She didn't see any exit doors in this wing. Her gaze was drawn to a metal catwalk at the end of the hallway behind her. Metal stairs descended from the catwalk. Above the surgical rooms was a glass bubble. Did people witness the surgeries?

A knocking sound came from up ahead. Sara cautiously continued down the hallway, stopping every few seconds to listen. Beyond the surgical rooms was a door. A closet? Storage room? Several other taps came from behind the door, then a hiss which sounded like a snake.

"Oh God, I hope it's a hologram." She patted her pocket. The sub-compact was still there. Slowly she pulled it out and hoped she still had bullets left. She didn't remember how many she had used up on the tanks. Her steps faltered as she reached the corridor. She stood for several seconds and listened. She didn't detect a heartbeat. Whatever it was, it wasn't alive. More tanks? The tapping was clearer now, quick tap-tapping. It was coming from around the corridor. She stole a glance over her shoulder wondering if she should go back outside, maybe try another entrance.

When Sara turned back around a spider with a body the size of a motorcycle helmet was fifteen feet in front of her. Another crept along the wall and paused. Sara heard a loud shriek and realized it was coming from her. She fired two shots but her hand shook so much the shots hit the wall. "I HATE SPIDERS!" she screamed.

A bullet whizzed by her head and struck the spider in front of her, blasting it into pieces. A second shot knocked the other spider off the wall. It broke into several pieces.

"Are you okay?" Dagger asked as a smile spread across his face.

"What are you laughing at?" Sara demanded.

Dagger used his foot to kick the metal pieces of the body away. "It's a robot." He bent down and flipped the body over. Sara crept closer. The underside had a power pack similar to the one the tank had. Two round black eyes shifted left and right as though the spider had some type of intellect and was searching for its attacker. "Pretty neat, isn't it?" Dagger was in full blown laughter now.

A sudden realization hit Sara. There was something all too familiar about these. Skizzy had helped Dagger create robot spiders last year, far more advanced than these. They were closer to the size of a normal spider and Dagger had used them for audio and visual surveillance.

"That's how you knew how to create those other robot spiders." Sara jammed her fists at her waist and waited.

"What?" Dagger straightened but the smile never left his face. He just gave a helpless shrug. "What else could they be? Everything else down here is either a hologram or a robot."

"Now I know I'm not leaving you alone. You want to threaten not to come back to Cedar Point…fine. But I'm not leaving."

Dagger's smile faded. So far they hadn't run into anything

life threatening but it was the unknown that was dangerous. Will something trigger a deadly gas? Are there fault lines in the area? He again considered punching Sara out and dumping her into the elevator if he could ever find it. Climbing up one mile of stairs carrying Sara wasn't something he looked forward to.

Dagger stared over her shoulder then moved slowly around her and toward a large metal door.

"What is it?"

The glass window on the door was frozen over. "Maybe all the inhabitants of this place have been frozen," Dagger said. He swiped a hand across the glass but it didn't do much to let him see what was inside. There wasn't a door handle or a latch, only a panel to the right of the door with an image of a hand.

"Place your hand over the image," Sara suggested.

"Why would my hand…" But Dagger never finished. Sara grabbed his hand and pressed it against the panel. There was a loud hissing and they both lurched back as though expecting something to emerge. A hallway led to another door which hissed open.

Frigid air blasted from the opening and as the frosty air cleared they could see a cave of ice with several pedestals jutting from the floor of the cave. Dagger waved her to follow but Sara shook her head. "The door might close on us. I'll stand here and hold it open. You go."

Dagger entered, wrapping his arms around him to ward off the chill. "It looks like a Doomstay Vault." He brushed a hand across one of the labels on a pedestal. "It gives a list of all the seeds that are being preserved."

"I thought the Doomsday Vault was in Norway," Sara said from her sentry post.

"There are fourteen hundred seed banks around the globe. But why here and why is BettaTec in charge of one of them?"

Sara stepped closer to see the size of the cave. "How do they keep everything running in this place?"

Dagger studied a panel on the wall inside the cave. "Photovoltaic technology. It converts sunlight directly into electricity."

Sara glared at him with one perfect eyebrow lifted. "You know about the tanks, the spiders, how the place is powered, your prints opened the vault yet somehow you aren't sure if you have ever been here before."

"Yeah, puzzling isn't it?"

Sara held up her hand to silence him. "Listen," she whispered.

Dagger stepped away from the vault and the two doors closed. He strained to listen but other than the faint hum of the ventilation system, he didn't hear anything out of the usual. Then he heard it. "Violin music?"

They moved cautiously down the hall, Dagger on one side, Kimber in hand, and Sara on the opposite side. The music slowly increased as they crossed a corridor. They stood at the intersection and listened. The music was coming from up ahead, in a sector marked *Central Control* on a brass sign above the hallway.

Dagger wanted to tell Sara to hang back out of harm's way but she was already several steps ahead of him. She was as stealthy as a cat with a curiosity to match. He hurried to catch up. They passed what looked like office doors to their left. Other than desks and chairs the rooms were bare.

Sara stopped abruptly. The marble wall was replaced with floor to ceiling glass panels. They stepped into an empty room with one high-backed chair facing a blank wall. The violin music was coming from this room. But from where?

"I don't see any dials on the walls," Sara said. "No radios, CDs." She stared at the ceiling. "Do you think there are speakers up there?"

Dagger stepped forward, curious about the one square of

black marble near the center of the room and to the right of the throne-type chair. Sara tugged on his arm.

"Don't." She scrutinized the walls, studied the ceiling again. "We're being watched," Sara whispered. "I can feel it."

Dagger could feel it, too, but couldn't find any monitors. He pulled Skizzy's toy from his pocket. It was still operating. Two things happened simultaneously. A podium rose from the black marble and a large computer monitor appeared to hang from the ceiling. Dagger took a step back as a faint light started at the top of his head and flashed down his body.

"Oh my God," Sara gasped. "It gave you a retina and full body scan."

A message appeared on the monitor.

Welcome home 617

32

Dagger took two more steps back but then a woman appeared on the screen. She had dark hair and brown eyes. It was the same woman they had seen with the baby but she appeared older. Fine lines etched the corners of her eyes. Her hair had hints of gray.

"I knew you'd come back, darling."

"Darling?" Sara whispered. "I told you she was your wife."

`Mother`

"Your mother?" Sara said. "Maybe she's the Connie that was mentioned on Demko's computer hard drive."

On the lower right side of the screen the word *KONRAD* flashed.

"The computer is answering your questions," Dagger said. "The computer is Connie."

`She created me`

"You must have been the baby we saw her holding. What do they do here?"

The monitor displayed what looked like a sleep clinic. Boys had wires attached to their scalps as they slept.

`Training and reprogramming`

"Programming for what?" Dagger suspected the answer. The remote facility, the surgical room, the high tech equipment. He was starting to get a picture.

Pursue and exterminate

"Exterminate whom?" Sara almost shouted the question.

"S…" Dagger hesitated, not wanting to mention her name. "Don't use our names," he whispered to Sara. He wasn't sure if anyone was monitoring their words and feeding it back to another location. The image on the screen vanished, replaced by what looked like a training camp. All of the boys had shaven heads and were dressed in white karate outfits. It progressed to boys a couple years older dressed in black uniforms shooting at small robot tanks as target practice.

"No wonder you knew the tank had an energy pack," Sara said.

Sara was too eager to ask questions when he had too many questions of his own. First and foremost was the tracking device in his neck.

"How are the explosives ignited?" Dagger asked.

Explosives?

"You don't know that others were vaporized when their missions weren't completed?"

A cursor blinked on the screen, as though Connie were searching for facts, or waiting for instructions.

You compromised site. Corporation moved to undisclosed location. If modifications were made it was after you left, to prevent future defections.

"That doesn't make sense," Sara blurted. "If you were given instructions, how could you deviate? And it's the computer that gave you the instructions. Why is it cooperating now? After all, Demko was following Connie's instructions."

All computers named Connie.
Mother reprogrammed directives.
Changed some sentries. Changed you.

"What happened to her, the mother?" Sara asked.

Eliminated

"Where are the other locations?" Dagger remembered three lights on the map. One had been in a location pretty close to where they stood now. Two were in Europe and one in Asia. If he could only get exact locations.

Unable to retrieve

"Of course you can't," Dagger said, the frustration building. If this facility had been vacated, probably all the rest had been moved, too. "If you aren't supposed to be online then you aren't connected to the rest of the computers."

"Why is it you don't remember her? You don't remember anything." Sara asked.

He erased your memory

"But you remembered the numbers," Sara told Dagger. "The coordinates that led you here."

"No, I only recognized the numbers as coordinates. Big difference."

"But you remember destroying their satellite."

"I did that right before I escaped…I think."

Dagger rubbed his eyes. The light from the monitor was blinding. None of this made sense and if he had heard it all yesterday, he wouldn't have believed it.

"Wait." Sara grabbed Dagger's arm, remembering the family in the director's home. "Who is he? Who's the director?"

The computer was silent for several seconds as the cursor blinked in the middle of the screen. Was it searching through videotape? Searching its stored information? After several more seconds one word appeared on the screen.

`Father`

Dagger stumbled back remembering that brief image of shoving a gun against a man's head. "Is he dead?"

Several more seconds passed before a response appeared.

`Unknown`

Dagger was beginning to doubt Connie's memory. How could it not have a record of everything that happened down here? It wouldn't be hard for someone to erase a hard drive and replace it with fabricated information.

"So I'm supposed to believe a computer just sat down here dormant until I walked in. That no one destroyed you when the place was evacuated." Dagger felt even more like an idiot addressing the computer as though it were human.

```
They gave me the command to destroy
all backups. Mother assumed their next
step and gave me a counter-directive.
```

"She took a big chance," Dagger said. "It was possible I would have never come back."

Eventually someone would have found
your computer chip. Mother made sure
coordinates were on the cover.
I am patient

"Why all the special effects?" Sara asked. "The park, the people, dogs, sun, rain. What was all that about?"

I was lonely

For a while neither one said anything. This computer was so advanced it had the emotions of a human. It had the desire to surround itself with familiar faces, sights, and sounds. Suddenly the screen filled with the same phrase, repeating *I was lonely* hundreds of times.

"What's happening?" Sara yelled. She looked at Dagger but his eyes were entranced, jerking left to right as though reading every line.

Sara studied the words filling the screen. She called on her enhanced eyesight and could see they weren't just words but also snapshots of people. But everything was moving too fast for her to read. Then the alarm sounded followed by the tramping of heavy feet coming from above.

"STOP! TURN OFF!" Sara wasn't sure what command could get the computer to stop but whatever it was doing it was doing it to Dagger. Had the computer kept them there until guards could arrive? Had it notified someone that they were there? And was the computer giving Dagger new instructions? She had to do something to stop it since she couldn't get any response from Dagger. She wanted to yell out his name but Dagger had cautioned not to use their names. Sara looked for a switch on the wall, something to turn off the computer. A box the size of an air purifier hung in the corner of the room. She doubted it would house the hard drive. It was too small for a computer that controlled as much as it did. But the entire facility was so advanced that nothing would surprise her.

Sara pounded at the buttons, checked the screen. "MOVE AWAY," she yelled at Dagger. Now the clanging of heavy boots against the grated staircase grew louder. Sara kicked at the unit and three doors popped open. Small key fobs were inserted in the CPU. She yanked out the fobs and kicked the CPU off the wall. It clattered to the ground and the computer monitor disappeared.

A loud voice sounded over the speakers. "THIS FACILITY WILL SELF DESTRUCT IN FIVE MINUTES."

Dagger shook his head, feeling a stabbing pain behind his eyes. "What the hell is happening?"

"We have to get out of here. Someone's coming."

Dagger joined her at the doorway. In the next sector, past the surgical rooms, four men marched in swat team garb, helmets concealing their faces, body armor covering every inch of exposed skin, boots heavy enough to rattle the thick glass walls. The lead guard raised a dull black metal object. A bright stream of light shot out, disintegrating the door frame.

"Holograms?" Dagger asked.

"No."

"Aim for the weapons," Sara said. "There isn't any part of their bodies that's exposed."

"Their necks. I see a small segment where the body armor meets. It's not all one piece."

Sara aimed the gun at the second guard as Dagger took care of the first, firing at the guard's hand, sending the weapon sprawling across the hall and the hand shattering into several pieces.

"More fuckin' robots," Dagger said. "Which means they don't die."

"Which means," Sara clarified, "that they have to have a

power pack somewhere."

"THIS FACILITY WILL SELF DESTRUCT IN FOUR MINUTES."

"Where to?" Dagger whispered.

"Back to the hallway. I think the office with the elevator is by the exit door at the end of the hall."

"Four minutes," Dagger reminded her. He let Sara lead the way while he covered her.

They charged out of the room and down the hall. A blast of hot air skidded across the wall to Dagger's right. He fired several shots.

"Shit, they have bulletproof everything. And what the hell kind of guns are those?"

They rounded a corner and ran right into another guard. Dagger charged the guard but was knocked away like a pesky fly. He hit the wall feeling all the air rush from his lungs. The guard raised his gun but Sara kicked it away, ducked a blow from an arm the size of a tree trunk, drove a hard kick at his chest and sent him flying fifteen feet. She grabbed the guard's weapon, found the trigger and fired. A stream of white light lit up the man's suit.

"What is this?" Sara stared at the gun.

"This way." Dagger said pressing a hand to his ribs. Sara glanced across the aisle and recognized the office. "No, this way." She rushed across the hall, firing the weapon at the pursuing guards. Dagger fired several shots as Sara crossed the threshold. Dagger stumbled in after her, feeling a blast of heat at his side. For some reason his fingers lost their grip and his gun dropped to the floor.

Sara said, "I think that's all of them."

The office door slid shut like an air lock. Then Dagger's legs gave way and he slowly slid to the floor leaving a trail of red along the wall.

"Dagger?" Sara wrapped an arm around his waist and felt her hand slide into his side which was warm and sticky. She pulled back her hand. It was covered in blood. "Oh my God."

He struggled to focus, tried to reason why he didn't feel any pain.

"THIS FACILITY WILL SELF DESTRUCT IN THREE MINUTES."

"Don't you die on me."

"Go." His breath came in ragged gasps. "This is where I belong."

"I am not leaving without you." She wrapped her arms around him in an attempt to lift him from the floor. "You can't die. Think of all the things you have left to do. You are the only one who can expose BettaTec."

What exactly did he have left to do? Destroy BettaTec? Seems impossible now. He is only one man and he hadn't been able to even slow them down. No, he could only think of one thing he would want to do before he died. Dagger stared at Sara's face, wanting to remember those fabulous eyes, those lips. Yes, there was one thing he wanted to do before he died. Where he found the energy he didn't know but he reached up, placed a hand around the back of Sara's head and pulled her toward him. He kissed her and for several seconds forgot that there was a ticking time bomb, that his blood was seeping from his body and spilling onto the floor. He didn't care. All he wanted was to taste her, remember the smell of her hair, the feel of her skin. She clung to him as though she were the one dying. The one memory he would take with him would be a kiss from a beautiful angel.

His arm started to feel heavy and he felt it slip from Sara's shoulder. And then everything went black.

33

"NO YOU DON'T!" Sara cried. She grabbed the belt at the back of Dagger's pants, lifted him from the floor, and with the guard's weapon under one arm, she half carried, half dragged him across the room to the waiting elevator. As the cylinder-shaped door closed, she heard the parting announcement:

"THIS FACILITY WILL SELF DESTRUCT IN TWO MINUTES."

Sara felt the whoosh of air and silently prayed that they made it to the surface in time, that the guards hadn't somehow destroyed the elevator's controls. She didn't want to die trapped in the shaft. She counted away the seconds until the door finally slid open. It had taken ten seconds for the elevator to rise one mile.

"Dagger, stay awake." Sara dragged him through the store to the street outside. The Cobalt was parked several doors away. Sara quickly settled Dagger in the passenger seat, tossed the weapon into the back seat, then rushed around to the driver's side. How many minutes left now? Seconds? She didn't see a key, didn't even see an ignition. Just some type of print pad. Sara grabbed Dagger's hand and pressed his thumb against the pad. The car rumbled alive. "Skizzy and his toys." The dashboard clock said it was just after nine o'clock. The sun had just dipped below the horizon, but dusk provided enough light so Sara could avoid maneuvering her way through pitch dark.

She continued to tick off the seconds as she floored the accelerator. The Cobalt shot off like a rocket. Sara didn't know what Skizzy did to the car but it was the fastest thing she had ever driven. She looked over at Dagger. He was leaning against the door, his face gray in the dim street lights. His shirt and jeans were wet with his blood. He wasn't responsive enough to put pressure on his own wound. Maybe he needed water but they had left the gym bag in the lab.

Sara's eyes kept watch on the clock, losing track of exactly how much time they had left before the explosion. And what kind of explosion would it be? Would two miles be a safe distance, or did she need to be one hundred miles away, a goal she couldn't possibly achieve. The speedometer pulsed at 140 miles per hour.

Her eyes scanned the road looking for signs designating a hospital. She looked for houses along the way but the area was a flat, desolate piece of land. She felt the pockets of her jumpsuit to make sure she still had the sub-compact. That's when she noticed the blood on her hand, her arms, and now on her clothes.

The ground started to shake. The console said the Cobalt had traveled four and a half miles. Sara checked her rearview mirror. A huge cloud of sand had kicked up but it was getting too dark to see if the ground had opened up. At least there wasn't any fire or a mushroom cloud, not that she would have been surprised to see one.

A couple blocks ahead off of the main road Sara saw two houses. She slammed the gear shift into second and peeled around the corner. As she got nearer she saw a ranch style home. The detached building a couple lots away was a smaller one story building with a sign out front that said, *Animal Hospital, Doctor Judith Engles.*

"We have help, Dagger." Sara looked over at him as she slammed the car into park and laid on the horn. His eyes were closed. "DAGGER?" She saw the outside house lights flick on and blew the horn several more times. Sara ran around to the passenger side and helped Dagger out of the car and up the sidewalk to the hospital.

A woman in stone-washed jeans and a blouse came running toward them. "Excuse me. The hospital is closed."

"He's injured," Sara said. "Are you Doctor Engles?"

The woman gasped as she saw the blood streaking his arm and Sara's clothes. Since Dagger's clothes were black, it was difficult to tell the extent of his injuries. "Get him inside." Doctor Engles opened the door to the reception area. A blood trail followed behind them. She led them through a doorway and turned on the overhead lights.

Sara hefted Dagger onto the examining table. Doctor Engles stared in shock at Sara's ability to lift Dagger by herself but she didn't say anything. The doctor peeled Dagger's shirt away from his chest and gasped.

"How did this happen?" She opened a cabinet and pulled out a stack of white gauze pads. She pressed a mound of them against the wound.

"He was shot. I don't think the bullet lodged in him." Sara wasn't sure of anything. The weapons didn't appear to shoot bullets. She felt nauseous looking at all the blood.

"He needs a blood transfusion."

"Do it."

"I can't. My hospital is closed. I don't have any supplies. Besides, this was an animal hospital, not a normal hospital."

Sara reached into her pocket, pulled out the gun and pointed it at the woman. "I said to fix him." The doctor's eyes grew wide as she stared at the gun. Her hands froze above the gauze pads that were turning red with Dagger's blood. Sara looked at the gun as though wondering who put it there. Her hands started to shake and tears ran down her face. "I'm sorry," she sobbed as she slowly lowered the gun. "Please, please make him better."

Doctor Engles averted her eyes from the gun and pulled

more pads from the package. She tossed the bloody pads onto the floor and pressed clean ones to the wound. She flicked stray hairs from her face leaving a bloody stripe across her forehead. "Damn," she said in frustration. "He needs blood, lots of it, and I don't have any."

"Take mine."

"You don't understand. He needs LOTS of blood."

Sara pulled a second examining table over and butted it up against Dagger's. "Take as much as you need."

"You don't..."

"DO IT!" Sara closed her eyes. "Just take whatever you need."

More bloody pads hit the floor. "There's a reason people only give one pint of blood at a time."

The vet pulled tubes and catheters from a drawer. Sara wasn't sure what all of the supplies were and had only been in a hospital one other time. She didn't remember a needle that large.

The vet worked quickly, wrapping a blood pressure monitor around Dagger's arm, then doing the same to Sara's arm. "He's lost way too much blood."

"I've heard of people losing ten to twelve pints of blood and surviving," Sara said.

"Yes, but those patients usually get immediate attention in an E.R. This isn't an E.R."

"Close enough."

"Listen," the doctor said with a hint of exasperation, "I don't have extra blood lying around to give him. And I can only give one pint of my own blood but that is provided we are the same blood type. Are you a blood match for him?"

"Yes," Sara said but she wasn't sure. When she had been in and out of consciousness in the hospital she vaguely remembered Dagger saying his blood type was universal donor. That's fine for him, but would her blood kill him? All she knew for sure is if he didn't get any blood he would definitely die.

Engles ran water in the sink until it started steaming, then scrubbed her hands, all the time keeping an eye on the gauze pads that continued to soak through with blood. "Damn, I should have been in Montana already. My son wants to open a wildlife sanctuary, not that the damn government gave me enough money when they bought this place from me. Eminent domain. Damn bureaucrats." She shut the water off with her elbow and slipped into latex gloves. Turning back to Sara, the vet said, "Please tell me you two didn't rob a bank or something that I'm going to get into trouble for."

"We didn't. I promise you who did this to him was the bad guy, not us."

"Fine. I don't care to know the details."

Sara didn't want to see what the vet was doing. She turned her head to study the animal prints painted on the walls. There were different paw prints for each animal. The pinch in her right arm felt like a metal pipe going through her vein.

"The most I can take from you is 1.42 liters."

"How much is that?"

"Three pints."

"Take four."

"It will kill you."

"No it won't. I promise."

Engles laughed softly. "You are making a lot of promises."

"How long will it take?"

"About thirty minutes per pint. But I warn you, if your blood pressure starts to drop dramatically, I'll stop."

In her peripheral vision, Sara could see the vet starting to work on Dagger's injuries. The doctor looked like she knew what she was doing. Her hands worked without thought. Salt and pepper hair was pulled back in a casual bun with little care for smooth and tidy. Sara could imagine Engles working in a sanctuary, hair and makeup of little concern as she cared for the animals she so obviously loved.

Sara forced herself to look at Dagger. His eyes were closed and damp hair clung to his neck. He appeared unresponsive to everything the doctor was doing. Sara started to feel lightheaded and wondered what would happen if she passed out. Would the good doctor call the police? Would they be arrested? She didn't have any identification on her. Did Dagger? She watched as her blood flowed down the tube and into Dagger's arm. She had no fear of losing a lot of blood. Her body could regenerate blood at a faster speed than it could regenerate limbs. But if it killed Dagger she would never forgive herself. She slowly reached over and brushed Dagger's arm. It was cold to the touch.

The medicinal odor was the first thing that broke Sara's sleep. She felt weak and barely able to open her eyes. A veil of light streamed through the window. Was it daytime? She tried to remember where she was. At home? In the car? In the control room of BettaTec? Then she saw Dagger lying on the table next to her. His shirt had been stripped from his body. Doctor Engles appeared to be changing Dagger's bandages. Of course. Now Sara remembered finding the vet. Was it just last night or had they been there for days?

Doctor Engles stared in shock for several seconds as she inspected the wound. "How can that be?" she whispered. "There aren't any scars. It's as though there wasn't an injury."

That was when it hit Sara. Her blood gave Dagger's body the ability to regenerate. She could almost read the same realization on Engle's face. Dagger had come in torn and bloody but it wasn't until he received Sara's blood that he had healed. Engles flicked her gaze to Sara. Maybe out of fear or preservation instinct, Sara could feel her eyes change, the lens become spherical, the pupils enlarge. They didn't change color but an experienced veterinarian would recognize the eyes of a hawk. It wasn't enough of a true shift to place the doctor in danger from the wolf.

Shocked, Doctor Engles stumbled back against the sink.

"It's okay," Sara whispered, raising up on one elbow.

"Who are you people?"

"We don't mean you any harm. I just want to get him back on the road and out of your hair."

"But how? This just isn't…" The scientist and researcher in her struggled for logical answers. She shook her head as though trying to clear the image from her mind.

Sara slowly rose from the table and tested her legs. The jumpsuit was gone. Instead she was wearing a pink sleeveless blouse and plaid shorts. She even had on underwear and the blood had been cleaned from their bodies.

"They are my daughter-in-law's clothes. You are close to her size." Engles nodded at Dagger. "Both of you had so much blood on your clothes." Her voice was shaky as she tried to gather her composure. "My son is a little bigger but his clothes will do." A clean shirt was hanging on the back of a chair. Engles held up a roll of tape. "If you can help him sit up, I'll tape his ribs. I don't have an X-ray machine but I think he has a couple bruised or cracked ribs."

Dagger groaned as they tried to move him. "How is his blood pressure?" Sara asked.

"Better but not as good as yours." She wound the tape several times around his sternum. "And to think I was going to be bored spending my last week in this house."

"You're leaving so soon?"

"The van is half packed. I was just taking my time packing the last few boxes until you two showed up." Engles cut the tape with scissors and had Sara help her slip Dagger's arms into the shirt. He winced at the effort but they finally got it on him. "You never did tell me your names."

Sara smiled. "No, I didn't."

Dagger struggled to open his eyes. "Where…?"

"Shhhhh." Sara pressed a finger to his lips. "You're fine."

He took in his surroundings, settled his eyes on the stranger, then at Sara. A car rumbled up to the curb outside. Sara turned toward the window thinking the worst. It was a black car, mid-sized. Police? Two men climbed out. They were dressed in camo pants, green tee shirts and sported dark glasses and baseball caps. She breathed a sigh of relief. After making sure Doctor Engles could handle Dagger on her own, Sara walked through the reception area and out to the street.

34

"Am I glad to see you two." Sara hugged Simon, then Skizzy whose main source of contact was his computer so he wasn't quite sure what to do with his arms. "You must have left the GPS on the Cobalt," Sara told Skizzy.

"Hey," Simon interjected, "when it comes to Dagger, we can't trust him not to walk into a pile of trouble."

"The doctor was very helpful." Sara leaned in close. "But don't use any names."

"Roger that," Skizzy said but stopped abruptly when he saw the sign in the lawn. "You found him a horse doctor?"

Simon hung back, checking the inside of the Cobalt. "Holy crap. Hope that wasn't your blood."

He had the passenger side door open. Blood pooled on the seat, the door frame, and floor. "Aw, man," Skizzy whined. "That was a sweetheart of a car."

Simon pulled the weapon from the back seat. "What the hell is…?" His finger accidentally hit the trigger, firing a flash of light. A tree thirty feet away toppled over, the trunk sizzling and smoking.

"Suweeet!" Skizzy grabbed the weapon. "What the hell did you bring me, girlie?"

"We're hoping you can figure it out."

"My pleasure." Skizzy caressed it like a new found kitten.

"We had to detour around a huge sink hole about five miles back," Simon said. "You wouldn't know anything about that would you?"

"Lots, but first we need to get out of here."

Simon followed Sara back into the hospital where Dagger

was sitting up drinking orange juice. “Well, well. What have we got here.”

Dagger scowled at him and continued drinking the juice.

“This is Doctor Engles,” Sara said.

Engles shook his hand. “And you are?” Engles prompted.

Simon smiled. “Someone who is going to take your problem child off your hands.”

“Of course.” Engles retrieved the empty glass from Dagger and headed for the door.

Simon stopped her and held out his hand. “Sorry, can’t let you do that.” He pulled the glass from her hand.

“I wasn’t going to…” Engles looked from Simon to Sara, then walked outside and crossed the lot to her house.

“I don’t think I can sit in a car for that long ride home,” Dagger said, eyeing the compact sitting at the curb.

“Nah, that’s just a shuttle to your Learjet,” Simon said.

They got him outside and into the car just as Skizzy hauled his Land Warrior from the trunk. “What are you going to do?” Sara asked when she saw that Skizzy had pulled the Cobalt onto the drive next to the hospital’s door.

“Destroy any and all evidence,” Simon said.

Skizzy stood in the hospital’s doorway. A stream of napalm shot out of the modified machine gun. Next he torched the Chevy Cobalt. The car exploded in a ball of light. He shook his head with regret as his favorite car went up in flames. Doctor Engles came running out of her house.

“What are you doing?” She clasped both hands over her mouth and took a step back from the heat. “That’s my hospital.”

Simon looked apologetically at her and shrugged.

“My God.” Engles legs gave out and she dropped to her knees. “Why?”

Sara knelt in front of her and stared into her face. “No one can know we were here,” Sara said. “The clothes, the car, the blood evidence. It all has to be destroyed. But to avoid anyone asking questions, I would suggest you leave for Montana at your earliest possible convenience."

"Yeah," Skizzy snarled, "like in the next ten minutes because my toy is all fired up and ready to destroy something else." He looked toward the house.

Engles gasped. "He's kidding, isn't he?" She looked again at Sara and pleaded with her eyes. No one said anything. Engles rose abruptly and stumbled to the house.

Sara stood and watched her leave. Doctor Engles had been very helpful and now they were going to destroy the few things she valued in her life. Sara turned her attention to the Taurus. "That's one of Dagger's cars, isn't it?"

"Yeah. Skizzy hacked into your front gate access code and we stole the car. Said since Dagger already had one of his, he was taking one of Dagger's."

"Good, pop the trunk," Sara ordered. Simon pushed a button on the fob and the trunk popped open. Sara pulled up the rug in the trunk then pulled out a satchel.

Simon said, "You mean we been driving halfway across the country without a spare?"

"Worse yet," Sara smiled, "you've been driving with a quarter of a million dollars in the trunk."

Simon's eyes widened and his jaw slacked.

When Sara had stored clothes in each of Dagger's cars, she had discovered by accident that Dagger supplied each of his vehicles with a satchel just so he had money should he need to get away quick. She walked up to the front door and knocked on the screen.

Doctor Engles opened the door and stepped out. "Guess it's a good thing I was pretty much packed. Just wasn't planning to leave so soon. At least those bastards with the bulldozer won't have the satisfaction of leveling my house. "Here." She handed a slip of paper to Sara. "It's a prescription for pain pills, should he need them."

"Thanks." Sara handed Engles the satchel. "We want to thank you for your help and offer a little something to get your wildlife refuge up and running."

Engles hesitated, unsure of what she was being handed. She cautiously peered into the bag. "Hush money?"

"Is it working?"

Engles appeared to deliberate for several seconds. Then said, with a slight smile pulling at her lips, "I don't remember a thing."

Sara turned and walked back to the car before Engles could change her mind.

Simon and Skizzy helped the vet load the remaining boxes and suitcases into her van. They waited until she was several blocks away before Skizzy fired up his toy again. Once they were sure everything would burn, they high-tailed it out of there.

Several miles down the road Skizzy steered the black Taurus up a ramp and into the back of a thirty-five foot motor home that was parked under an overpass. Simon and Skizzy helped Dagger into the motor home and settled in the back bedroom.

"His color sure ain't good," Skizzy said.

"Kinda looks like warmed over oatmeal, if you ask me." Simon pulled pillows from an overhead compartment.

Sara sat on the edge of the bed and placed the pillows behind Dagger's back and head. Doctor Engles had said that Dagger might feel more comfortable sleeping sitting up. "Where did you get the motor home?"

Skizzy just smiled. "Has all the comforts of home."

Simon tossed a blanket onto the bed. Nodding toward Dagger he said, "What's he doing?"

Dagger's body shook as though chilled. "The doctor said he might show signs of shock. We just need to keep him warm." But there was something else going on. His eyes were open but moving slowly from left to right and back, as though reading a teleprompter. Sara realized it was the same reaction he had when standing in front of the computer monitor. Had the computer been spitting out subliminal messages?

Skizzy stepped closer. "Looks like he's communicating with the mother ship."

Simon slowly straightened, his hands clenching and unclenching. "If you don't get up there and get this boat in motion, I'm going to kick you from here to that mother ship."

Skizzy retreated to the front and soon had the motor home in gear.

Simon braced himself against the doorway as the vehicle rocked onto the road. "You look like you could use some sleep, too," he told Sara. "When you wake maybe you can come up front and fill us in on what happened, if you feel up to it."

Sara nodded. She couldn't argue there. Although she should be feeling a lot worse than she did after losing four pints of blood, she still wasn't back to normal. But were Simon and Skizzy ready to hear what happened one mile underground?

35

Sara caught the phone on the first ring. "How's our boy doing?" Simon asked.

"He's been sleeping for two days. Guess his body still needs time to recuperate. He lost a lot of blood." Sara had explained everything on the drive home but played down the part about Dagger's injuries. She didn't want any curious eyes wanting to see scars he didn't have.

"Well, Skizzy has some interesting theories he's trying to prove."

Sara held up the morning paper which pictured Cardinal Esrey and Donald Thomas in an exclusive written by Sheila. "I'm surprised Skizzy has had time after the hatchet job he did on Father Thomas. Or I should say Mister Thomas, or whatever his name is."

"He's like a kid in a candy shop. For one thing that plasma gun is years ahead of its time. Skizzy could't even find a prototype when he hacked into the military web sites. He thought it might also be argon gas, microwave or electromagnetic pulse. He checked those two BettaTec satellites and neither one was homed in on that missile silo in Nebraska. Guess BettaTec did assume it was already destroyed so why monitor it. And the reports of an earthquake and sinkhole were just another ho hum news report."

Sara heard water running in Dagger's bedroom and quickly said her good-byes promising to let Simon know when Dagger was well enough for visitors. She heated up a mug of chicken broth in the microwave, grabbed a spoon, then carried it to Dagger's room. Pressing an ear to the door, she confirmed sounds of movement, knocked softly, and carefully nudged the door open with her elbow.

Dagger was standing in front of the bed shoving clothes into a suitcase with one hand, the other hand gripping a cane Simon had given him. He was dressed in gym shorts, his hair wet and dripping beads of water on his shoulders. Dagger had removed the tape from around his ribs. Sara was surprised Dagger had been able to stand long enough to take a shower. Dagger looked up, then quickly turned away and hobbled over to the dresser. A tightness radiated through her chest. She shook it off and walked over to the bed. Dagger always did travel light. He had packed a shaving kit, some slacks and underwear. Dagger hobbled over with several black tee shirts.

Sara set the cup and spoon on the nightstand. "Sit and drink your soup. I'll finish that." She removed the shaving kit and returned it to the bathroom. "Simon called." She told him about their conversation, the article on the front page about Father Thomas and the story buried on page sixteen regarding the suspected earthquake. She returned to the bed and pulled the black tee shirts from the suitcase.

Dagger leaned on the cane as he sipped the hot broth, all the while watching her movements. "Sara, you're supposed to put the clothes in, not take them out. You saw the computer do a retina scan. They know I'm still alive."

Sara placed the tee shirts back in the dresser drawer. She saw the cane tremble under Dagger's hand. "I think you better lie down before you fall down. You need another week or two to get your strength back. Then if you still want to leave, I'll help you pack." Just saying the words twisted that knife in her heart.

Dagger gave up and sat on the bed. He seemed to watch her with resignation. That warmed over oatmeal color Simon had described was still evident in Dagger's face. "How's Einstein?"

"Quiet, nervous. I had to assure him you were here by bringing him in to see you while you slept. He dropped a cheese curl on your bed."

Dagger smiled. "I think I might miss him."

Sara ignored his comment. "Do you recall how long after you met me and Grandmother that you thought BettaTec had managed to get their two satellites in orbit?"

Dagger rubbed a shaky hand over his face. A stubble was growing and it would be thick in a day or two if he didn't take a razor to it. "Yeah, about three or four months. Why?"

"A month before we met you Grandmother took off her necklace and restrung it. This time she used strands of copper wire. All she would tell me was that it needed to be safer which I thought was an odd term for her to use. I remembered this after the clasp broke outside of Skizzy's shop. For those brief few seconds when the necklace fell to the ground, you were exposed. Then we stepped into Skizzy's shop with his copper lined walls." Sara smiled at how Skizzy's phobia just might have saved Dagger's life. Dagger was paying close attention now. "Then Doc Akins came by, removed part of that chip and was taking it to California when…" They didn't have to be reminded of what happened to Akins. "Anyway, Skizzy repaired the necklace, practically soldered it onto your neck, no clasp, no reason to lose it unless you get into an accident and someone in an ER somewhere cuts it off, which is probably why you should never be out of my sight," she added under her breath.

Sara closed the suitcase and returned it to the closet. "Demko showed up at our doorstep and I think it's clearer now how he changed from being a rather pushy client to wanting to kill you. Somehow he did a retina scan or was programmed to recognize defectors. That's when he tried to kill you. We figured you two exchanged retina scans. You saw Cardinal Esrey on his itinerary and assumed you were the one who had known him and might have killed him. The second Demko was a backup in case Number One didn't complete his mission which was to retrieve the flash drive Father Thomas had stolen from the guy at the airport." She took his empty glass to the bathroom, filled it with water, and returned to the bed with the bottle of pain pills.

"As far as BettaTec is concerned," Sara continued, "you died on the plane. As far as Demko Number One, Skizzy placed a fictitious accident report on the police department computers stating Demko Number One had a whiplash and refused hospitalization other than to accept a neck brace. This, we hope, will have BettaTec suspecting the reason why his chip went haywire. Then Skizzy booked him on a plane to Vancouver, again in the hopes that BettaTec assumes this is why they can't locate him through the chip."

"You and the boys have been busy."

Sara smiled as she shook out a pain pill. "It was a long ride back from Nebraska so we spent the time bouncing ideas off of each other."

"But what about Demko Number Two? Wouldn't he be expected to return the flash drive?"

She gave a shrug of indifference. "Don't you think BettaTec would have given instructions that Demko destroy it even if it means destroying himself? As far as they know, he accomplished what he set out to do."

Dagger sank back against the pyramid of pillows. Worry still left tracks across his forehead. "Provided BettaTec doesn't send someone to retrace Demko's steps before he flew to Vancouver."

"Such a worry wort. Now take your pill." She handed him the pain pill.

He dropped the pill on the nightstand. "Is Padre sniffing around for answers?"

"Padre's been busy. He discovered that Father Thomas isn't a priest much less Donald Thomas. Cardinal Esrey had met some people several weeks ago who had gone to the seminary with Father Thomas. Only problem is the real Father Thomas died in a car accident right after graduating from the seminary. What better way for a BettaTec assassin to get close to the Pope. What they have against the Pope one can only guess. Skizzy thinks it might not even be the current Pope they are after. Could be the next one, that it's all a move in BettaTec's giant chess game of manipulation. Either way, Father Thomas wasn't going with the program. Skizzy figures there was a break in the ranks and the leaders have chosen up sides. Unfortunately, Father Thomas was on the wrong side."

Sara walked over to the jalousie windows and cranked them open, bringing a waft of floral odors from the garden. She kept the blinds closed but slices of sunlight managed to seep through.

"Remind me to ground you for coming after me."

"Right," Sara grumbled. "After I remind you to thank me for again saving your life. You might still be at the bottom of that sink hole if I hadn't dragged your bleeding body out of there."

No argument there. She was right but then the memories of bleeding out on the floor came back to him. "Why is it I remember bleeding all over the car and a doctor stitching me up but I don't have any scars? Did I dream it?" Dagger asked.

"I was wondering when you were going to get to that." She pulled the sheet up to Dagger's waist. Her fingers grazed the area where he had been injured. Skin as smooth as a baby's had replaced the damaged skin. "You were pretty badly injured. That futuristic weapon sliced into you pretty good. You lost a lot of blood so I gave you four pints of mine."

Dagger blinked several times as though trying to remember details. "I can heal my wounds as though nothing happened?"

"If anyone needs that ability, it's certainly you." Sara rummaged through the bathroom cabinet and returned with a roll of tape.

"But why aren't my ribs healing?"

"You only have four pints of my blood. Not all of it so don't expect miracles." She motioned for him to sit up as she re-taped his ribs. "The doctor said NOT to remove the tape. Got it?"

"Can I…?"

Sara knew what he was thinking. "No, I'm pretty sure you won't have any shifting abilities. That isn't something you can get from my blood." She returned the tape to the bathroom. Once she was sure he was comfortable, she made her way to the door.

As her hand reached for the doorknob Dagger said, "Stay."

Sara's breath caught in her throat and she heard her pulse pounding in her ears. She looked over at Dagger to make sure she had heard right. In the past she had thought nothing of waking him by walking into his bedroom with a cup of coffee and sitting on his bed. Why does it feel different now?

"I don't know what's real and what isn't anymore," Dagger said.

Sara released her hold on the doorknob saying, "And lying next to a shapeshifter will give you a grasp of reality…how?"

Dagger gave a weak laugh to the irony of his statement. Then his face turned serious and he stared at her with an intensity that frightened and thrilled her. "You're one of the few real things in my life."

"On one condition," she replied. "You take your pain pill."

"You know I don't like those. It makes me sleep too soundly. Then I can't wake myself from dreams of being stuck one mile below the surface or stuck in the Doomsday Vault."

"I'll wake you out of the nightmare, if that happens. You need as much sleep as possible in order to get your strength back."

Dagger relented and took the pain pill, washing it down with half a glass of water. Sara kicked her sandals off and carefully climbed in next to him, fearful of moving the bed too much. His major injury might be healed but his body still showed bruises and his ribs were still tender.

She stretched out next to him and propped herself up on one

elbow. "Is there any part of you that doesn't hurt?" she asked.

A slight smile tipped the corner of his mouth as he lifted the baby finger on his left hand. Sara slipped her hand into his and squeezed. If she was fearful of anything, it was what the visit to the city might have done to him.

"What did Connie show you?" Sara asked.

"Connie?"

"The computer, when it was repeating the phrase, *I was lonely*, it was like you were hypnotized. You just stared as guards tramped down the metal stairs and the minutes ticked off until total destruction. You just stood frozen in place. Afterwards, when Simon got you settled for the ride home from the vet's, your eyes were shifting left to right as if you were reading instructions."

"I did?" Dagger's puzzlement swiftly changed to relief. "My memory. Connie was starting to give me back my memory."

"Your memory?" Sara slowly sat up. "And I cut the power to the computer before it finished? I can't believe I ruined your only chance..."

"Don't blame yourself. With the guards and the bomb, we didn't have much time to hang around." Dagger thought of the few snippets he had been able to grasp. The memories hadn't been in chronological order. He remembered some of the training; he remembered his mother telling him not to reveal that he wasn't like the others. And he remembered his father finding out that his mother had tampered with the program. Exactly what was his father's role? Did his father have something to do with his mother's death? Was that why Dagger had a memory of pressing a gun to his father's head? So many questions and so few answers.

"What if she also planned to give you the identities of the players? It was your one chance to expose all of them and I screwed it up." One lone tear made a lazy trail down her cheek.

He reached up and wiped the tear away with a finger. "Don't

worry about it, Sara. What's done is done. Maybe a face in the crowd or a name in the paper might trigger something someday. Maybe I know more than I can grasp at the moment."

"What about your real name? Did the computer reveal that?"

He tugged at her arm and she reluctantly lay back down. "I kind of like Chase Dagger." He blinked slowly, either the fatigue or pain pill taking its toll. "Has a nice ring to it." Then again, all he would ever be was a number...617. That's all anyone had been. His words were slow and labored. "How do you know the vet won't say anything?"

"Because we paid her off."

Dagger swung his head toward her. Obviously the pill hadn't taken that much effect yet since the mention of money always got his attention. "You what?"

"I gave her the satchel of money for all of her help. She's in Montana by now scoping out a new animal sanctuary, thanks to you."

Dagger gave a weak laugh. "Easy come, easy go." Blinking started to become an effort. Memories of Connie and the security guards flooded back, the wound he suffered, and his last thoughts as he felt his life drain away. "How old was the vet?"

"I don't know, maybe late fifties, early sixties. Why?"

Dagger took a deep breath and winced as his ribs protested. "I had the strangest dream that I kissed a beautiful angel. She didn't have gray hair, though." He closed his eyes, giving up on the effort to keep them open. "I knew when I died I definitely wasn't going to Heaven so I thought, 'if this is Hell then I'm definitely staying.'"

Sara smiled secretly. "They say when you are close to death you are prone to hallucinations."

* * *

A figure made his way slowly across a dark London street. The rain was a light mist which played havoc on his body. His slight limp was more pronounced than usual. Later the police would blame it on poor visibility that the man didn't see the vehicle barreling down on him at sixty miles an hour. It hadn't left skid marks and it was only because of the distance the body had been thrown that authorities could gauge how fast the vehicle was going. The man had died instantly. As yet the victim had not been identified.

The Cedar Point Police Department was at a loss to explain how a prisoner being transported to the county jail at the crack of dawn had been abducted by three men in a black SUV. The police van had been run off the road by the SUV and tipped over on its side. Witnesses say Donald Thomas, who was due to be arraigned in court at nine o'clock, was reluctant to leave with his rescuers and had screamed for assistance from the police officers who lay unconscious from the accident. Witnesses were unclear as to which direction the SUV had driven. Authorities had yet to locate the vehicle.

Skizzy stayed up all night searching the Internet for photos from a list he had made of certain names that had popped into his head. Given enough time, he could probably make a lengthy list. At seven o'clock he sat staring at two computer monitors struggling whether to believe he was a genius or totally off the deep end. If anyone would believe him it would be Dagger.

John Wilkes Booth, Lee Harvey Oswald, Sirhan Sirhan, and Khalid Islambouli who had assassinated Anwar Sadat, were just a few photos he had examined closely, assassinations that affected the course of history. He even found photos of Charles

J. Guiteau who assassinated James Garfield in 1841. When it was difficult to find photos from all angles, he was successful in finding autopsy reports.

Where to go from here, though. Newspapers? They probably control them. Politicians? Some of them are probably members. You Tube? The Internet? Would only force them underground. No, he and Dagger needed to outmaneuver them, to be patient and unpredictable.

Skizzy returned his attention to the photos on the monitor. What did the future hold for mankind if their lives were in the hands of a select few? Although he wanted to congratulate himself on his brilliance, there was a chill that tamp down any attempt to be too smug. He was still having a hard time believing what he could see right before his eyes.

Skizzy discovered the one thing these assassins had in common: They each had a scar on the back of his neck.

Printed in the United States
118328LV00005B/25-30/P

9 780978 540296